Advance Praise for *Ash Ridley and the Phoenix*

"Lisa Foiles has created a fantastical world where every reader will dream of being just like Ash and will want a phoenix of their own just like Flynn. This delightful book is full of inspiration, excitement, mystery, suspense, and heart. I highly recommend *Ash Ridley and the Phoenix* for any reader who is ready for a new adventure!"

—Ashley Eckstein, *Star Wars* actress, founder of Her Universe, and author of *It's Your Universe: You Have the Power to Make It Happen*

ASH RIDLEY
and the
PHOENIX

ASH RIDLEY
and the PHOENIX

LISA FOILES

A PERMUTED PRESS BOOK

ISBN: 978-1-68261-903-2
ISBN (eBook): 978-1-68261-904-9

PERMUTED
PRESS

Permuted Press, LLC
New York • Nashville
permutedpress.com

Published in the United States of America

For my dad, Steve, who better not have too many adventures without me before I get to be with him again.

PROLOGUE

The five beasts roared, shrieked, howled. Not even the booming thunder could compete with their deafening battle cries. Had the animals been uncaged that night, they would have torn through a hundred innocents—and one guilty.

But the witch pressed on. Her shriveled hands gripped the reins tightly, peeking out from the sleeves of a hooded cloak. Lightning struck the horizon. A skeletal claw reached from the sky. This was not a night to be traveling alone, especially if your horses were pulling deadly cargo.

The five carts behind the hunched witch shifted and rocked with the rage of the magical creatures they contained. A half-lion, half-tiger in the front cart shot a paw through the bars,

LISA FOILES

revealing switchblade claws. It swiped for the hag, but struck only raindrops.

After sixteen miles of muddy road, a light appeared up ahead. A small settlement with a wooden sign read *McElliott Inn and Goods*. Another sign had been hastily nailed on top that said *No Vacancy*.

A man and woman desperately packed up vegetables, fruits, and supplies from their roadside stand. The wind had destroyed most everything, but there was still some to be salvaged.

"I need a room," the witch said to the man.

"Haven't got any," the merchant yelled through the rain. "We're booked, I'm sorry. The nearest town is eight miles north."

The witch pointed a crooked finger at the man's face and drew a counterclockwise circle in the air.

"Now that you mention it, we do have one," the man said stiffly. "You may take our room."

"Joseph!" exclaimed his wife, shocked.

The witch drew the same circle in her direction.

"Yes, it would be our pleasure," the wife said pleasantly.

The animals in the cages eyed the merchant and his wife with wide, hungry eyes.

The witch cracked her whip. Her horses pulled the convoy toward the inn, but a red flash abruptly caught her eye. She yanked on the reins.

"What...is that?" said the mesmerized witch, hopping from her seat.

She walked with trepidation toward a display of swinging wooden cages. Most contained ugly cats, small dogs, or various rodents for sale, whining and yipping to be freed, like a miniature version of the witch's caravan. But the witch only had eyes for the last cage.

"It's a red fowl of some kind. Perhaps a parrot," shouted the man as he packed up the last box of vegetables. "We found him lying in our patch of dormanberries."

Tilda sneered at such simplicity. These ignorant bumpkins had caught the creature with a common sleep-inducing medicinal plant, when not even a magical spell could have done the job.

Thunder shook the ground.

"How much?"

The merchant wiped rain from his face. "Perhaps... thirty gold?"

The witch flicked her hand.

"Twenty gold?" the man said again, unwittingly.

The witch retrieved a handful of gold coins and slammed them into the man's hand. She snatched the wooden cage as if someone was going to steal it from her at any moment. She set it in the supply cart and returned to the driver's seat.

"I was never here!"

With a final wave of her hand, the witch sent the man and woman flying backwards with a magical gust of wind. They landed hard in the mud. When they sat up, rubbing their heads with amnesia, the witch had already galloped away.

The red bird softly cooed and blinked open an eye.

CHAPTER 1

THE TRAVELING CIRCUS

TEN YEARS LATER

ree-sleep is a peaceful sleep, especially under a Cascadian Apple Tree on a warm September night. Even the twitchy squirrels, hustling ants, and diligent spiders that have made the tree their residence will often tolerate visitors. Their curiosity is worth the opulence of a springy grass bed and a star-speckled sky peeking through a canopy of leaves, while distant howls act as a haunting lullaby. This tree-sleep was precisely the kind of sleep Ashtyn Ridley was enjoying.

Bonk!

Right before a rotten apple bounced off her noggin as if she sported a painted-on target.

Ash remained fast asleep.

Bonk!

Another one, larger this time, smacked her in the forehead. Blinking open her tired eyes, she could make out the marshmallow clouds in the blue sky and two large howler monkeys in their cage staring at her with obvious impatience.

"Spare me the morning torment, you imps," she mumbled, grabbing a fallen apple of her own and lobbing it toward the primates.

She squeezed her eyes shut again and rolled over, away from the hairy alarm clocks and toward the tree's trunk, hoping for just a few more precious moments of rest for her growing twelve-year-old bones.

Thud!

Another object landed on the back of her head. This one felt softer than an apple. It crumbled on impact...and brought a stench with it. *Eww.* Ash hated those monkeys.

Ash was next roused by a thick wooden walking staff, whacked against her spine. That was worse than the apples and the...*not*-apple.

"Get up," barked an old woman's raspy voice. "We've got a full day of traveling if we're to reach Rosedale City in time to have a show tonight. That's gold in our pockets. Get up, you lazy girl! Up!"

"All right, all right," Ash whined, motioning for the old hag to cease her incessant staff thumping. "That stick's got pokey parts."

"Feed the beasts and pack up," the ugly, decrepit woman demanded as she disappeared into her personal tent.

For a crotchety, ill-tempered old witch, Tilda sure wasn't very pleasant. Supposedly, her name had once been Matilda the Wondrous for her dazzling works of magic and acrobatic broom flying. But that was when Tilda was much younger. Now she did nothing more than slap gnats out of her mangled, gray hair and enchant poor, aging animals with charms of beauty and illusion.

The monkeys let out high-pitched screeches in Ash's direction.

Ah yes, the animals, thought Ash as she finally pushed off the ground and hobbled onto her skinny legs. She brushed whatever crumbs were left from the monkey projectile out of her light-brown hair and straightened her raggedy, brown smock and olive-green pants. She threw on her boots (after dislodging a wayward snail from the left one's toe) and shot the howlers an evil glare as she walked toward the supply cart.

There were a total of six cars in Tilda's Traveling Circus of Mythical Beasts: five cages on wheels housing the animals and one cart in the front that carried provisions, all drawn by two docile Clydesdales.

Ash started with the end cart, gripping a bucket of grain. The cart housed an old unicorn, his once-shimmering white coat had become tinged with yellow as the years had gone by. His back was swayed and his mane was tattered, but his aging eyes still sparkled with the youthfulness of a foal every time he saw Ash.

"Good morning, Hero," Ash greeted, as she scooped grain into his feeding bucket. She had named him Hero because of the grand deeds she imagined him performing as a young, spry unicorn. Such exceptional caliber deserved to be recognized.

"Let's shine up that horn of yours."

Ash snatched a rag from her belt and polished the elderly beast's horn. The dirt spots disappeared, leaving only nicks and scrapes.

"And I would never forget your ear scratches. Come here, pretty boy. You itchy thing!" Ash scratched and rubbed Hero's long ears as she did every day. Hero leaned all of his body weight into it, closing his eyes and enjoying his favorite part of the morning routine.

"Hurry up, girl! We've got to get a move on to Rosedale!" Tilda yelled.

Normally, Ash hated getting up early and rushing the animals' breakfast, but today was different. Today, they were traveling to the last city on their tour before heading back to Oatsville. Her home. She'd get to see her father for the first time in six months.

She continued to the fourth cart, which held Perry the peryton, a skittish, shimmering turquoise stag with large wings. He began eating as soon as the grain hit his bucket.

Ash quickly tossed grain into the third cage holding the obnoxious monkey duo. The two hyperactive Ash-haters immediately flung their food back in her face, and at that moment she wished she'd named them something nastier than Benny and Bobby. Maybe Awful and Awfuler.

"Fine. No breakfast for you, then," she snapped, sticking her tongue out as she walked by. They howled and bounced around their cage as usual.

Next was the second cart. Ash slowed her gait. This cage held a very large kludde, a dark gray wolf with wings and a blue flame that always hovered above his head. His eyes glowed red, and his movements were intense and deliberate.

"Are we going to be friends today, Maurice?" she asked softly.

Maurice's slivered eyes locked on her like a target as he rested motionless on the floor. Ash took a deep breath and very carefully added grain to his bucket. The moment her arm reached through the steel bars, the dog's lips rumbled with a growl.

"...Maybe tomorrow then," she said with a nervous smile, removing her arm from his cage and moving to the next.

Finally, the front cart held a single bird, twice the size of a peregrine falcon. The creature sported breathtaking scarlet and orange plumage, with whirling amber eyes and a golden beak. This was a phoenix. Or at least that's what Tilda had told Ash. It was difficult to confirm the witch's claim when no one in twelve counties had seen a phoenix bird in over four hundred years. There were only vague descriptions and amateur drawings to compare it to. In all the books Ash had read and picked up on the road, she'd never found one that even mentioned the creature.

Ash was sure the bird was real. There was something regal about the way it behaved, as if the creature knew it was over-qualified as a circus attraction. Feeding him was Ash's favorite part of the morning.

"And a very good morning to you, Flynn."

The phoenix, resting on a wooden perch, cooed at the sight of her.

"How'd you sleep?" she asked him.

He tilted his head to the left.

"Good dream? Nightmare? Did you imagine floating in the wind, looking down on the countryside, scanning the fields with your keen eyes for the perfect worm to slurp up?"

He tilted his head to the right. Ash smiled softly and rested her head against one of the bars.

"You have no idea what I'm saying, do you?"

Flynn let out a single hiccup. It was so abrupt that it shook his whole body, and Ash couldn't help but laugh.

Ash reached for him and he leaned forward toward the bars. She softly stroked his head and picked moss and bugs out of his feathers. His plumage was rough to the touch, and Ash wondered if it had been like that his whole life or only now that he was older. When scratching behind his left wing, Ash noticed a small area with no feathers—just red, irritated skin.

"Miss Tilda, Flynn's got a bald spot on his back."

"Don't give the creatures names. I told you that," scolded Tilda, loading up the last of her tent pieces in the front cart. "The minute you name an animal you become attached, and they're nothing but horrid mongrels that would devour you in a heartbeat. They're not your friends. They get too old and lazy, I get rid of them."

"Yes, but Tilda, Fl—I mean, the phoenix has been so tired lately. And now his feathers are falling out."

Even as she spoke, four feathers from the bird's chest fluttered to the ground.

"He's fine. Come, get in the cart. We're late."

The journey to Rosedale was relaxing—the road was smooth and the sky was clear. Ash rested in the supply cart, listening to the clip-clop of the Clydesdales and flipping through the tattered pages of *Griffins & Hippogriffs: Differences & Similarities*. It was an old book she'd read maybe fifty times. Her small library consisted mostly of educational textbooks, but whenever she could acquire a book about magical creatures, it moved to the top of her reading list.

They turned onto a wide road that snaked through a shallow valley, but the route soon turned challenging. They were forced to traverse a gorge—a narrow, slippery road high up on a steep mountain that threatened a rockslide with their every step. Tilda snapped the whip on the Clydesdales' hindquarters as an order to push through their hesitation.

There was a loud *crack*. The convoy jolted. It sent Ash, Tilda, and the animals into a panic.

"The wheel! On the peryton's cage!" Tilda shouted, pointing to the problem.

The wooden wheel had severely fractured after hitting a sharp rock. The peryton inside the now-slanting cage bleated with fright. The other animals began panicking as well, and soon all the cars were wobbling to and fro on the edge of a cliff that did not allow for a lot of to-ing and fro-ing.

Tilda frantically searched the front cart for her wand, while Ash ran to the peryton's cage.

"Perry! Shh, calm down," Ash said. Then she sang, softly.

> *The road is long, for my darling dear*
> *The wind is cold, the sun's disappeared*
> *But don't be 'fraid, for this, too, will pass*
> *We'll lie soon down on green, silky grass*
> *We'll lie soon down on green, silky grass*

As Ash sang, the peryton became enthralled, almost hyp-notized. Even the other animals calmed and listened to Ash's soothing voice. Tilda quickly repaired the wheel with a zap of magic and they were ready to carry on.

"You're a good boy, Perry," Ash whispered. She slipped him a carrot from her pocket, where she always kept them.

"You done warbling then? Let's get moving," Tilda said.

Rosedale was a vivid sight, made even more beautiful by the glowing sun sinking into the hills behind it.

Every town and city in the land of Cascadia was named for whatever plant, animal, crop, or tree was the most plentiful in that region. Oatsville, the closest city to Ash's family farm, was where more oats were harvested than anywhere else. Just south of Oatsville was a small village known as Mosquito Swamp, which—well, it was not a very sought-after vacation spot.

But oh, Rosedale! What a vibrant, colorful city—a painter's palette. She couldn't imagine a lovelier place to live. Tilda and Ash had just entered the city through its wooden archway and already Ash had identified fifteen different types of wild roses. Yellows and reds were the most abundant, with every shade of pink as an unyielding second-place competitor. If it weren't for the hundreds of thorns that acted as little sentinels relentlessly protecting each innocent flower head, Ash would have swept up a bouquet of them in her arms. But she resisted. She never did like pokey things.

As their caravan rolled down Main Street, townspeople gathered. Confused and astonished, they ceased their business to chatter and gossip about the unusual visitors. Children ran beside the carts, *ooh*-ing and *aah*-ing at the fantastic creatures and arguing over which one was the most dangerous.

"Is that a unicorn?"

"Mummy! Can we go see the monkeys, please?"

"That be a kludde dog, it is. Never seen un, m'self!"

With a wave of Tilda's crooked wand, glitter magically rained down on the crowd and banners unrolled from the top of every cart:

Tilda's Traveling Circus of Mythical Beasts
A Spectacular Display of Dangerous Creatures!
Performances Every High Noon and
Evening at Sundown

The spectacle fed the crowd's curiosity perfectly. This wasn't the first time Tilda had lured an audience to her sideshow.

"You must set up for the show quickly tonight, girl. None of your dilly-dallying," Tilda whispered to Ash, still smiling and waving to the onlookers. "We've got them in our grasp."

Indeed, a large portion of the crowd had followed them all the way to the south edge of town, where they would set up camp and perform their show for exactly three days.

"Welcome, my friends! My lovers of magic! My darlings of danger!"

The witch greeted the salivating Rosedale onlookers, all dressed in clean suits and fashionable dresses. Tilda and Ash had parked the carts in a semi-circle and immediately proceeded with their show. Ash's first job was to close the red curtains on each cage, hiding the animals. She then scurried over to help Tilda get dressed in her performance garb, a pointy purple hat and black velvet cloak. Like a trained animal herself, Ash scurried backstage once more.

LISA FOILES

"Tonight, you will see not through your own eyes, but through eyes which may deceive you.... Is it real? Is it true? Is this the devil's work? Or is it the kind of magic in which only a child believes?" Tilda said.

Good, the fireworks from Tilda's wand were right on cue— Ash could tell by the excited audience reaction as she hid behind the cages. She threw on her own costume: a floppy green hat and matching robe with star and moon symbols, both about three sizes too big. Ash's least favorite part of the show was keeping that stupid hat from falling down over her eyes.

Tilda continued her opening speech. Ash had heard the monologue so many times, she mouthed the words while gathering her props.

A faint squawk came from the phoenix's cage.

"What's wrong, Flynn? You nervous?" Ash whispered. "I'm the only one who should be nervous. Have you seen that giant hound next to you? I'm crazy enough to take him out of his cage tonight. And he *hates me*."

More applause from the audience. Was that Tilda's joke about a dragon eating her spellbook and her taking the words right out of his mouth? No, that would be laughter, not applause. Ash still had a few more minutes before her cue.

"Let's see, harnesses, rope, ribbon hoops, baton..."

Ash heard some chatter from the monkey cage. She smiled devilishly.

"Ha! How could I forget my favorite part of the show?"

Ash snatched a bucket of water from the supply cart and faced the monkeys. "Terribly sorry I have to do this, but you know. Show business."

10

She tossed the bucket of water on the horrid twins, who jumped and screeched with displeasure.

The monkeys were the only members of the animal circus who were not, in fact, creatures of legend. They weren't magical, rare, mythical, any of those things. They were simply two howler monkeys from a jungle somewhere in North Cascadia. They were a fairly new addition to the circus, filling the center spot ever since Tilda's liger died. She had been a beautiful half-lion, half-tiger mix with a roar that could be heard for five miles and a purr that could be heard for two. Ash had named her Betty.

When Betty passed away in her sleep one night, Ash cried for six hours straight. Tilda, calloused and uncaring, spent that time seeking out someone who could bring her a replacement beast. She was promised two rare, magical water monkeys in exchange for three hundred gold pieces by a man named Jinpa. Though outraged at such a high price, Tilda agreed, planning to dupe him with copper coins and a simple spell when he came through.

But there was no need. Jinpa brought her two normal monkeys instead, claiming water monkeys had drowned three of his men while attempting to catch them. Tilda accepted the monkeys, cursed Jinpa with mule hooves as he ran from her, and continued on with her day. For Tilda, this was a standard transaction.

As a result, Ash splashed the howlers with water before every performance, then Tilda enchanted them with fangs, yellow eyes, and claws to look believable. No one had ever questioned it, so they continued the ruse.

"...and as I reached into the fiery dragon's massive jaws to retrieve my spellbook..."

Oh! That was Ash's cue. She ran to Hero's cage.

"...I took the words right out of his mouth." Tilda finished the joke, and the audience erupted with laughter.

"I have encountered every type of beast, both alive and undead, in Cascadia," Tilda continued, "but I will never again come across anything as beautiful...as the unicorn."

Ash unlatched the unicorn's cage, threw a rope around the horse's crooked neck, and led him out to the crowd.

With a wave of Tilda's wrinkled hand, she cast a spell on Hero before he came out to soften even the most cynical non-believer. The audience gasped. Hero was beautiful again. He pranced with the spunk of a horse half his age, and whinnied like a king among subjects. His mane and tail flowed untangled as he cantered in a circle before the crowd, and his coat was as white as the first snowfall of winter.

Ash felt goosebumps spread down her arms, as she did during every show. She never got used to seeing it. A real unicorn. A fairytale come to life.

The unicorn act was simple. Hero trotted around for a bit, jumped over Ash's baton, then touched Tilda's wand with his horn to create a giant beam of white light that illuminated the dark sky.

Next, the kludde act, by far the scariest. Ash didn't care how many times Tilda impatiently assured her that she cast the calming spell as soon as the curtain was opened. Ash was still leading a massive dog around by a thin piece of rope. A dog that could slice her body in half with one swipe of a toenail.

The kludde cooperated, growling at the audience and howling at the moon, then went back in his cage. His tail almost got caught in the cage door as Ash closed and locked it as fast as humanly possible. Ash released her stress with an exhale and moved on with the show.

The monkeys were next, and much easier to enchant due to the fact that they were just normal, boring animals. In fact, Tilda had them doing all sorts of tricks: somersaults, backflips, cartwheels, balancing acts like standing on each other's shoulders, then standing on each other's shoulders on top of Ash's shoulders. It was all very silly—and a bit degrading.

Next was the peryton, the beautiful stag with the large bird wings. Tilda enchanted his metallic coat to change colors, from blue to green to red. It reminded Ash of rainbow fish scales, shimmering beneath clear water. The peryton then reared up on his hind legs to show off his impressive wingspan. He flapped his wings twice and blew all the hats off the audience members. Ash would've seen it if her own hat hadn't fallen down over her eyes. Again.

At last, it was the finale. Ash's eyelids were already getting heavy. She let out a yawn before remembering she was more or less on stage. Tilda shot her a disapproving side-eye.

"Alas! We come to the end of our spectacle," Tilda announced. "You've seen fantastic, rare beasts, but not the rarest. Oh no, my children. These were all animals you could see flying in the night sky. Prancing through an enchanted forest. Lurking in your local swamp."

Three children in the front row widened their eyes to the size of dinner plates.

"But not this last beast. Adults claim he is a tall tale; little ones say he lives only in dreams. Rumors speak of magical powers that no wizard or warlock can match. The fairies whisper sightings, the trolls brag of recipes, and..."

She leaned in close and pointed south, in the direction of the ocean.

"Not even your beloved Regal Kin have one to boast."

A few words could be heard in the crowd. *Lies! Impossible! Can't be true!*

"The only one of its kind in all the world: the magnificent phoenix!"

Ash already had the bird's harness ready, and on cue, she flung open the cage door. The phoenix flew out of the cell. Fire burst from his wings, leaving a flaming trail in the air. He circled the audience three times, not spooked by their whoops, gasps, and wild applause.

Tilda had never been able to put a spell on the phoenix in all her years. Not that the bird actively resisted; he simply sat there as she tried spell after spell. Magic seemed to have no effect on him. This had been most unfortunate especially in the last five months, during which the bird started to show signs of age and frailty. The witch went on and on about how no one with half a mind would travel for miles or pay loads of gold to see a sleepy bird with wilting plumage.

The only thing that outraged Tilda more than the ugly phoenix was Ash suggesting they contact a Regal Kinsman for help. Tilda cursed the name of the Kin, calling them rich bigots and pompous warmongers, and, without explanation, sent Ash to her tent with no meals for two days. She survived only on the carrots in her pocket and anything edible the monkeys threw at her.

Ash hadn't the slightest idea why the Regal Kin were such a touchy subject. She'd grown up hearing fascinating stories about them from her father, about their great battles and triumphs throughout history. She could only imagine such a sight: an army of men, women, and beasts sworn to protect the King of Cascadia. Real people soaring on dragons, swimming with serpents, galloping on griffins—she had only seen these things depicted in paintings and books.

She desperately wished to see the beasts in action, but it didn't seem likely that any great wars would take place near the little farm town of Oatsville. During her travels with Tilda, Ash swore that she had once seen a man flying through the clouds over Granite City on a horse with a chicken's head. Tilda whacked her on the noggin with her walking stick as punishment for making up lies. Two days of scrubbing the cages from top to bottom.

The phoenix landed on Ash's arm and jerked her out of her thoughts. The show!

Ash trembled as usual while holding up the heavy bird with just one skinny forearm. "Pale and frail," the kids in Oatsville used to call her. Sadly, by the looks of his diminishing feathers and weight, it appeared Flynn the phoenix was joining her in that description.

Ash tuned out Tilda's final speech about the "fabled phoenix of fantasy" and turned her eyes to Flynn instead. He looked even worse than earlier. His eyes seemed to be glazed over, and a few of his talons had even fallen out. Ash felt more than just sadness for the creature. She felt guilt. She wished she'd spent more time before the show cleaning him up, maybe oiling his wings. No bird that regal should be paraded around looking so pitiful. He was a legend, after all.

After one more flight, Flynn returned to his cage and Ash locked him in. She stroked his head a few times before returning to Tilda.

The crowd erupted in applause for Tilda's final bow and last thank you to each of her celebrity beasts. Ash wondered why she never got a thank you in the finale. Maybe she needed to be hairier with a few more hooves. Or sprout a pair of wings. It seemed unlikely.

Tilda snapped for Ash to assist her as the satisfied show-goers reached into their pockets for gold and silver pieces. A wealthy town like Rosedale would undoubtedly turn a hefty profit for their first show of the weekend. Ash could only imagine how much they'd amass after Saturday and Sunday.

Tilda and Ash both turned their hats upside down as coin collectors. A few townspeople attempted to shove past the two performers for a closer look at the animals.

"Paid viewing hours are tomorrow, mid-morning! No one is allowed in tonight," Tilda barked, using a much harsher tone with her adoring fans than just moments prior during the show. Performer Tilda and Real Tilda were vastly different individuals.

Ash sometimes wished the show would never end.

The calmness of post-performance set in. The crowd had gone home. The animals rested. The only movement was a rat that scurried about the wheels of the carts.

"Show's over, bub," Ash said to him. The rat snatched a piece of grain from a feed bucket and hurried away.

Ash had erected Tilda's tent, fed all of the animals, replenished their water, and quietly slipped them vegetables from Tilda's food supply before the old hag even finished counting the money. The witch was in a trance. There was nothing she loved more than glittering stacks of coins.

"Looks like a lot tonight!" Ash said with a smile.

Tilda exhaled loudly, suppressing her frustration at being interrupted.

"Yes, child."

"That's even more stacks than all of last weekend's shows combined! I suppose Rosedale really is a wealthy town. Could you imagine living here? With all these beautiful roses?"

"No. This isn't a place for people like you and me," Tilda replied. "We don't belong."

Ash fetched her rolled-up tent from the supply cart and stood it on its end. Before building, she leaned against it and gazed at the stars. "Maybe not now. But maybe someday."

Tilda finished counting and began scooping the coins into a canvas bag.

"Enough of that, girl," she said. "Know your place in this world. You weren't born into royalty or riches. You'll never be part of those families. Your father is a poor oats farmer, his father was a poor oats farmer, and when you're older, you'll be a poor oats farmer."

Ash looked toward the south. Somewhere out there was a castle. And the Regal Kin. And all sorts of adventures.

"You have to be born special, Ashtyn," Tilda said. "It was never in the cards for you."

Ash wondered if Tilda meant metaphorical cards or the actual tarot cards she used to predict peoples' futures when moonlighting as a charlatan psychic. Perhaps it didn't matter.

"Well, at least we did well tonight. Will you send my father my portion of the earnings tomorrow morning, straight away? I know he'll be thrilled to receive it. He pays rent end of September. It's always a tough month for him."

Tilda quickly mumbled, "Yes, yes, fine," as she took the bag of coins into her tent.

"Tilda?" Ash said, pushing her luck with the witch in hopes she'd be too consumed with money thoughts to punish her impertinence.

"What do you want, you horrid girl? Out with it."

Ash bit her lip. "Do you ever wish you were one of the Regal Kin?"

This was a question that under normal circumstances would reward Ash with no meals for several days or even a beating. But Tilda indulged her.

"To wish is to be a fool," she replied. "The Academy is for the rich and privileged. And we're nothing but peasants."

Ash looked down at her feet. Rips in her pants, holes in her boots...she could even see her toes wiggle. She wouldn't be able to afford new ones for years. Not with her father needing all the money she earned.

"I will hear nothing more about this as long as I'm living, do you understand?" Tilda said, back to her usual stern tone.

Ash nodded.

Tilda disappeared inside her tent for the night and Ash finished setting up her own. The animals were dozing, even the usually energetic peryton.

Maybe the old witch was right. Maybe she would never be privileged. But in just six more days, she'd be somewhere she knew she belonged: at home with her father in humble Oatsville.

CHAPTER 2

THE UNFORTUNATE VISITOR

sh thought that waking up to the pungent aroma of roses was even more delightful than waking to the smell of breakfast. Not that Ash had enjoyed a home-cooked meal in months. She concluded that eating bacon would have been more delicious than the ant-infested rose petals of Rosedale.

She skipped having a meal entirely and went straight to work tending to the animals. Best to get a jumpstart on chores, knowing Tilda would likely be cross with her after last night's conversation. She'd lie low today.

The enchantments placed on the animals from the show had worn off, leaving the beasts looking unkempt, per usual.

Hero shook some bees off his face and whinnied with frustration. He'd just discovered the downside of having a city overrun with flowers: bugs. Lots and lots of bugs.

Ash was brushing Perry's hind legs when he was spooked by Tilda's sudden exit from her tent. The witch gripped her bag of coins, threw a tattered scarf around her neck, and headed toward Main Street.

"Are you going into town to send my father the money today?" Ash blurted. *Oops, so much for lying low,* she thought.

Tilda turned and walked slowly toward her.

"Tell me, do I constantly interrupt you?" she asked.

Yes. "No, ma'am."

"Do I question how you care for these animals? Do I poke a nose into your business?"

Yes and yes. "No, ma'am."

"Then keep your insolent nose out of mine!" Tilda barked. "Perhaps I shouldn't send your father any of this money as a result of your prying?"

Ash stiffened up and bit her tongue.

"That's what I thought," said Tilda. "I'll get a courier while I'm in town. Clean up this awful mess! There are props lying everywhere from last night, have you no sense?"

Tilda glanced toward a family of four—wealthy, from their attire—waiting nearby. She immediately forced a smile and waved.

"Take admittance for viewings. I'll return shortly," she whispered through grinning teeth. "And smile!"

Tilda thrust her walking stick at Ash's toes. Ash yelped, then quickly smiled at the family.

LISA FOILES

Once Tilda hobbled off down the bustling city streets and
Ash regained feeling in her two smallest toes, she approached
the mother and father. They had two small children, a boy and
girl, weaving in and out of their legs. They growled at each
other like very small, non-threatening lions.

"It's two gold pieces each to see the animals, or twenty
silver," she said.

The father smiled and reached for his pockets. "Quite rea-
sonable to see such incredible creatures." He handed her the
money. "Which shall we see first?"

"Oh, it's not a tour," Ash said nervously. "You can just see
them and say hello. Keep your hands outside the bars."

"Nonsense!" the father replied as they approached the carts.
The two children grew less and less courageous with every step
toward the beasts. "We'd like to hear about them from their
caretaker."

Ash blushed. Normally Tilda talked to the customers and
everyone treated the "caretaker" as if she didn't exist.

"Well, I don't know much," she began. "But I suppose it's
interesting to know that the peryton—that's Perry, here—
loves music. He'll stop anything he's doing to listen to music,
no matter what the situation. In fact, all the animals really
respond to music and singing."

Except those wretched monkeys.

"Oh, and he can change the colors of his coat to blend in
with his surroundings."

"Yes! We saw that in the show last night," said the mother.
The kids were now clutched to her calves, eyeing the kludde.
The kludde eyed them back.

"Actually, that was a bit of a spell by Miss Tilda. Normally, they change colors much more slowly and not quite as vibrantly. Most commonly, they turn their bellies light blue—so that when they're flying, no one can spot them against the sky."

"Fascinating!" said the father.

Ash started to gain confidence. She never knew how much she loved talking about the animals.

"And the kludde is over here," Ash walked toward the large dog. The children did not. "I call him Maurice. He's actually small, believe it or not. According to rumor, he could grow to be two, maybe three times his current size."

Maurice growled. The children gasped, and one started to cry. The parents were too intrigued to care.

"Is he a baby?" asked the father.

"Oh, no. He's only small because of the cage. Like a fish, he'll only grow as big as the pond he's in. Or cage, I guess. Also, he loves eating rabbits, ground squirrels, and carrots. They all love carrots. Would you like to feed one to the unicorn?"

Those were the magic words that brightened the faces of the frightened brother and sister. They cheered and ran to the unicorn's cage. Ash handed the mother a carrot.

"He's really quite friendly. Just hold out your hand flat, like this."

The mother smiled, took the carrot, and joined the children by the unicorn. The father remained with Ash.

"I'll let them play," he said. "I'm more interested in you telling me about this red bird."

The father walked toward the phoenix and studied it intently. Ash had plenty of fun facts about the bird. His wingspan reached from one end of the cage to the other. The texture of his feathers never allowed him to stay wet. His eyes changed colors from yellow to red when he was upset. He liked eating worms but not spiders, berries but not apples, sunflower seeds but not corn seeds. His body was always warm to the touch, even in the coldest weather.

But she couldn't bring herself to say any of it, not when three of his hind feathers drifted to the ground as he shifted. He was tired and weak, and let out what sounded like a human child's cough.

He shouldn't be seen by people, she thought. *Not like this.*

"Sorry, sir, I don't really—"

She was interrupted by two boys, about ten, running into the semi-circle of the caravan, kicking up dust with each step.

"Dad! Mum! Did'ya see her fly in?" said one of the boys to the couple, out of breath. He turned to Ash. "You, girl! Did you see her?"

"I don't know what you're talking about, and you can't be in here without paying," Ash said sternly.

"On the northeast end of town, by the big weepin' fern!" said the other boy, as if Ash were stupid.

"Boys, slow down, what are you both going on about?" asked their father.

"There's one of the Regal Kin!" They spoke in perfect sync.

Regal Kin. In Rosedale? It was so far from the kingdom. It couldn't be.

"It's a girl!"

"A pretty girl."

"A woman, actually."

"Yes, a very pretty woman. And tall."

"She's got a pegasus!"

"I wanted to tell them that part!"

"Then talk faster!"

Ash couldn't process it all with the back-and-forth chatter. "Quiet, both of you! You mean it? A Regal Kinswoman? Here?"

The first boy spoke up, barely edging out the second. "We saw her! They said she's here to pick up a relative to take to the Academy tomorrow morning! Mum, Dad, come on!"

"We want to see her!"

Ash's heart beat so hard she thought it would break loose from her chest and go hopping down Main Street. After a lifetime of bedtime stories and reading countless books, could she actually meet one of the Regal Kin?

The two excited boys ran back into town, followed by their briskly walking parents and siblings.

"I can't go.... I have to stay and work," Ash whispered to no one.

She stood in a trance, wondering if there was any miracle on earth that would allow her to leave her post and catch a glimpse of the Kinswoman. A real member of the Regal Kin. With a pegasus.

Ash blinked her eyes and instantly returned to reality when she saw an enraged Tilda rushing back to camp, like an old, pudgy bull that had just been jabbed by a cattle prod.

"What's wrong? Did you get the courier?" Ash asked, wincing as she said it and knowing she shouldn't have. She noticed the witch was sporting a brand-new hat, robe, and leather boots...and they looked rather expensive.

"The bird! The bird!" Tilda shouted. "Hurry, that meddlesome, snooping tart will be here at any moment! That awful wench!"

Ash had never seen Tilda so rattled. She began sifting through the supply cart like a madwoman, tossing items over her shoulder, not caring if they broke.

"Where's the robin?" she screamed at Ash, grabbing her by both shoulders.

"In my tent," she replied. "I always keep it with me."

"Switch the birds now! No time to waste!"

Oh! Now Ash knew what Tilda was ranting about.

When Ash entered into Tilda's employment years ago, one of the protocols they'd discussed was what to do when someone visited their camp with the intent of ridding them of their beasts. "Threatening to steal them" was how Tilda put it. The simplest way to persuade someone not to steal a magical beast was to convince the individual that the beast was not magic at all. That, or Tilda would just zap the thief with a spark from her wand. Ash suspected the latter wouldn't be an option in their current scenario.

As a precaution, Tilda and Ash always traveled with a birdcage containing one small robin. When any threatening parties asked about their most valuable animal, Ash would stealthily switch out the birds. Tilda would then cast an illusion spell on the unknowing fowl while Flynn sat quietly in Ash's tent.

That is, if "sat quietly" translated to "squawked and flapped his wings in terror-stricken hysteria."

They'd only performed the switcheroo thrice prior, and all three times, Ash ended up wrestling the frantic Flynn to the ground in a feather-flying frenzy. Once Ash got a grip on his beak and tackled the rest of him to the floor, the bird would stay fairly quiet for the remainder of the operation.

It was that time again.

Ash burst through the floppy cloth door of her tent and quickly but tenderly snatched the robin from the birdcage. She'd been taking care of Gertrude along with the other animals for so long, she'd nearly forgotten the little thing's very important job.

Ash set Gertrude inside Flynn's cage and quickly grabbed the phoenix, rushing him back to the tent. She didn't wait around to see Tilda place the spell on the tiny robin; she was much more preoccupied with the wild beast she was hiding.

But Flynn didn't wriggle this time.

Ash could only hear what was going on outside her tent, but it sounded like a crowd of people had gathered. A very large crowd. Larger than their show last night.

Still gripping Flynn, Ash peeked through a slit in her tent's door.

"Welcome to Tilda's Traveling Circus of Mythical Beasts!" Tilda shouted to the crowd with an affected smile. "I do believe we have a special guest?"

Out of the crowd stepped a most exquisite sight.

It was a tall, pale woman. She had platinum hair down to her waist and she glowed as if she were not human. She looked neither young nor old, but the wisdom of many years was reflected in her eyes. Her airy, white dress was accented with gold and Ash noticed her feet were bare as she stepped forward.

"Wow..." Ash uttered under her breath.

"I am Odetta. You must be the woman in charge of this carnival."

The lady spoke slowly and softly, in a most peaceful tone. The crowd went silent as she spoke, gawking at her beauty. One girl about Ash's age hid slightly behind Odetta. She wore a similar white dress and had curly, light blonde hair. A cute girl, save for the scowl.

"Why yes, my child," Tilda replied, quite disingenuously. Her raspy voice complemented Odetta's like claws against silk. "What an honor to have a warrior of the Kin at our little sideshow."

She's Regal Kin! Of course!

Ash completely forgot about the phoenix she was holding, partly because of the commotion outside and partly because Flynn was too tired to budge.

"I've heard great things about your show, Witch Tilda. That it is an enjoyable performance, showcasing your rare creatures," Odetta said.

Tilda appeared to grow more and more uncomfortable. "The show is at noon! Why don't you come back then and see it for yourself?" Tilda barked.

Odetta smiled softly, unmoved by Tilda's disrespect. "If the rumors spreading through Rosedale are true, Miss Tilda, then you are in possession of a very rare and very dangerous creature. In fact, the only one of its kind. A phoenix. As Kin, I have a great personal interest in magical creatures. If it is not too much trouble, I would like to see it."

Tilda's grimace turned to an eerie grin. "Of course, my child. Right this way."

Tilda extended her hand for Odetta's, looking like a decaying shrew hoping to suck some youth and beauty from the enchanting woman. She led Odetta to the phoenix cage and pulled back the curtain. Inside was a large red bird, the size of an eagle, with bright red feathers and flames shooting out from its wingtips. The bird screeched and flapped its wings, sending a wave of heat over the crowd.

Odetta smiled and turned to Tilda. "You are very clever, old woman. But that is not a phoenix you possess."

She looked to the other cages. "I see now that this show is made of nothing more than simple charms cast on poor, aging animals. I pray you use discretion, dear witch. Be wise in your jesting. It would be heartbreaking should any of them drown in the wake of your financial agenda."

Tilda heard the rebuke in Odetta's voice. She furrowed her already wrinkled brow. Ash waited for steam to shoot out of her hairy ears.

"You've spoken your mind, now leave an old woman in peace!" Tilda shouted. "I'll already lose half a month's profit because of your snobbish meddling and careless bean-spilling! Leave me! Leave!"

Most of the crowd backed away and returned to their bustling, while some stayed with Odetta, perhaps hoping she would make the grumpy witch vanish.

Odetta smiled and nodded a thank you to Tilda, then she and the scowling girl headed back into town.

Once the crowd cleared, Tilda let out a shrill string of curse words and threw her new hat onto the ground. Ash slipped out of her tent to return both birds to their original cages.

"The nerve of that impudent hussy! How dare she!" Tilda kicked the grain bucket, spilling the animals' lunch onto the dirt. Ash began scooping it back in.

A bell rang out from deep within the city.

"Noon! Noon already! Do you realize what this means?" Tilda continued. "No one is here for our noon show, no one will come to our night show, no one will come the rest of the weekend!"

Tilda cast her walking stick to the ground, causing dust to fly in Ash's eyes.

"Maybe they will...maybe we'll just give people a few hours—"

"No, you foolish girl!" Tilda screamed. She took a moment to think. "We will pack up tomorrow."

"Tomorrow? But—"

"This town is ruined for us. We'll move on."

"And go straight to Oatsville?" Ash asked, hope in her voice.

"No," Tilda answered. "We're still short half this month's profit. We'll leave straight for Toadberg in the morning."

Toadberg! That miserable, frog-infested mudtown was eight days' travel in the opposite direction of Oatsville. Even if weather allowed, the journey would be over sixteen days of slogging through marshlands before returning home.

"But Tilda, we can't—"

Tilda reared back and slapped Ash hard across the face.

"Enough!"

Ash's eyes welled up with tears from the sting of her cheek. She blinked them back and nodded.

Ash dared not speak the remainder of the day. They proceeded with their two remaining shows, but hardly a dozen townspeople came. They hadn't even properly finished the evening show before Tilda shooed the crowd away, frightening a small girl holding a toy unicorn. She flung her staff across the campsite and disappeared inside her tent for the night.

The visit from the Regal Kinswoman had been bittersweet. Odetta's beauty was unmatched, a living, breathing work of art who would float through Ash's dreams for weeks to come. But her inquiry regarding the phoenix had cost Tilda her gold, and Ash her brief freedom.

It had been a long five years since Tilda had rolled into Oatsville and offered Ash's father, Landon, a proposition. He was a penniless farmer with a waning business and a young daughter. Taxes were high and making ends meet was becoming impossible. Ash's mother had died in childbirth, and Landon had been forced to educate Ash at home because he couldn't afford schooling. Most people would have seen their situation as a tragedy—Tilda saw it as an opportunity.

Tilda needed an assistant; Landon and Ash needed money. Landon refused at first, but Ash insisted, and the deal was struck. She'd go on the road with Tilda as her stablehand. Half of her earnings would be sent back to Landon and the Ridleys would stay afloat. As an additional part of their arrangement, Tilda would return Ash to Oatsville every March for one week and then again in September for the last two weeks of the month.

Just the thought of those breaks kept Ash going, and gave her something wonderful to look forward to.

CHAPTER 3

LANDON RIDLEY

TWO YEARS AGO

The sun is a cruel adversary when trying to be invisible. Ash refused to let shadows give away her position as she ducked behind the back of her farmhouse, heart pounding so vigorously it was practically audible. He would be there any moment. He would find her.

With her back against the splintered wooden siding, she scanned the area. A parade of chickens weaved through the legs of a dusty mule. Goats bleated to be let out of their barbed wire pen. Two hogs slurped from the water trough.

Ash gasped as she heard the rickety screen door around the front of the house bang shut. She darted behind a stack of crates, crawled over a rusty wagon, and narrowly escaped landing on two skittish cats. They hissed their disapproval, but Ash was already on the move.

She glanced behind her. No one seemed to be coming around the side of the house yet, unless they were spying from a hiding place of their own. Ash's eyes were set on the large chicken coop nestled between the cow pen and the grain bins. Her bare feet, calloused from years spent outdoors, kicked up dust as she darted toward her destination. The whinnies, clucks, and snorts of the bustling farm did well to conceal the sound of her soles slapping the dirt.

A lazy hog turned into her path, and Ash had to think fast. She dove over the pig and landed with a somersault in the mud on the other side. The mess didn't faze her; after all, her sundress was just a cut-up burlap sack with a twine belt. Easily replaced.

The clash of falling equipment behind her confirmed exactly what she'd suspected: he was close.

Ash didn't bother with the squeaky coop door—she crept up its side ramp and squeezed through the window. She curled into a ball on the pine-shavings-covered floor, while shelves of hens above her gossiped and bickered. He'd never find her here.

A brown duck appeared in the window where she entered. *Quack.*

Ash raised her eyebrows.

Quack quack.

"Hey, quit it," she whispered. "Go away!"

QUACK QUACK QUACK!

Someone grabbed the outside handle of the coop. Ash clapped her hands over her mouth.

The door swung open and blinding sunlight poured in.

"A-HA! The prisoner has been located!"

Ash sighed and rolled her eyes. She looked at the duck. "Thanks. Thanks a lot."

"Now, before I free you...you must answer my riddle," her captor said. "Until I am measured, I am not known, yet how you miss me when I have flown. What am I?"

Ash concentrated. She was no prodigy at ten years old, but riddles and logic came much easier to her than traditional arithmetic problems or scientific equations.

"Time?" she replied.

Her father, Landon, grabbed her waist and lifted her out of the smelly henhouse. Ash erupted in giggles as he spun her skinny frame around until she was nearly sick. Her answer must have been correct.

He set her down and she dizzily stumbled into Jemima the mule.

"The chicken coop? Really, Ashtyn? We've played hide-and-seek together for so long, and after ten years of practice, you choose *the chicken coop?*"

Ash placed her hands on her hips. "Hey, last time I dove into the barn loft and was picking out hay splinters for a week afterward. I wanted something less pokey this time."

Landon smiled and shook his head. His messy, chestnut hair fell over his wrinkled eyes, and he brushed it aside with the back of his hand.

"Sit down, will ya?"

Ash's brows furrowed. "In the mud?"

"You're already muddy."

He had a point. She shrugged and took a seat near the water trough on the dampened dirt, courtesy of post-slurp droplets from animal snouts.

Landon untied a sack from his waist. "Your Highness, Princess Ashtyn Ridley, I present you with a gift on this fine holiday. May you continue to rule your kingdom with grace, wisdom, and a pronounced aversion to horseflies."

Ash was conveniently swatting one away as he finished his speech. Landon placed the sack in Ash's lap.

"Wait, what fine holiday is it?"

Ash could see her father mentally reaching. "It's Random Gift Wednesday! Obviously."

Ash giggled. "What's Random Gift Wednesday?"

"I think it's fairly self-explanatory," Landon said, smiling. His grin faded to a serious one. "We miss so many holidays together while you're on the road with Tilda, Ash. Maybe this can be all of them rolled into one...if that's all right."

Ash returned a half smile. She hated Tilda's name even being mentioned during her short vacation away from the witch. She had a full week to spend with her father—no cage cleaning, no fussy perytons, no manure shoveling, and, most importantly, no Tilda.

"Well? Open it already!"

Ash reached into the sack and pulled out two pocket-sized paperback books. "*Proper Grammar and Punctuation Workbook* and *The First Sea Serpents of Cascadia!*"

"One for your brain, one for your imagination," Landon specified.

Ash had never read a book about sea serpents before—she was thrilled to add it to her collection. It would be another perfect distraction while traveling the countryside.

"There's something else," her father said with a twinkle in his eye.

Ash reached inside the sack to find another sack. A smaller one this time—a velvet, purple pouch with a yellow drawstring. Landon nodded for her to proceed. From the pouch, she drew an odd, wooden musical device.

"A flute?"

"A pan flute," her father corrected. "See, it's got five pipes, each a tad longer than the previous. The smallest pipe will make the highest pitch and the longest, the lowest."

Ash examined the weird instrument, feeling the smooth pipes with her fingers. "You made this?"

"I carved it, yes," he answered. "You have such a natural talent for music, Ash. You love singing to the animals, and it even calms them down and lulls them to sleep. Unless you're just boring them..."

Ash playfully punched him in the shoulder.

"Now you have an instrument to master. Try to match my pitch."

Landon whistled a sustained note. Ash blew into the flute. After a few tries, moving her lips horizontally across the pipes, she hit the right note. Landon whistled a higher note. Ash matched it. Landon trilled a beautiful, complex little tune, fit for a songbird. Ash chuckled.

"Don't think I'm quite there yet," she said with a smile. Her father was a fantastic whistler. She knew that she got her musical talent from him.

"You like?"

"I love," Ash replied. She pursed her lips. "I don't have a gift for you, though."

Landon gasped. "How dare you not come prepared to a holiday celebration you knew nothing about!"

Ash frantically looked around the farmyard. She saw grain buckets, watering cans, that brown, tattletale duck—no, those would be terrible gifts. She sprang to her feet and returned to her chicken coop hiding spot. With an "excuse me, sorry," she snatched an egg from one of the hens. On her way back to Landon, she picked a yellow dandelion from a patch of weeds.

She sat down and began rubbing the dandelion head all over the white egg, staining it a bright yellow. She inspected her work and presented it to her father.

"For King Dad, a most rare offering on Random...what was it?"

"Random Gift Wednesday," he whispered.

"Random Gift Wednesday! For this is a golden dragon egg, stolen from a mother dragon most foul. It will hatch and then you can start breeding dragons. And people will come for miles to see your dragon farm! I mean, kingdom."

Her father accepted the yellow egg with a kingly bow. He held it up, opened his mouth to make a royal speech, but stopped. Something caught his eye in the far distance behind Ash and his entire demeanor changed.

"What is it?" Ash asked.

Landon rose to his feet, stuck the egg in his back pocket, and grabbed Ash's hand.

"Come on, hurry!"

Ash wasn't sure what her father had seen, but she was sure that she should have grabbed shoes before sprinting across a freshly-cut field. Even on her calloused soles, the dried crop remains were still pokey.

Landon led her down a hill toward a clump of tall trees. Ash knew the spot well—it was a peaceful little grove with a small pond. It was a popular gathering place for moose and deer, and many fawns were born in its shelter each spring.

Her father signaled for Ash to slow her movements and keep quiet. They crept behind a large boulder and peeked into the trees.

There, drinking at the pond with a herd of deer, was a griffin. A real, live griffin. An actual magical creature stood twenty feet in front of them, mingling with common fauna, like a prince among peasants. It was so rare to see one up close.

"Wow..." Ash uttered to herself.

The griffin was a mesmerizing sight. He had the body, back legs, and tail of a lion, and was the size of an average horse. Its head, however, was that of an eagle, with a rounded, golden beak. He had sharp front talons that dug into the grass and enormous eagle wings folded to his side. He was simply majestic.

Ash had read all about this animal in her *Griffins & Hippogriffs* book and she couldn't understand why the beast wasn't tearing the deer limb from limb. He was a beast of prey and they were easy dinner. But no, they were co-existing and leaving each other be. He only seemed to be thirsty.

As the grand creature dipped his beak into the pond and threw his head back to swallow, Ash turned to her father.

"So he's what you saw!"

"He flew into the trees behind you and I knew those weren't average wings," he whispered back.

"Why is he so calm?" Ash asked.

"Well," Landon began. "I'm guessing because he's exhausted. He limped away from a great battle with a narrow victory. I believe just this morning he had to defeat a hideous mother dragon in order to retrieve her golden egg. For a desperate princess desired to give it to her father."

Ash smiled. It was a lovely daydream.

The griffin suddenly jerked his head up from the water. The deer pricked up their ears, as well. They shot panicked looks toward the top of the hill. A clamor echoed through the valley, a distant pounding and a loud, angry voice. It was coming from the farmhouse.

As the griffin looked up, he noticed Ash and Landon. They tensed. The griffin's gaze was locked on the duo. Even from their distance, they could see the creature's black pupils narrow into slits, as his focus cut through them with piercing intensity.

The blood drained from the faces of the father and daughter. They could see nothing but the razor sharpness of the griffin's beak glistening in the sunlight—a beak that could be plunged into their throats in a matter of seconds.

Another loud pound came from the farm. It broke the griffin's eye contact and he looked once again toward the hill. The deer scattered. With one final warning glance to the pair, the griffin's lion legs pushed off and he bolted away, deep into the trees.

Ash and Landon immediately ran for the farmhouse. There was no time to discuss what had happened—they were alive, that was all that mattered.

The two entered the house through the back door, but not without Ash first sweeping her books and pan flute off the ground to bring them inside. A fist brutally slammed against the front door and a gruff man's voice demanded he be answered.

Ash stuttered with panic. "Who is that, Dad? Is that—"

"Stay inside, Ash," Landon said intensely.

"But I—"

"Stay inside!"

Ash backed away from her father and stood in the kitchen. Landon exited the front door. Before he closed the door behind him, Ash heard the man shout, *"You dare keep a royal tax collector waiting, Ridley?"*

It was all muffled after that. Landon's voice argued, the man's voice returned no sympathy. Landon seemed to beg; the man seemed not to care.

Dust exploded from the door as a body was forcefully slammed against it. Ash gasped. She always suspected the tax collectors pushed her father around, but she'd never witnessed it.

The shouting ceased. Boots stomped off the patio and a horse galloped away. It was over, whatever it was.

A clearly shaken Landon returned inside. Ash remained frozen in the kitchen.

Landon reached into his back pocket, which was now dripping with thick, slimy liquid. He retrieved broken pieces of yellow eggshell.

"I...I guess we'll have to postpone the dragon farm," he said with forced optimism.

Tears poured from Ash's eyes.

Landon rushed to her, grabbing her by the shoulders.

"Hey, hey, shh, shh," he reassured sweetly, sitting her down at the rickety kitchen table. "Hey, it's all right. You think that ugly guy scares me? Nah. Now that griffin, that scared me."

Ash wasn't having any of his humor. Landon cut the act.

"Do we have enough?" Ash uttered through the sobs.

Landon sighed and took a moment to collect himself. "No. No, we don't. And he'll be back."

Ash scrunched her face with anguish.

"They keep raising our fees, I don't know why. But I can't change it. I just need to put in a little more work to make ends meet, that's all."

"But you already work so hard! You work all day and all night and never get a break! You work harder than anyone in Cascadia! I'll do it, Dad. I'll stay with Tilda through September, I won't take time off. I'll pick up small jobs in towns we pass through, I can earn extra—"

Landon laughed and hugged her close, her eyes dampening his dirty white shirt. "It already kills me that you have to work in the first place, Ashtyn."

"I don't care. I want to."

Landon broke the hug and straightened her shoulders. He looked her right in the eyes, even though she refused to look back. He softly sang to her, the ending of a lullaby he'd always sung to her.

"But don't be 'fraid, for this, too, will pass..."

She finally met his gaze.

"We'll lie soon down on green, silky grass."

And with the final lyric, he smiled at his beautiful daughter, and wiped the tears from her cheeks.

CHAPTER 4

A LEGEND REBORN

Ash was lost in the memories of her father while serving the animals their dinner under the pallid moon. She didn't even stop to make a face at the awful monkeys reaching through the bars in an attempt to grab a chunk of her hair.

Her trip home was delayed a few weeks, but Ash wouldn't cave to heartbreak. She'd still get to see her father in the near future. She wished she could send him a message via a courier or a carrier pigeon, but Tilda would never lend her the money, and she'd get in trouble just for asking. Her only option was to be patient. Perhaps she'd find some activities to help the time pass. Maybe she'd weave a necklace out of strands from Hero's tail as a gift for the next Random Gift Wednesday. Or maybe she'd see how many slimy, warty Toadberg frogs she could fit inside Tilda's boots.

A loud hiccough snapped Ash out of her thoughts. It was the phoenix.

"What's wrong, Flynn? You thirsty?"

Ash glanced to his water bucket. Full.

Flynn coughed three times as a dozen feathers shed from his back. He was losing his reddish color and there was oozing around his eyes.

Ash reached in the cage to stroke him. He was cold. He was never cold. Since the day she'd first felt him, he'd been warm, almost hot to the touch. Flynn quivered as she stroked his back, as if the mere contact were painful.

She searched the supply cart as quietly as possible to not wake the sleeping witch, and gathered different types of food. Apples, grain, lettuce, carrots—he didn't want any of it. In fact, the seed in his feed bucket hadn't been touched all day. How had she not noticed?

Flynn's coughing turned to desperate wheezing. He shivered. Ash knew she couldn't leave him—not tonight. She thought about bringing him into her tent, but he seemed too delicate to move. Instead, she fetched a blanket and curled up in the dirt beside the cage. It wouldn't be the most comfortable sleep, but no one, not even a bird, should be alone when they're sick.

Hours passed and the night sky was at its blackest. Nothing but crickets and distant howling could be heard. Ash had somehow drifted to sleep with her head resting on the cart's wheel. Not exactly the most un-pokey of pillows.

It took Ash a few groggy moments to realize that she wasn't dreaming of loud gagging sounds. They were coming from Flynn.

Ash quickly woke. She got to her knees to be eye-level with Flynn, who had left his wooden perch and was now on the floor of his cage, shivering even more violently. He was sitting in a pile of his own molted feathers, gagging, hacking, coughing—over and over.

"Shh, shh, Flynn," she whispered, "It's all right, Flynn. Just...breathe. Lie down."

She reached through the bars to gently nudge his body to a prone position. He was freezing, and his entire right side of feathers fell off as she touched him. Nearly all his feathers were gone now.

He wheezed and gasped, trembling against the ground. Ash felt her heart rate double. A tear ran down her cheek. She couldn't even think of what to do. Wake Tilda? Take him to a doctor? Find Odetta somehow?

As her mind raced, Flynn began to convulse. His body jolted and jerked. He contorted grotesquely, as if some unnatural force was trying to rip his frail body apart. He screeched loudly with pain.

With a blinding flash of white light, Flynn burst into a brilliant fire. Every part of him was ablaze with orange flames that licked the air. The bright flare lit the entire campsite.

Ash gasped and squinted at the light. She could make out Flynn's silhouette amongst the flames. His eyes were closed and his chest expanded, as if he were breathing in the heat. He spread his wings and straightened to a stand, looking not like a withered old fowl, but like a supernatural, heavenly being.

The light began to fade and the flames shrank, quickly. The bird shriveled, smaller and smaller, until he disappeared.

The camp was dark once again. All was quiet. Ash gripped the bars. Nothing was left in the cage except a pile of black ashes. The phoenix was gone.

Ash covered her mouth, as hot, stinging tears poured from her eyes.

"Oh, Flynn!" she whispered.

The unicorn, the peryton, the kludde, even the monkeys—all were motionless and silent, as if they understood the gravity of one of their own dying.

Ash was crying harder now, not caring if Tilda woke to her wails. Let Tilda beat her, take away her food, leave her here to rot. Nothing mattered. She was as trapped as the phoenix in that cage, never to fly, never to live again. Such beauty, such a kingly beast turned to nothing but dust in Tilda's toxic circus of the damned and unwanted. Was not every animal and human in this traveling masquerade simply a shell of their former selves? An infirm unicorn? A stunted kludde? An ugly old witch and a lonely girl reduced to shoveling waste?

It would be understandable if the sick bird had ended his own existence, unable to take another day as a rat in a trap, paraded around from city to city to slack-jawed gawkers. He deserved better.

Ash rested her head against the bars, angry thoughts still whirling in her head.

Until the pile of ashes began to move.

CHAPTER 5

THE MENACE WITH WINGS

sh rubbed her teary eyes, unable to believe what she was seeing.

Ember crumbs slid to each side as the mound of ashes shifted. She leaned in as closely as she could without getting her head stuck in the bars. The pile trembled and shook, more and more rapidly as she watched. Then, something tiny, something very tiny, poked through the blackness.

It was a wing. A red wing. The length of Ash's forefinger.

It couldn't be, she thought.

A second wing popped up, followed by tiny, yellow, wriggling feet. Whatever it was, it was on its back. Ash heard the tiniest coo, almost a purr, and out popped a tiny, red head with a tiny, gold beak.

It was a baby phoenix, and it looked Ash straight in the eye as it rose to its feet.

"Flynn? Is that you?" Ash whispered.

The little thing looked at her as if he'd never seen such a silly looking bird in all his eight seconds of living, tilting his head to the left and right. Ash didn't have feathers or a beak. He seemed to find that very interesting.

Ash smiled, but the tears kept falling. It had to be Flynn!

The baby bird took his first steps toward Ash, not without a bobble or two. As he stepped fully out of the burn pile, his tail was revealed: six inches long, split into two strands. It started out red and faded to bright yellow at the tip.

Ash laughed as little Flynn got right up next to her face, investigating her unbirdlike features. He pecked her nose once.

"Ouch!" Ash said with a laugh.

Flynn shook his head and hopped around. He then stretched his wings out for the first time and flapped them twice. The wind from the flaps sent a portion of the cinder pile flying, which, naturally, was the scariest thing baby Flynn had ever seen.

He cheeped and ran toward Ash, taking refuge under her chin. Ever so slowly, Ash placed two fingers on his back and caressed him gently. He not only allowed her to do so, but closed his eyes and began to purr, very quietly. He gave her hand a nudge with his beak, then looked up at Ash and cooed.

He must think I'm his mother! Ash thought.

Flynn interrupted his back scratch with a sneeze—a sneeze that shook his entire little body and shot a fireball three feet out of his nostrils. It left a black burn mark on the wall of the cage.

"Whoa."

What happened next in the few hours before sunrise was the beginning of an unusual friendship. Flynn was a very energetic hatchling who wanted nothing more than to hop around, blow smoke rings out of his nose holes, and experiment with his brand-new wings. He tried and failed several times to fly before Ash simply picked him up and carried him where he wanted to go, which, incidentally, was everywhere.

Ash introduced him to Hero, then to Perry, then, briefly, to the monkeys. Flynn was so comically animated, it was easy to see he thought the long, pokey thing on Hero's forehead was peculiar, Perry's wings—enormous in relation to his own— were quite peculiar, and the monkeys' big goofy ears were *especially* peculiar.

Lastly, Ash pointed out the very large doggy, Maurice. Before Ash could get a good grip on him, the excitable Flynn leapt out of her hands and into the kludde's cage.

"Flynn! No, come back!"

Flynn glanced back at her with a look as if to say, *What are you doing out there? Come in here with me!*

Flynn hopped over to investigate Maurice's large nose, resting on the ground as he slept. Ash tensed up, her brow beginning to sweat. That dog could swallow Flynn in one chomp.

The little bird bounced right up onto Maurice's snout and tilted his head, as if to say, *Hello. Are you a bird?*

Maurice opened one eye, as if replying, *No. I'm a dog.*

A dog! How peculiar. The bird sprung up onto Maurice's head. *Would you like to play?*

No. I'm trying to sleep. Please go away.

Ash had never been so uncomfortable and stressed in her life. But soon enough, Flynn grew bored with the tired pooch and bounced back into Ash's hands.

Flynn also discovered that he enjoyed perching on Ash's shoulders—particularly her right shoulder. He liked perching on her head, too, but Ash made that spot off-limits due to potential droppings. This led to Ash realizing that the chick would likely be hungry as soon as his excitement of being alive wore off, so they spent a bit of time digging through the dirt to find worms. Flynn thought this activity was strange, but found his first earthworm delicious.

Ash and Flynn spent the last pre-dawn hour inside her tent, where Flynn desperately tried again and again to get his wings to work. Whenever Ash giggled at his failed attempts, Flynn gave her a scolding look to say, *This is very serious. Please stop laughing.*

Ash was no bird, but she figured the best way to fly was to learn by example. She opened the door of Gertrude's cage. She could always find another robin. Flynn watched with saucer eyes as Gertrude zoomed out of the cage and fluttered around the tent several times before zipping out the door flap. Ash and Flynn peeked their heads out to watch her go, flying higher and higher until she disappeared from sight. It was that exact time that light began creeping over the mountains, and Flynn sat on Ash's right shoulder as he witnessed his first sunrise.

Sunrise.

Oh, no! Ash thought, ducking back into the tent. Tilda would be awake any minute, barking at her to load everything up so they could start en route to Toadberg. What would she say about Flynn? She couldn't tell Tilda. The witch would surely make poor baby Flynn the newest attraction of the circus, probably charging twice as much and starting a new tour immediately. Forget Toadberg, that meant no Oatsville at all!

Ash's heart sank. It was obvious: she needed to let Flynn go. As soon as he learned to fly, Ash would send him away. He wouldn't be trapped in a cage like his former self. He would be free.

Flynn chirruped happily as he hopped down Ash's arm and into the pocket of her shirt. He curled into a fuzzy ball inside the deep pouch and closed his eyes to nap. It was a perfect hiding spot.

That was it. She'd hide Flynn, for now. Figure out the rest later.

"Ashtyn! Wake up!" bellowed Tilda from outside.

Ash took a deep breath. *Oh, Flynny. Please stay asleep.*

Ash emerged from her tent, like a nervous squire about to face the evil dragon that terrorized the kingdom, ready to dig its wrinkled claws into her frail spine.

"Where were you last night?" Tilda asked, standing next to the empty phoenix cage.

"I was...in my tent," Ash said. It was a partial truth.

"Did you see this happen?" Tilda pointed to the spot of charcoal in the center of the cage. Ash walked over to get a closer look at the black spot on the floor and on the side where Flynn had sneezed.

"He's gone," Tilda said, shaking her head. "I suppose those damned legends are true, then. Bloody bugger. My biggest attraction next to that unicorn."

"Legends?" Ash asked, genuinely curious.

"Yes! Yes! The legend!" Tilda snapped back, grabbing Ash by the front of her shirt. "Are you stupid, girl? The phoenix! He kills himself in a fire every five hundred years and rebirths himself from the ashes!"

Ash winced from Tilda's horrid breath so close to her nose and hoped with everything inside her that Flynn remained asleep.

"Then do you know what happens, child?" Tilda asked, mocking Ash's ignorance. Ash shook her head. "Then he's small enough to hop through the bars and out of my circus! Blasted creature! Hellish fowl!"

Tilda let go of Ash with a shove. Ash stumbled backward. With the jolt, she felt movement in her pocket. Flynn was awake.

"Fetch that robin," commanded Tilda. "We'll use it as a façade until I can get ahold of Jinpa for another beast."

The robin. Ash had released it from the cage.

"I—I don't have the robin," Ash said. "It escaped when I swapped the birds yesterday. I didn't want to bother you with it."

Tilda fumed and yanked a supporting pole from her tent, causing it to collapse.

"You foolish girl! Fetch me another! Nay, fetch me a cat. We'll say it's a young mngwa cat for the show in Toadberg. Don't make me wait!"

Tilda's screeching stirred Flynn into a frenzy. Ash clasped her pocket shut to prevent him escaping.

"Go!" screamed Tilda, and Ash ran into the city.

Flynn was buzzing in her pocket like an angry hornet as Ash entered the loud streets of Rosedale. Townspeople were bustling in every direction, with horse-drawn wagons and merchant carts populating the street. The commotion piqued Flynn's curiosity greatly, and he seemed determined to investigate.

Ash ducked into an alley behind a cart selling woven baskets and briefly let go of her pocket.

Flynn immediately flew into the air, ten feet above Ash's head. He soared up and down the deserted alley. He zigzagged and loopity-looped, sending Ash into a panic.

"Flynn! Come down this instant!"

Ash said Flynn's name three times before he listened, and even then, he swooped down in front of her face as if to say, *Lookie, Mum! I'm flying!*

Ash was nearly at wit's end before she noticed a stray cat tracking Flynn's every movement from the back of the alley. A cat! Perfect!

She glanced back to the cart selling baskets. The merchant was busy with a customer, and there was a small handbasket with a latching lid hanging from his display. Ash crept up and snatched it. She couldn't let Flynn go free—not in the middle of the city. She opened the lid and swung the basket toward the whirling bird.

Missed.

She tried again when he swooped closer. *Got him!* She latched the lid.

"Hey! Ye need ta pay fer that basket!" called the merchant, but Ash was already sprinting down the alley and around the corner after that cat.

Ash dodged and weaved through crowds of people and behind stone buildings, chasing the gray tail of an uncooperative feline. She winced every time she stepped in a thorny patch of roses or bumped the basket against something.

"Whoops, sorry, Flynn. Hang on!"

The frisky cat leapt from a fence to a cart to finally the roof of one of the shops lining Main Street. It darted in the opposite direction: back toward the campsite.

Ash, with a grunt, turned on a dime and dashed back down the busy street. She tracked the cat from roof to roof, running parallel.

"Got you now, furball!" said Ash, just before being yanked off the street by her sleeve. Flynn's basket flew from her hand.

"I told ye, ye need ta pay fer that basket or I'll 'ave ye arrested, ye dirty thief!" threatened the angry basket merchant, with a firm grip on Ash's shirt.

The basket! It was being kicked around by boots and horse hooves in the middle of the street.

"Let me go!" Ash yelled.

After a brief struggle, she let her shirt rip and lurched for the basket. She was just in time to save it from being flattened under the wheel of a wagon.

"Watch it!" yelled the wagon driver as Ash tore off once more.

She could still see the cat, leaping from roof to roof toward the campsite. Ash sprinted to catch up, but the cat reached Tilda first.

Tilda saw the cat spring from the last rooftop before fleeing town through their campsite. Tilda pointed her wand at the cat, uttered a spell, and out came a zap of lightning. Ash arrived just in time to see the spell miss. And miss again.

But that was the least of Ash's problems.

Little Flynn had been busy at work on the basket while Ash was preoccupied chasing the feline. He had pecked a hole in the wicker just big enough to fit his tiny body through.

Flynn soared out of the basket and into the air. Tilda and Ash both gasped.

The bird, thinking it all very exciting, chased the cat around the campsite, nipping at its tail with his sharp beak. The annoyed cat turned to attack the bird, but Flynn was far too nimble. Round and round they went, even knocking over Ash's tent and spilling their only buckets of grain. The animals in the cages were very aggravated by it all, especially the monkeys who screeched and howled and rocked their cart back and forth. If they could talk, they'd surely be cheering the chase on.

"Catch them! Catch them!" Tilda screamed at Ash.

Before she could even try, Flynn, having a marvelous time, chased the cat through the kludde's cage, atop the supply cart, and onto the rump of one of the Clydesdales, claws-out.

Tilda, quite unfortunately, had already hooked up the Clydesdales' harnesses in preparation for departure. When one horse reared up from the piercing cat claws, the other was forced to rear up as well. The spooked horses took off at a run, pulling the entire caravan of carts behind them. Fast into the field they went and down a steep slope.

"No!" Tilda cried, as the carts turned over on their side, crashing hard against the grassy ground.

The wooden tops of the carts split open, giving enough leeway for Hero, Perry, and Maurice to break through. Off they ran, through the field and toward the nearest forest. The kludde growled as he raced, the peryton spread its wings and flew into the blue sky, and Hero—he'd never looked so handsome as he did galloping through that lush field. Not even one of Tilda's spells could duplicate such majesty.

Tilda crumbled to her knees. Her long, spindly fingers grasped chunks of her matted hair and ripped them out. Her leathery skin doubled its wrinkles as she scrunched her face with agony, and her spine curled over like a shepherd's hook.

"My babies! My babies! Come back to mama, my lovelies! Come back!" she wailed, voice like knives on porcelain.

Ash snatched Flynn out of the air and gripped him tightly. He warbled.

With her back to Ash, Tilda heard the hatchling's noise behind her and instantly stopped crying.

"Ashtyn...my darling..." she said in a deep, wheedling tone. It was otherworldly. "Come to me...come help an old woman to her feet, won't you?"

Ash backed away. "I—I don't—"

"Musn't be afraid of Mummy Matilda...my sweet, sweet child..."

Ash held Flynn close, fear pumping through her veins.

"You must give me that bird, child."

"No," Ash whimpered.

Tilda slowly twisted her head around toward Ash, her skull seeming disconnected from her spine. "Give me that bird!"

Tilda's eyes glowed red. Her entire body seemed to swell with rage as she gripped her wand so tightly that her quivering knuckles turned white. The wand sparked, as if warming up to deal a vicious spell.

Ash knew Tilda could still perform just enough black magic to be dangerous. She backed away a few more steps. Quickly, she turned and ran full speed away from Tilda, back into town.

"Give me the bird! Give me the bird! The bird is mine!" Tilda screamed.

The old woman's voice got further and further away as Ash sprinted back up Main Street.

She slipped Flynn into her pocket and gripped the fabric tightly. Was Tilda behind her? How close? She didn't stop to find out.

Adrenaline quickened her pace. She knew she had to escape, but where would she go? Running, faster and faster, she gasped for air and felt her eyes well up with tears. Tilda would find her. Tilda would catch her.

She reached the northeast edge of town. A weeping fern canopied a crowd of people. The area buzzed with excitement and the ground was blanketed in white rose petals—something important was going on.

Ash jumped as high as her legs would spring her to see what the commotion was about. She caught a glimpse of what looked like a winged horse and a white-haired woman.

Odetta!

"Excuse me! Please!" Ash cried. "Let me through!"

No one listened. She attempted to squeeze through, but no one complied.

"Please! I must see Odetta!"

"You think you're special? We all want to see the pegasus. Wait your turn like the rest of us, peasant girl!" said a gruff man, who reeked of whisky and spit when he talked.

Ash couldn't help but cry now. She tried once more, desperately, to squeeze through the crowd. "Please, it's important, you've got to—"

What happened next would be Rosedale's only topic of gossip for the next three months. The gruff, smelly man slammed his hands against Ash's shoulders and shoved her to the ground. The forceful jolt caused her to fall backward, hard on her rear end, on the cobblestone street. Ash remembered what happened next fuzzily, but it seemed Flynn was very displeased with this angry fellow for pushing his favorite new friend.

As quick as lightning, he flew from Ash's pocket and met the lout at eye-level. He sent a fireball blasting from his tiny beak that not only engulfed the man in flames, but blew him back eight feet through a wooden fence. The attack also set several others near him ablaze, unintentionally but unfortunately.

One townsman threw a bucket of water on the smoking individuals. Ash thought it was safe to assume they would remain singed for the next few days.

But aside from the water thrower, no one at the time was paying any attention to the victims. The crowd had parted into a circle and stared slack-jawed at Ash and her tiny, terrifying firebird in the center.

Most intrigued of all was Odetta. She stood in white robes next to a pegasus, large as a Clydesdale, elegant as a swan. The horse's body was so brilliantly white, it was almost blinding to behold. Its wings were a glittering silver. It was harnessed to a white and gold sleigh, decorated with ceremonial garlands and wreaths made of white roses. Inside the sleigh was a pony-sized unicorn. Beside it stood the scowling blonde girl from the day before.

Flynn ignored the crowd of stunned onlookers and fluttered beside Ash, still lying on the ground. He landed on her chest and pecked twice at her chin. *Hey! Get up!*

Ash blinked her eyes and came to. She scrambled to her feet when she realized the setting of one hundred people staring at her, including several men who had clearly just been set on fire.

"What is your name, girl?"

It was the soft voice of Odetta. She stood next to the pegasus, the pair of them almost glowing.

"Ash. I—I mean, Ashtyn Ridley," Ash responded.

"Does that bird belong to you, Ashtyn Ridley?"

She wasn't sure how to answer. Odetta had asked to see the phoenix the day prior. Would she be in trouble?

"Yes, ma'am," Ash admitted. She was tired of deceiving people. "He died in flames and was reborn yesterday. I've taken care of him since. Are—are you going to take him away?"

Odetta laughed and placed a hand on the neck of her pegasus.

"Take him away? Child, you were with him when he was birthed. He is bonded to you now, as this pegasus, Odessus, is bonded to me. Nothing in the world could take him away from you."

The crowd murmured. Flynn nestled on Ash's right shoulder and crooned.

"There must be a mistake," Ash said. "I don't come from a family of Regal Kinsmen. I'm just...my family is poor..."

Odetta stepped toward Ash, and Flynn immediately flew up to this white-haired stranger to investigate. Odetta uttered an inaudible phrase and lifted her finger. Flynn perched on it— the first human he'd touched who wasn't Ash. Odetta looked the bird in the eyes, then lowered her hand. Flynn circled round her head once and returned to Ash's shoulder.

"Magical beasts make no mistakes," she said. "This phoenix belongs to you now, and you to him. A bond between human and beast is precious and powerful, and will never be broken. You should feel very special, Ashtyn."

It didn't seem possible. She had a Bonded Beast, an extraordinary partnership between man and animal. If everything she'd heard about this phenomenon proved true, then her life would not, and could not, ever be the same.

Ash's surprise quickly turned to worry. She had no money. She had no food. She was far from home. How could she possibly care for such a kingly bird in the way he deserved?

As if reading her mind, Odetta grinned. "My niece Farrah there, in the sleigh," she said, gesturing toward the blonde girl with the small unicorn. "You must join her and leave at once."

Ash felt her hands begin to quiver. She'd read about the bonding process. She'd dreamed of being one of Cascadia's privileged few. But it couldn't be happening, not to her.

"Leave...where?"

Odetta's eyes sparkled as she laughed. "To the Academy! You didn't think you could control a magical beast without the proper training, did you? We must enroll you as a student at once, there's not a moment to spare."

"*All hail the Regal Kin! Praise be to the Regal Kin! Saviors of Cascadia!*"

The shrill voice's mockery was punctuated by a blood-curdling cackle. The crowd parted and there was Tilda, with a ghastly grin of fractured teeth peeking out from her hooded cloak.

Ash gasped. She held Flynn close.

"Another brat for your precious Academy, how *marvelous*." Tilda's bloodshot eyes targeted Ash. "Give me the phoenix."

Odetta stepped in front of Ash. "You are not welcome here, old woman."

Tilda cackled once more, throwing her head back and revealing a grotesque, leathery face warped by greed. "Your grasp on this land may be strong, but you tyrannical puppet masters will not jerk my strings so easily! I want what is right-fully mine. I want it!"

Ash looked down at Flynn. Tilda could acquire any beast she wanted. Why was her desire for the phoenix consuming her? Why *this* animal?

Odetta remained unmoved. "Take your hysterics elsewhere. You are sick."

"The bird belongs to me!" Tilda hissed.

"Not anymore."

"I will make the girl suffer with a pain not even death will end!"

"You have no power here."

Tilda shrieked like a demonic screech owl. Thrusting her wand forward, the witch uttered an incantation. Three braided crimson beams shot toward Ash. Odetta calmly flicked her wrist and the spell blew to the side, missing them completely. She whispered a command to Odessus and the beautiful horse reared up. With a whinny and a powerful flap of his wings, the pegasus hit Tilda with a continuous gust of wind. The wind deprived her of oxygen, and the hag choked. Asphyxiated, her bony fingers clawed at her throat. Her skin seemed to shrink around her skull. When the wind stopped, the air violently returned to her lungs, depressurizing her body. She grabbed her eye sockets and wailed.

"Be gone, old woman. May you never forget my restraint."

Tilda screamed in anger and pain and ran, far away. Far out of town.

Odetta extended her hand to the trembling Ash and smiled. "Come now. We mustn't waste a moment."

Ash returned Flynn to her shoulder and took a deep breath. She shook her head. Everything was happening so quickly.

"But...Miss Odetta, I'm afraid I can't pay to go to school," said Ash. "And, I'm not sure if my father will approve, and—"

"You lovely, silly girl!" said a plump woman, who bustled out of the crowd and up to Ash. She flung a shawl over her shoulders, causing Flynn to briefly hop up. "Here, doll, you'll need this. It gets cold in the air!"

"Hope you aren't afraid of heights," said a black-haired man, nearby.

"Oh, hush, George," the plump woman said to her husband. "You'll be fine, love. Our daughter, Farrah, will teach you how to breathe inside heavy clouds."

"I'm just sayin', Vivian, Edmund got sick his first time flying to the Academy," said George.

"Ignore him," said Vivian with a reassuring smile. "Well, what are you waiting for? Get in that sleigh!"

Ash took one more look at her surroundings. A crowd full of anxious faces watched the astonishing scene unfold.

She smiled and grabbed Odetta's hand.

Everyone cheered. Vivian picked out a white rose from one of the ceremonial wreaths and handed it to her as she stepped into the back seat of the sleigh next to Farrah, whose unicorn

was curled by her feet. Flynn b
around the sleigh like a sprir
bird quite knew what was hap,
stop and ask questions.

George hooked up Odetta's pegas
ness. Odetta waved a thank you and sat c
front seat. She picked up the golden reins and .
time to her brother, George, and his wife, Vivian.
parted to allow the pegasus and the sleigh to enter .
petal-covered road.

George and Vivian waved goodbye to Farrah, who returnec
the gesture with a half smile. Before the crowd could finish
their "so long!" cheers, Odetta snapped the reins and the pegasus galloped off. Ash waved to the jubilant audience and Flynn
flew circles around her head.

"Excuse me," Farrah said sternly to Ash. "You'd best
hold on."

Ash faced forward as the sleigh picked up speed. She
gripped her seat and they lifted off the ground. Higher and
higher the sleigh climbed as the pegasus flapped his enormous silver wings. The townspeople of Rosedale looked like
ladybugs from their height! She barely caught a glimpse of
the crashed carnival cages before the sleigh ascended into the
white, fluffy clouds.

CHAPTER 6

THE BODAS BUMBLE TRAINING ACADEMY OF BEASTS AND MAGIC

he clouds met Ash's face with a refreshing mist. The sleigh dipped down through thick cumulus bundles, riding the line between stratosphere and mesosphere. The earth became visible again as they soared over mountains, meadows, and streams. While gripping the sleigh with her right hand, Ash extended her left arm and released the white rose into the wind. Like a wing, she tilted her hand forward and back to feel the airstreams. She closed her eyes and inhaled the crisp air.

Flynn, on the other hand, wouldn't close his eyes for a second. He flew beside the sleigh keeping pace, his long tail dancing in the wind like two red streamers. He'd zip high out of sight, then glide back to their level, turning barrel rolls like his entire life—consisting of about six hours—led up to this moment. At full speed, he could fly up to meet Odessus the pegasus. He swooped under the horse's neck as if to say, *We're flying! Isn't this wonderful?*

Odessus would whinny and shake off the annoying bird, then return to his important task at hand: flying his passengers safely. Odetta couldn't help but laugh at the vivacious little phoenix and the stoic, proper pegasus.

They continued dipping in and out of clouds—stratus clouds, now—and Ash smiled uncontrollably at the gorgeous overhead view of the countryside.

"I knew Cascadia was pretty, but never like this!" shouted Ash, expecting agreement from Farrah.

Instead, Farrah gave Ash a half-smirk and returned her gaze forward. Ash got a very cold feeling from Farrah, and it wasn't from the elevation. Since the moment she saw her at the circus, the girl looked annoyed, as if her face was cursed with a permanent scowl. Ash thought perhaps her curls were pinned to her head too tightly, or maybe her white dress had itchy seams.

A flock of geese soldiered on below them in triangular formation. Flynn joined their group for a few moments, before getting honked at and returning to the sleigh's side. The rush of flying was better than anything Flynn or even Ash had ever dreamed of. So much so, that she couldn't help but spread her arms and laugh out loud.

Now standing beside her, Farrah's unicorn let out a very quiet whinny. Farrah placed her hand on the horse's neck.

"Is she okay?" Ash said to Farrah, speaking loudly over the wind.

"She doesn't like flying," Farrah replied, keeping her gaze on the animal.

"I'm Ash and that's Flynn," Ash said, offering a handshake that was awkwardly received. "He's a phoenix!"

"I've heard," Farrah said. "He seems...elated."

Ash glanced at Flynn, who was irritating Odessus again.

"Yes! He is!" she replied with a laugh. "What's your unicorn's name?"

"Fiona."

"She's beautiful! Can you ride her?"

"Yes, she just turned four, the proper age for a unicorn to allow a rider. I'm sorry—but Fiona is very nauseated. Would you mind if we didn't speak anymore? The loud talking perturbs her."

Ash nodded an apology and returned her attention to the sights below. Out of her peripheral vision, she couldn't help but notice that Fiona jerked her face away every time Farrah tried to rub her nose.

"Her ears—you should scratch her ears. Unicorns love it," Ash said, remembering her time spent with Hero.

Fiona shot Ash an irked glance, suggesting that her advice was not welcome. Ash bit her lip and went back to minding her own business.

A few uncomfortable moments passed before Farrah spoke up, as if she just couldn't hold her tongue any longer.

"You do realize that all of those people there today were gathered for me, don't you?"

"Oh?" Ash said. "I supposed they were there to see the pegasus."

"Well, yes, I mean, of course they wanted to see Odetta and Odessus. My aunt is Regal Kin, after all. But every child leaving for the Academy for the first time gets a ceremony," she informed Ash, with an edge to her voice.

"And that...that was yours?"

"Yes. And you ruined it."

Ash understood why Farrah had looked so cross with her. "I'm terribly sorry. Really, I didn't know."

"Well," Farrah said, "now you know."

Farrah spoke no more that trip, concerned only with Fiona. Ash figured the lack of conversation was probably for the best, as it allowed for fewer foot-in-mouth opportunities.

About a half hour into their trip, Odetta called to Ash.

"You mentioned your father. Where does he live? We will visit him before proceeding to the Academy."

Despite the chill atmosphere, Ash was filled with warmth. *Her father.* She couldn't wait to tell him everything that had happened.

"Oatsville. It's near middle southwest Cascadia, in the farmlands. North of Cottonbridge and Lentilton."

Odetta adjusted the sleigh's course and they veered left toward Oatsville.

For Ash, the next forty minutes was a blend of two incredible feelings: flying, and the anticipation of seeing her father.

With her new best friend, Flynn, still soaring beside her arms-length away, things were looking up.

The sleigh reached the middle southwest region of Cascadia. Odetta directed Odessus to drop down out of the clouds and fly in sight of the ground. As they glided over farmlands, Ash could see farmers—the size of termites from her height—look up from their morning chores at the pegasus-drawn sleigh. A few rubbed their eyes in disbelief. Ash giggled, remembering all the times on her father's farm that she thought she'd seen unusual animals in the sky.

With some directions from Ash, Odetta guided Odessus to a farmhouse on a small hill, far away from the dirt roads that led to Oatsville. Next to the house stood an old oak tree where Ash used to play as a girl. Beyond it were hundreds of acres of oat fields, the long golden strands topped with florets bending in the breeze.

The sleigh had barely touched the ground before Ash had jumped out and ran up the dirt entrance to her house. She hurdled over some barrels and scrap wood on the porch and swung open the front door.

"Dad!" she yelled, tripping on the entryway rug as she entered. "Dad! It's me! I'm home!"

Flynn zoomed in through an open window to investigate the strange, musty house.

There was no one in the living room to the right, no one in the kitchen to the left. Ash skipped over to the two bedrooms. Both empty. Back to the kitchen, she peeked out the window to check if he was working in the back garden. Nothing. He wasn't there.

"Dad?"

Still no answer.

When she finally stopped to catch her breath, something seemed odd. Her feet had left dirty footprints all over the floorboards, as if the place hadn't been swept in months. In fact, there was a thick layer of dust and dirt on everything in the house. And where were the animal noises?

She opened the creaky back door to the garden and animal pens. They were empty. No goats, no pigs, no cows—no animals to be found. Even the shelves of the chicken coop were vacant. The farm equipment was rusted, the garden was horribly overgrown and infested with weeds, and all the troughs were dried up.

"Dad.... What happened?" she whispered to herself.

Stepping back into the house, Odetta stood by the front door.

"Is something the matter, Ashtyn?" she asked.

"I—I don't know," she answered.

Walking through the kitchen, she noticed rats in the cabinets, which were filled with old, stale food—food she remembered being there six months ago when she visited for the week in March. In the rusty kitchen sink, dirty plates had been untouched for a very long time, evidenced by one with a half-eaten blueberry muffin. Or at least it could have been. It was dark green and black with mold and was hard as stone.

"Ashtyn?" Odetta said.

Blinking out of her trance, she turned to Odetta.

"He's not here. He hasn't been here for a while," she said, the words requiring an effort as her throat tightened. Her entire body felt tense, crippled with worry.

"Would you know where to find him?" Odetta asked, her soft voice a calming sound in the turbulent ocean of Ash's confusion.

"No. He would only leave to go into town for food and to sell his crops. He'd always come right back. But our house has never looked like this. He's been gone for months."

Ash couldn't comprehend the silence, the emptiness. The house had always been a ruckus of animal noises, laughter, and music. The two of them loved to sing and whistle together.

Ash headed into her father's bedroom. The unmade bed was sprinkled with leaves and dirt, blown in from an opened window. His clothes were still in the drawers. Wherever he was, he had gone abruptly and hadn't packed for the occasion.

She opened the drawer of his bed's side table. It was still there: a purple velvet pouch with a yellow drawstring.

Flynn glided into the room and perched on Ash's right shoulder. He tilted his head at the unfamiliar velvet bag. She opened it and withdrew its contents. It was the pan flute, the one he'd given her two years ago.

She had once brought it with her on the long journeys with the circus to play songs for the animals. That is, until Tilda decided she despised the sound and threatened to smash it. After that, she'd left it home with her father.

Ash blew into the flute slightly, and it responded with a beautiful, airy tone. Flynn cooed in response.

She returned the flute to its sack and stuck it in her pocket. It was no use waiting around—her father was not coming back. She grabbed a shoulder sack from her room and packed a few personal belongings: clothing, several of her favorite books, a writing pad, a hairbrush, a blanket, and a small wooden box with the name "Ashtyn" carved in the top. It had been her surprise gift for Random Gift Wednesday the previous year. He had promised that this year he would find her the perfect piece of jewelry to fill it.

Ash walked beside Odetta on the dirt path back to the sleigh. Her head was hung low and she remained silent.

"How much do you know about the Academy, Ashtyn?" asked Odetta, seemingly changing the subject.

Ash shrugged. "Nothing, really. I've heard stories, but who knows if they were true."

"The Academy is overseen by four Elders, who have each student's best interest in mind. I am one of these Elders. I will speak to the others about your father, and we can even present the situation to the king. We will find a way to help, Ash. I can assure you."

Ash nodded, but couldn't find a response.

Leaving the house was bittersweet. The excitement of seeing the Academy was tempered by the gut-wrenching feeling that something bad had happened to her father. But there was nothing gained by worrying about it now. The Elders would help. And there were far more present things to focus on, like riding in a sleigh with a girl who disliked her and going to a strange school full of children who might also dislike her. She'd never been to a school before, nor had she ever really associated with children her own age—and she wasn't off to a great start. She sighed.

Ash barely had time to arrange her thoughts before the sleigh swooped down out of the clouds. In an instant, all of her worries melted away once more.

Below, she saw the ocean for the first time, a sparkling, restless reflection of blue sky and bright sun that consumed the horizon. On the land's edge, nestled between two high cliff walls was a grand, green valley—and there, in the valley's center, was the Academy. The stone-gray school looked massive, even from their height. Green ivy blanketed the towers and spires that encircled a central keep. The front boasted an enormous clock over the entrance. The school faced inward toward the valley, with the ocean at its back, as though the threatening clock requested this positioning to be a constant warning to tardy students.

Encompassing the valley at the base of the surrounding rock walls were two bodies of water creeping in from the ocean. On the left was an inlet that hugged the grounds. At its end was a small bay and a very, very large tree. Ash squinted and saw that small houses lined the inlet, some even built into the side of the rock wall. There were caves, as well—Ash estimated nearly forty.

To the right of the valley was a river. It outlined the valley similar to the inlet, but rather than coming to an end, it kept flowing far into Cascadia. This was the Steelhead River, as those were the most common type of fish inhabiting it. Above, waterfalls from the neighboring mountain spilled down the cliffside and poured into the Steelhead. They were known as the Underspring Falls, since the source of the water was caused by underground springs in the mountains.

In fact, the name Cascadia had been given to the land because of the rampant streams, springs, and waterfalls that decorated the country. There was never a shortage of water in Cascadia, sometimes surprisingly so, as tributaries and brooks tended to creep into areas without explanation.

The moist, salty air from the ocean kissed Ash's cheeks as they flew closer and closer into the air space of the Academy. She looked to the left as a man in uniform riding a massive purple dragon rose up next to them. The beast's two turquoise wings must have each been the size of Ash's farmhouse. Ash was so mesmerized, she had to remind herself to keep breathing. It was one thing to catch a glimpse of a dragon zooming across the night sky—it was quite another to have one so close that you could almost reach out and touch its glistening scales.

The man waved to Odetta with a smile and motioned her downward toward the entrance of the valley. Odetta nodded and the man broke away. Odetta spoke a command to Odessus and they descended straight down, nose first.

They leveled off just in time to land gently on the road leading into the valley. They were back on earth now. A tired Flynn perched himself on Ash's shoulder.

"You're a good boy, Flynny," she whispered, patting him on the head.

Odessus trotted and high-stepped merrily as he pulled the sleigh through open gates and under a grand archway. To the left of this entrance was a statue of a man atop a bumblebee that was, quite literally, the size of an elephant. Ash read the carved writing on the archway:

The Bodas Bumble Training Academy
of Beasts And Magic
Founded by Bodas Bumble, Age of
King Theonidas, Year CDXIX
Dedicated to Blightey Bumble, Elephant Bee and Loyal Friend

The Academy had been founded by a man with an oversized bee? she thought. *What a fascinating history this school must have!*

Past the gates, Ash and Farrah wobbled in their seats as the sleigh slid over bumpy, uneven cobblestone. A swinging sign read *The Shoppes.*

They soon found themselves on a busy street with tall narrow buildings on each side. Through one shop window, Ash saw human clothing for sale in vibrant colors, but inside the next window were horse supplies in all shapes and sizes: harnesses, lead ropes, bridles, saddles, and hoof picks. The next shop had aquatic supplies, such as plastic masks for diving under water, flippers, nets, and swimming trunks. Beside that was a shop that boasted *Over Four Hundred Types of Rawhide Bones and Chew Toys!*, which was about three hundred and ninety varieties more than were offered by any feed store Ash had ever been to.

They passed several carts on the sidewalk selling fruits, vegetables, breads, and grains, as well as an entire cart selling berries and worms. Ash snatched Flynn out of the air before he could zip over for a sample.

"Nice try," she said, placing him back on her shoulder. He chirped at her with a disapproving bird-word.

Each store was more bizarre than the previous one. One window displayed terrarium supplies. Another advertised a brand-new flea and tick control that was "sensitive enough for griffin fur." For every normal shop, selling cages, kennels, leashes, and litter, there was an abnormal shop that sold ten-foot tall currycombs or one selling live goats as "free-range manticore feed."

Ash was so enthralled looking at the goodies for sale—one store even sold a "Dragon Talon Grooming Kit"—she was oblivious for a while to the fact that the overwhelmed shopkeepers, boisterous children, and multitasking parents had ceased bustling at the sight of Flynn. Some children cheered and pointed, one mother dropped both her jaw and her bags, and an elderly merchant selling "Granny Elm's Hairball Formula" fainted right on the sidewalk.

"Look there, Ashtyn," said Odetta. "The shop at the end."

The last store on the left was painted green with a red door. Its red awning was speckled with white spots, which looked like droppings rather than decoration. A wooden sign read:

Flanagan's Feathers
A One-Stop Shop for Bird Things

"You'll go there if you ever need supplies," she said. "Flanagan is a sweet man, and very knowledgeable. He'll ensure you have everything you need for the health and wellbeing of Flynn."

Ash nodded and examined the storefront. Even through the window, the merchandise looked expensive. She'd have to worry about that later.

The cobblestone ended and before them were acres of green grass—and a sight not even the most imaginative poet could have described.

Children, everywhere, were standing unprotected near beasts that under normal circumstances would tear their throats out and eat them for a pre-dinner snack. But no—students were playing and frolicking with these magical animals! Playing tag and hide-and-go-seek! As a man would play fetch with a beagle in the park, so was one fifteen-year-old student playing catch with a wolf the size of a hippopotamus. Two girls, probably seventeen years of age, cantered together on white horses that had spiraled goat horns.

"Kirins!" Ash exclaimed, recognizing the horses from a painting she once saw in a village near Violetbrook.

One boy, about Ash's age, was chasing a small beaver-like creature while being chased by a massive rabbit at the same time. Another boy looked on, laughing so hard he was turning blue in the face.

Farrah waved to a dark-haired girl with deep-set eyes trying to keep a large gray cat under control. The girl waved back to Farrah, then noticed Ash and furrowed her thick brows in confusion.

Ash lifted her arm to wave hello, but was startled by a gust of wind overhead from two older boys racing a black pegasus and a hippogriff through the air at top speed. Ash recognized the hippogriff immediately, having read her *Griffins & Hippogriffs* book so many times. It was a legendary winged horse with an eagle's head and it looked exactly how she'd visualized it, only twice as stunning.

As Odessus trotted the sleigh forward, dodging children and maneuvering around parents hugging their sons and daughters goodbye, they fell under the shadow of the looming Academy—a fortress both intimidating and inviting.

There was a large staircase leading up to the burgundy and gold entry doors with that ominous clock overhead surveying the valley with unforgiving accuracy. On the grass just before the staircase stood what looked like very important adults in a semi-circle. The path leading to these individuals was lined with temporary white columns, and a short queue was formed by students, their beasts, and their parents.

Odetta commanded Odessus to halt. A man in uniform immediately rushed to the sleigh and assisted Odetta to her feet. Once Ash, Farrah, and Fiona stepped out, the man bowed.

"I'll have the students' belongings delivered to the appropriate corridors at once," said the man.

"Thank you, Lyle," Odetta responded.

Farrah slid a pink halter with matching lead rope over Fiona's nose. She combed the horse's mane, and her own, with her fingers.

"How do I look, Auntie? Is my hair frizzed from the flight? Is my dress smudged or wrinkled?" she asked. "Oh, I probably look a fright!"

Ash looked down at her own attire. It was both smudged and wrinkled...with a tear in the sleeve and bird droppings in the front pocket.

How different their lives were. Ash smirked at the thought of Farrah's repulsed expression were she to mention that she usually bathed in creeks.

"You look beautiful, Farrah," Odetta assured. "Come stand in line, girls."

The three stepped into line behind a young boy. His mother was licking her fingers and rubbing smudges off his cheeks, much to his displeasure. He held a small monkey—a monkey that had red eyes, fangs, and was dripping wet.

"So that's what a real water monkey looks like," Ash whispered to Flynn, shaking her head. Tilda's monkeys had looked absolutely nothing like it.

Flynn sat on her right shoulder and trilled along with her giggles before being frightened by a loud sneeze from Fiona. He zipped underneath Ash's hair.

Farrah grunted and stomped her foot. "I knew it! Fiona's caught a cold from flying! Auntie, I told you it was a terrible idea."

Farrah proceeded to spew whines and moans at Odetta as her patient aunt assured her everything was going to be fine.

Fiona did look a bit drowsy. The pony stood perfectly still with her eyes half open and her head bobbing toward the ground, about to nod off to sleep. She appeared as though she'd prefer to trade all of the commotion for a soft bed of hay and a handful of grain.

While Farrah was preoccupied with complaining, Ash slipped a small carrot chunk out of the pocket where she always kept them and quietly fed the bite to Fiona. She followed it up with a few seconds of precious ear scratches. The pony perked right up and leaned her itchy ears hard into Ash's hands.

As Farrah wrapped up her whining, Ash quickly pulled her hands away.

"The luck of it," Farrah continued. "Meeting my teachers for the first time with a tired, sneezy unicorn."

On cue, Fiona sneezed once more.

It was Farrah's turn next. The semi-circle of professors, five of them total, stood ready to greet her. One woman in the center took charge and motioned for Farrah to come forward.

It was an odd-looking group, to put it lightly. The woman in the center looked to be the oldest, with a face that suggested years of trying to keep students in line. Her hair was pulled back in a high bun and was dark brown with orange highlights, looking like stripes. Her skin was a light brown, almost bronze in color, and her fingernails were like claws.

Farrah lifted her chin. She marched Fiona forward to meet the woman with confidence.

From a distance, it looked as though Farrah was reciting some sort of elaborate pre-planned speech. Ash lip-read phrases such as "It's a great honor to be accepted" and "My performance will be impressive." A few minutes in, the skinny professor tried to disguise a yawn.

He had a very large nose and wore a floppy, green hat with a feather hanging from one side. He stood next to another man whose dark brown hair was pulled back into a ponytail, with a matching mustache-beard combo, looking almost burgundy in the sunlight.

The remaining two professors on the opposite side consisted of a short man in horse-riding attire and a very large, very muscular, very intimidating woman with golden eyes and brown freckles on her neck and cheeks.

All of them looked exhausted. They were clearly ready for the day of meet-and-greets to be over.

"Is there anything I'm supposed to say to the professors? Or, perhaps, not say?" Ash asked Odetta. Farrah had clearly rehearsed for weeks.... Ash, not so much.

"Just be respectful and kind, as you've been to me. You'll be fine."

Ash twitched from a tickle on her neck and remembered that Flynn was hiding in her hair. She shook her head back and forth until Flynn came zipping out, ready for playtime. He circled her head, brushing her nose with each flyby. She laughed and tried to blow him off course as he flew.

"Young lady!"

Ash straightened up and ceased her laughter. She scrambled to grab Flynn and set him on her shoulder, but he evaded her, thinking it part of the game.

Her stomach dropped. Was she in trouble already? How could she be so stupid, playing with Flynn during Farrah's introduction to the professors? This Academy was an incredible opportunity. She was blowing it.

The voice had come from the orange-haired professor who had been in the middle of handing Farrah some sort of welcoming certificate. Though she wasn't the only one staring at Ash. The other professors were, too.

"Is that...?"

"It can't be."

"Not for over four hundred years have we seen one!"

The professors were locked on Flynn, eyes and mouths agape. Farrah, however, glared at Ash with pursed lips and ears that were seconds away from spewing flames. Looked like Ash had ruined Farrah's second ceremony, too.

The orange-haired professor quickly shoved the certificate into Farrah's hands and walked straight to Ash. Flynn immediately investigated her face, making sure this new bizarre-looking bird meant Ash no harm.

"Professor Thorne," said Odetta. "I realize that presenting you with a new student on such late notice is against protocol, but—"

"Where did you find this bird, girl?" said Professor Thorne, smiling as Flynn hovered in front of her. Her age seemed to melt away as a look of childlike wonder replaced it. "Where, in all the corners of Cascadia, did you find this creature?"

"I—I just—" stuttered Ash.

"Professors, I bring you Ashtyn Ridley and her Bonded Beast, Flynn the phoenix. She rescued him from a traveling animal circus. She laid by his side as he performed his rebirthing ritual."

"It's true, then?" asked Professor Atlas, the small man in the riding clothes. "The phoenix does die in flame and rise again from the ashes? Bera, am I dreaming?"

"Of course it's true!" said Bera, the large woman. "You see the little bugger right in front of your face, don't you? Barnabus Talon! Get your beak nose over here. What do your eagle eyes see?"

The skinny man with the feathered hat and big nose was frozen, still as a statue, staring at Flynn as if the bird were a ghost. "Dear, gracious me. It's folderol. Poppycock. A wizard's cruel joke. Not in all my days...no, not in all my days...."

"Don't mind Professor Talon," said the man with the mustache and beard. "He gets a bit twitchy when it comes to birds."

He knelt down to Ash's level and took her hand. It instantly calmed her nerves. He spoke softly, and Flynn landed on Ash's shoulder to get a good look at him. "I'm Professor Suarez."

Suarez motioned toward Flynn. "May I?" he asked. Ash nodded. Gently, Suarez caressed the bird's head. Flynn cooed softly.

"Tell us, Ashtyn," asked Professor Atlas. "Where do you come from?"

"I'm from Oatsville, in the farm country," she said.

Behind the curious professors, Ash saw Farrah angrily stomp her foot in the grass and lead Fiona away with a yank.

"Can I—I mean, I would be most honored if I could stay. And attend the school," Ash continued. "If it's not too much trouble, and there's room for me. We don't take up much space and wouldn't require a lot—"

"My dear!" interrupted Suarez, with a laugh. "You have it all wrong! For we are delighted to meet you and your very special friend, and would be honored for you to attend the Academy. That is, if you'll have us." Suarez finished with a wink.

Ash smiled from ear to ear. She looked at her tiny Flynn. He was, at the moment, much more concerned with biting at an itch under his wing than with the news of being accepted into some silly school.

"When do we start?"

CHAPTER 7

THE TREEHOUSE
DORMITORIES

Professor Thorne walked Ash up the stone stairs and through the massive double-doored entrance of the Academy. She had shaken off her childlike whimsy of seeing a phoenix for the first time and was back to business, staring straight ahead with perfect posture and a matter-of-fact expression.

"Do you have a uniform? Books? A cage? Did Odetta take you to The Shoppes?"

Ash tried to listen to Thorne, but the gothic grandeur of the entrance hall had taken Ash's breath away: statues three times her height, intricately carved furnishings, elegant, royal-blue banners on stone walls. The ceiling must have been over a hundred feet high. At the top were stained glass windows, each depicting a great beast. Ash recognized two as a dragon and a griffin—just like the wild one she saw with her father two years ago on her farm. The others, however, were beasts she'd never seen before, even in books. A serpent with nine heads? A two-legged lizard with a rooster head? How could such creatures really exist?

"Speak up, child," Thorne pressed.

They carefully avoided a dwarf on a tall ladder replacing oil in a chandelier. Ash tried not to stare, having never seen a dwarf before, either.

"Um, yes, ma'am. We did ride through The Shoppes, but I'm afraid I didn't have money to buy a uniform, or books. Or a cage, did you say?"

"Yes, a cage for Flynn."

Flynn. Where was he?

While Thorne marched ahead of her, listing off required items, Ash frantically looked back and forth for Flynn.

There were several spiral staircases leading to different corridors of the school, as well as many hallways and open doors. Flynn could have ducked down any of them.

Finally, Ash spotted Flynn's tiny red shape sitting on the dwarf's ladder. He was pecking at the silver latch that kept the ladder locked. As he fought this shiny enemy, the latch buckled. The dwarf began to teeter.

"Oh, boy," Ash uttered under her breath.

Frightened of the wobbling equipment, Flynn zoomed back to Ash's shoulder. The ladder tipped...and crashed, shattering a mirror on the wall. The dwarf was able to jump for the chandelier in time, so there he swung.

Thorne turned toward the wreckage. "Oh, for heaven's sake, will one of you get him down?"

A nearby student, about sixteen years old, nodded and motioned for his large bumblebee beast to buzz up and rescue the dwarf. The dwarf swatted at the oversized bug, as if insects weren't his cup of tea, but the bee persisted. Ash thought it best to turn back to Thorne and keep walking.

"As I was saying," Thorne continued. "We tend to be forgiving your first year, but years two through five, you'd best show up to school prepared. For now, we'll find you a used uniform from the lost and found."

They entered a door with a wooden plaque reading *Administration.* Inside was a horridly cramped room even more chaotic than the entry hall.

Two more dwarves sat at desks with stacks and stacks of books and papers piled on every flat surface, including on the floor and on top of filing cabinets. All of their drawers were at maximum capacity and the messiness was made much worse by the fact that two saber-toothed lion cubs were chasing each other around the room, growling and hissing as they romped.

Ash quickly grabbed Flynn and clasped him inside her front pocket. He wriggled wildly, wanting desperately to chase the kitties.

"Oh, quit your horseplay, you savages! DeeDee! DumDum! Honestly now!" the male dwarf yelled at the cats. He scribbled in an oversized notebook and placed a document in his "In" pile, which far outweighed the "Out" pile. "Don't mind the smilodons. They're just kittens, after all."

"Yes, dangerous kittens that will grow up to be even more dangerous adults," said Thorne, trying not to step on the memos scattered on the floor.

"Goodness me, is that Dennis hanging from that chandelier?" said the female dwarf as she glanced into the hall.

"Students are retrieving him, fear not," Thorne said.

"He's deathly afraid of heights, that one!" said Donnie.

"And bugs," Dottie chimed in.

"Do you know him well?" asked Ash.

"Why, yes! He's my cousin," said Donnie.

"And he's my cousin, too," added Dottie.

"She's also my cousin."

"Yes, indeed, all three of us are, in fact, cousins."

One of the lion cubs jumped clean over Dottie's head and landed on Donnie's desk, nearly knocking over his mountainous "In" pile. On its heels was the second cub, who *did* knock over his mountainous "In" pile.

"DeeDee, sit! DumDum, stay!" yelled Donnie.

"Will you two assist me or must I stand here all day?" interrupted Thorne, sternly.

"We'll try," said Dottie.

"We're very busy!" said Donnie.

"I need a uniform from the lost and found. Have you any, Dottie?"

Dottie glanced at an overflowing basket of clothing in the corner. "A few. Aren't you a bit old to be wearing a schoolgirl uniform, Professor Thorne?"

"Changing policies again! Why weren't we informed?" added Donnie.

"It's not for me, it's for her!" Thorne exclaimed. "This is Ashtyn Ridley, a first year."

"Hello, Ashtyn," the dwarves said in unison.

"Just Ash is fine," Ash corrected.

"Hello, Ash," they said.

Thorne rolled her eyes.

"What size are you, sweet pea?" asked Dottie.

Ash looked down at her stained and ripped clothing. "Um, small?"

Dottie approached her with a tape measure and took three quick measurements. "A two-thirds medium-small youth, actually. I think I've got one of those!"

"And Donnie," Thorne said, shooing one of the cats off a shelf next to her. "Write up a syllabus for Ashtyn. Promptly, please."

Donnie adjusted his glasses and began flipping through files in a desk drawer. "Day before school starts and she brings me a new student. Promptly, indeed," he mumbled to himself.

"What was that, Donnie, dear?" asked Thorne.

"Nothing, nothing! What kind of animal do you have, Ash?" Donnie dipped his quill in ink.

"A phoenix, sir," she responded.

Both Donnie and Dottie halted their activities and looked at Ash. She sheepishly pulled Flynn out of her pocket. He squawked. She put him back.

"Hogwash!"

"Madness!"

"Truth," said Thorne.

"A phoenix? A phoenix!" exclaimed Donnie. "We've never had no phoenixes here before! How on earth do you expect me to write up a syllabus for an animal I've never before seen?"

"Donnie, you maddening buffoon, use your thick head," scolded Thorne. "Obviously the basics: Arithmetic, Grammar, History. Then Avian, Riding and Flying, Herbs and Healing, Introduction to Magic and Special Skills, and, let's see what else...Chemistry and Potions. No, wait, that's year two. Oh yes, Combat. And Beasts of Prey, but only if her schedule allows."

Donnie scribbled it all down at an impressive pace just as Dottie approached Ash with folded clothing. "Here you are! Two sets, dark brown and gray. Should fit you nicely. Sorry they aren't in flashier colors. Oh, and leather boots—these are nice! Arganian lambskin. Apprentice Rebecca Crump left 'em in her dorm her first year. We contacted her parents, but they said to just keep them. I was hoping they'd go to a good home! She's a fourth year, now. Beautiful girl, that Crump."

Dottie disappeared from Ash's view as she piled the clothes in Ash's arms. The lion cubs weaved through her legs and nearly toppled her.

"Speaking of dorms, Dottie, please find Ash a spot in the treehouse dormitories. I'll have Apprentice Jeffrey lead her there at once."

Dottie nodded and returned to her desk. Just as she attempted to pick up a black leather-bound book entitled *Student Housing*, one of the cats latched onto it with its chompers for a surprise game of tug-o-war.

"Excuse me, Professor Thorne," Ash said quietly. "You mentioned I'd be in a class called Combat. I've never fought anything in my life."

Thorne grinned. "That's why you must learn, child. With a bird like that, you'll be a valuable asset to the king's army someday."

The king's army, she thought. *Me? And...this little fuzzball?*

Ash peeked inside her pocket. Flynn let out a string of grouchy chirps.

"Pardon me," said a high-pitched, squeaky voice from behind Professor Thorne. They turned to see a young boy with a chimera on a leash, a beast with three heads consisting of a lion, a goat, and a snake, with bat wings. "My syllabus has me in three classes at the same time: Avian, Feline, and Serpent. Which one am I supposed to go to, huh?"

Professor Thorne looked at the beast and pierced her lips together. "Hm. Take it up with Professor Talon."

The boy shrugged and walked away.

"As you can see," Thorne said to Ash. "Class placement here at the Academy can be tricky."

Complete with her almost-new uniforms and a class schedule, Ash walked beside Apprentice Jeffrey down the steps of the school and onto the lawn. It looked as though nearly all of the parents seeing their children off had gone back home, leaving the Academy students to settle in.

Flynn was so pleased to be outside in the sunshine again that he whizzed and whirled every which way, flying as high as his wings would take him, then gliding back down to Ash.

"Lively little fellah, isn't he?" Jeffrey said with a grin, fixated on the bird.

Ash nodded. She felt her face blush. Jeffrey Ruxin was quite a good-looking lad. He was seventeen years old with short, light-brown hair and striking facial features. He was tall, charming, and polite—a combination that made not staring at him with puppy dog eyes a hopeless cause.

"You like him, then?"

Ash raised her eyebrows. "Hm?"

"Flynn. You two get along? My pal Gavin bonded to a bird and they hated each other at first. It was hysterical watching them bicker."

"Oh. Yes. Flynn and I get along so far. But I suppose he's only a baby."

"Ah, see, that's interesting. It's customary for first-year students to have spent between four months and three years with their animals before arriving, depending on the type of beast."

Jeffrey whistled loudly. Within moments, a lively, gray hippogriff with massive wings sped toward them out of the sky. It came in a bit too fast and landed with a skid next to Jeffrey.

"This is Jareth, my hippogriff. Been together about six years now, haven't we, you big oaf?"

Jeffrey lovingly punched the animal on its nose. It head-butted him right back.

It was fascinating—the two didn't just seem like a boy and an animal roughhousing with each other, they seemed like brothers. Like kin. Ash noticed that the two of them even shared the same eye color, bright golden hoops around dark pupils. Jeffrey had eagle eyes of his own.

"'Spose I should be showing you around, then. Wouldn't want old Thorne ringing my neck later," he said. "Far to your left over there, on the port side of the school—sorry, my father is a sailor—are the athletic grounds. That's where your Riding and Flying class will take place. It's also where we practice and hold the Beast Games, but you won't worry about that until next year."

As they walked, Ash noticed Jareth sniffing at her carrot pocket. Flynn also noticed, and took the liberty of distracting this strange horse-bird by perching on the top of his head.

"Here on the starboard side of school, we have the stables. There are about sixty stalls, I think, and they've talked about expanding. You obviously won't be needing one, with a bird and all."

Jareth was most annoyed at the tiny bird on his head, and desperately tried to shake him off. He even spun in a circle a few times, but Flynn clutched Jareth's thick neck feathers fast with his tiny talons.

As Ash pushed the beasts out of her line of sight, she locked eyes with Farrah, who was grooming Fiona outside one of the stalls with a mane-and-tail brush. Standing near her was the dark-haired girl from earlier, with a tiger-sized mngwa cat on a leash. The gray-spotted feline seemed to share the same permanent scowl as its sullen master, and Ash assumed it was a window into the type of company Farrah kept. Both girls glared daggers at Ash as she passed and whispered to one another. Ash quickly ducked behind Jareth and Flynn.

"Am I seeing things, or is Farrah Loomington looking at you rather unfavorably?" asked Jeffrey, with a smirk.

"You know her?"

"She's Apprentice Edmund's little sister. He's a mate of mine at times, and an enemy of mine at others."

"I sort of...accidentally...ruined her going away ceremony."

"Yikes."

"...And her introduction to the professors."

"Yikes again!" Jeffrey said with a hearty laugh. "You are quite the spoiler, aren't you? She'll get over it. I've known her since she sucked her thumb and crawled on all fours. If you ask me, all the Loomingtons are wound too tightly. Bloody brilliant students, but vainglorious human beings."

"I thought Odetta was very lovely," argued Ash.

"Oh yes, Odetta is an angel," he said. "But trust me, she's the only one."

Ash peeked back to see if Farrah was still staring at her. She was gone, much to Ash's relief. Unless, of course, that meant Farrah was waiting for her someplace else.

"On the far side of the stalls, as you can see, is the inlet. Now, it's forbidden—for first years, especially—to enter the water during the day without supervision. It's entirely forbidden at night. Not only is it reserved for students with aquatic beasts, but it's also connected to the ocean, so naturally sea creatures visit from time to time. Some friendly, some not so friendly. Best not to risk it."

As he spoke, a gigantic sea serpent popped his head up out of the water. It looked around, then dipped back below the surface. Jeffrey watched as if this was a normal occurrence, but Ash's jaw nearly dragged on the grass.

If the serpent wasn't enough, a beautiful, golden dragon emerged from one of the caves inset in the cliff, overlooking the inlet. A boy mounted it and they flew off into the clouds.

"A dragon!" Ash exclaimed, accidentally saying what she was thinking out loud.

"Well, of course," Jeffrey laughed. "Students with dragons have dorms in the caves. Those big socially inept lizards wouldn't feel comfortable anywhere else."

Ash squinted and was able to see stairs leading up to each cave, indicating living quarters. Below those were maybe a hundred small houses between the inlet and the cliff in rows lining the beach.

Now, Ash's time spent with Tilda's circus had been grueling, to say the least. But one benefit of traveling to so many regions of Cascadia was that Ash now considered herself an authority on trees. Oaks, chestnuts, redwoods, cedars—she'd seen them all. But nestled beside the inlet's bay, overlooking the area with an aura of wisdom, was one of the largest trees Ash had ever laid eyes on. It looked like a beech, but Ash couldn't be sure.

The tree, sporting golden autumn leaves, seemed to grow bigger with every approaching step. Even Flynn ceased his pestering of Jareth when he spotted this massive plant.

"And finally, we arrive at the treehouses," said Jeffrey. "Lovely beech tree, isn't it? Been here for ages. Up there is where you and Flynn will be living. Well, for the first two years at least. All third years move into the Academy dorms. They're much nicer, sure, but the outdoor dorms have more character, if you ask—"

"In the tree?" Ash interrupted, still focused on the sheer size of the beech tree. "We're going to live *inside* the tree?"

"Of course! Can't you see them?" Jeffrey pulled Ash close to the tree's trunk and they looked up, into its thick, weaving branches. "The dorms. There are about twelve up there, with two roommates per house. The professors place all students with birds and small forest-dwelling animals in the Treehouse Dorms. They're quite comfy!"

Looking up, Ash could only see the undersides of two houses sitting in the branches, and several walkways made out of planks and rope. Students living in trees? She didn't know whether to be excited or worried about termites.

"I'll leave you to get settled then," Jeffrey said, mounting Jareth. "Your papers should tell you which dorm is yours. Up the spiral wooden stairs you go and you'll find it. Good luck, Ash! And happy first day tomorrow!"

After hesitantly ascending the steps leading up the tree's trunk, and ever so carefully navigating the rope ladders and walkways through branches, leaves, and the occasional spider web, Ash arrived at a small house. The door indicated the numbers 11 & 12 in green cursive lettering. It was fairly high up, about three-quarters to the top of the tree, and looked like a human-sized wooden birdhouse.

Ash could already see why the professors had placed her in the treehouses. Flynn was right in his element. He flew circles around the tree trunk and weaved in and out of the branches. He ate three ants, discovered a squirrel's nest, and got bonked on the head by a falling beechnut all in the span of two minutes.

Ash reached in her pocket to double-check her syllabus. At the top was scribbled: *Ashtyn Ridley, Treehouse Dormitory #12.* She was in the right place.

She knocked on the door. No answer. Slowly she opened it and stepped into an entryway with a coat stand and a shoe cubby. A door on the left read *11* and a door on the right read *12*.

"Guess we're this way, Flynn," she said to her bird, who zipped inside to inspect the place. "Let's hope it's better than a tent and a blanket on the ground."

And indeed it was. Inside was a cozy cottage interior with a circular throw rug on a wooden floor, a dresser, and green curtains framing a window that overlooked the valley. Best of all, beneath the window was a small bed with a quilted comforter and a fluffy pillow. Stacked at the foot of the bed were three more folded blankets and her sack of belongings from Odetta's sleigh.

Ash ran over and belly-flopped on the bed with her face pressed into the pillow. "Oh, Flynn. This is the life," she said, muffled.

She looked up when she heard clanging and saw Flynn pecking at a birdcage on the desk. Ash rose to investigate. Sitting on her writing desk was a birdcage and a basket of bird supplies. Birdseed, a mineral block, cleansing solution, claw clippers, a bell toy, and a book called *The Proper Care and Feeding of Companion Birds*. Inside the basket was a note:

Dear Ashtyn,

Here are a few items from Flanagan's Feathers to get you started. Have a wonderful first week. The Elders and I look forward to your progress.

Elderess Odetta Loomington

Flynn flew inside the cage and immediately perched on its hanging swing. Ash smiled and sat down in the desk chair. She watched Flynn swing back and forth, really looking at him for the first time since that morning. His tail already looked longer than it did just hours earlier. His beak was still much too large for his tiny head, but he certainly seemed more confident in his little, red body.

"Can you even believe where we are, Flynny? You're only a day old and you've already experienced the biggest adventure of my life with me," Ash said.

Flynn cooed as he rocked. Ash wasn't sure if he was agreeing with her statement or simply enjoying the swaying motion.

"I hope I understand you better one day, you silly thing."

A poke in Ash's hip reminded her of the pan flute. She retrieved it and drew it from its velvet pouch.

"I hope you're all right, father. Wherever you are."

She blew into the flute. It returned a soft note, and then another.

But the third sound was more of a loud thud.

The entry door to the dormitory swung open, banging against the wall. A young, white fox sprinted inside. It had orange tribal-looking markings on its forehead and three tails, each with an orange tip. The hyper animal ran a lap around Ash's room, mussing her comforter, knocking her folded blankets to the ground, and sending a tall lamp teetering. Ash lunged for it and prevented a crash just in time.

The dog-fox-thing panted heavily and sniffed everything in sight. Once it spotted Flynn, who was still in his cage looking quite terrified of the pooch, it barked and lunged down to full play position.

Through the door poked the head of a twelve-year-old girl with short, dirty-blonde hair.

"Hello!" she said with a large smile and bright eyes. "I'm Marni Mayberry! I'm your roommate!"

She dragged a large, expensive-looking trunk inside the entryway and shut the door behind her. "Can you believe I dragged this thing all the way up here?"

Ash would have responded if the fox hadn't tackled her to the ground and started licking her face. Ash couldn't help but giggle.

Marni gasped. "Mitzi! Come here! Sit!"

The fox ignored her. Marni rolled her eyes and pulled the dog off Ash. "Sorry about her! She loves meeting new people. You should have seen her today meeting the professors. She stuck her snout right between Professor Talon's legs! Couldn't you just *die*? I've never been so embarrassed in *all* my *life*! Here, let me help you up."

"Thanks," Ash said, shaking hands with Marni after she pulled her to her feet. "I'm Ash. That's Flynn."

Marni pushed Mitzi aside. Flynn took the opportunity to quickly fly out of his cage. He perched on top of the window's curtain rod and cheeped angrily at Mitzi. Mitzi, of course, barked happily back.

"Wow! A real phoenix! Everyone all over school's been talking about you, you know," said Marni.

"Talking...about me?" Ash asked.

"Well, I mean, they're talking about the phoenix, so consequently, they're also talking about you," Marni said. Marni spoke at such a quick pace that Ash could hardly keep up with her. "Apparently, Flynn—it's Flynn, right? What kind of name is Flynn if your name is Ash? It's tradition to give your Bonded Beast a name with the same first letter as your own."

Ash raised her eyebrows. She had named him Flynn because she'd read in a book that it meant "ruddy" or "red-haired." Now that she knew he was so important, perhaps she should've named him something more regal and starting with an 'a.' Like Alexander. Or Augustus. Archimedes.

"I guess I didn't know," Ash replied, sheepishly.

"It doesn't really matter. Anyway, apparently Flynn is the first phoenix anyone has seen in something like four hundred years, and everyone's stunned that he was found by a peasant girl of all people!"

Ash blushed, wishing she'd changed out of her filthy rags before meeting her new roommate. Especially since Marni was dressed in such a beautiful, clean button down coat with a plaid pattern and matching hat.

"No, no! I don't mean it like that," Marni rushed to say, not missing a beat. "Just that all of the eggs and newborns of magical beasts normally go to trusted families who have been Regal Kin for generations. It's very rare that someone is allowed into the Academy who's never had a relative attend."

"I've never even seen the Academy, let alone have someone in my family attend it," Ash said.

"Exactly! So, just a heads up, that's probably something you should prepare for," Marni said, removing her traveling coat, hat, and gloves to reveal a very cute—and likely very expensive—purple dress and white stockings.

"What do you mean?" Ash asked.

"Oh, you know. Stuffy families who don't think an outsider should have a Bonded Beast. I think it's fantastic! It's a tight-knit society, so I've known bunches of other students attending this year since I was little. And I'll be honest, I only like about twelve of them. But I can already tell I'm going to like you. Aren't you excited to be roomies?"

Ash's brain was trying to process the fact that this girl—a girl her own age—actually liked her, when she realized that this pause in Marni's dizzying chatter meant it was time to respond. "Um, yes! Very excited!"

Mitzi continued to bark at Flynn, who zipped down to hide underneath Ash's hair. Ash leaned down to pet the dog and noticed a charm on its collar.

"Mitzi the kitsune?" she read.

"No, no, not *kit-soon*. It's pronounced *keet-soo-nay*," Marni corrected. "My parents are world-renowned travelers. They normally never let me go with them—too young they say, I don't agree—but when they met a Regal Kinswoman in the Oriental Regions with a pregnant kitsune, my parents had me flown there immediately to bond to one of its cubs. There were five, and I got the best one. She's from a thunder clan, with magical lightning powers!"

"Really? That's incredible," Ash responded, amazed that such a hyper little puppy could actually possess magical powers.

"Well, she *will* perform magic. When she's a bit older and more trained. Lately, I just try to get her to sit. Sit!" Marni commanded. Mitzi simply looked at her with a big smile. "Dumb dog."

Suddenly they heard whispering.

"Is that her?"

"Where's the bird?"

"I don't see anything!"

"Ow! That's my foot!"

Marni and Ash shared a confused look. They looked to the window and saw three heads crowding each other for a peek inside.

"Excuse us! Privacy, please?" yelled Marni.

But the door swung open anyway and in hopped a bildad, a dumb-looking creature resembling a beaver with a hooked nose, webbed feet, and long hind legs. Mitzi immediately chased him.

"Dickon the Great, at your service!" said a boy, entering the room with a flamboyant pose.

"Dickon! Get Dudley out of here! I just got Mitzi calmed down!" Marni said.

Another boy appeared in the doorway. He was a visibly nervous child and carefully avoided Mitzi and Dudley as he slipped in.

"This is why you should've left your animal in your room like I did, Dickon," he said. "Lucky is curled up quietly on my bed as we speak."

"Who are you?" asked Marni, desperately trying to wrangle her barking fox.

"Ooh, a kitsune!" said the boy, ignoring Marni's question.

"*Keet-soo-nay*," she corrected.

The third intruder was a cute, dark-skinned girl with a friendly grin.

"Sorry, Lokey," she said to the nervous boy, "but Lucky actually hopped out your window and followed Nettles and me here. Hope you don't mind."

Lokey glanced to the window to see a nearly human-sized rabbit scratching at the glass and looking comically gloomy. "Aw, man! Go back to sleep, Lucky! Why didn't you stop him, Naomi?"

Without a sound, Naomi's animal of prey, Nettles, glided inside and perched eerily on the windowsill. Ash immediately recognized this beast from a picture book she'd owned about winged creatures. It looked like a flying reptile the size of a hawk with wings like a bat. Its head was long and narrow, with about fifty conical teeth. It was known as a kongamato, hailing from the desert. Ash gulped at the sight of it.

Lokey's big, sad rabbit finally joined the group and hopped right onto Ash's bed.

By now, Ash and Flynn—who was still hiding in Ash's hair—were quite overwhelmed by the barking, squawking, out-of-control menagerie that had overtaken her previously empty room.

"All of you live in this tree, too?" asked Ash.

"Yes, plus a few students who are second years. And they're all *leaving now*," Marni hinted loudly.

Dickon sauntered over to Ash and crossed his arms. "Ash, is it? Everyone says you have a phoenix. But I don't buy it. So, let's see him then."

The other children voiced their agreement. Ash looked to Marni, who shrugged.

Carefully, Ash reached into her hair and got ahold of Flynn. She drew him out of her hair and held him up. The kids widened their eyes and their mouths fell open.

"Wicked awesome!" said Lokey.

"No way," said Dickon.

"Adorable!" said Naomi.

After a nod of approval from Ash, Dickon reached out his hand and stroked the bird's back. He quickly pulled his hand away.

"Ouch!" he said, holding his fingers. "He's hot! And his feathers are so scratchy and coarse."

"Not to me," Ash said, petting him. "To me he feels as soft as cotton. And just a little warm."

"How sweet," said a condescending voice from the doorway.

It was Farrah, standing with the dark-haired girl from the stables. "Having a party, are we?"

Ash tensed up, but Marni approached her face to face. "What are *you* doing here, Farrah? Shouldn't you be back with your pointy-head pony in the smelly stable dorms?"

"Tell me, Marni, did your mum and dad even stop their sleigh to let you out today? Or did they just fly over and push you off so they could go on another vacation without you?" Farrah snapped back.

For the first time since Ash had met her, Marni was speechless.

Farrah strolled into the room, surveying the variety of students and animals.

"I guess my brother Edmund was right," she said. "Treehouse kids really are a bunch of freaks."

"That's rude," said Ash, once again speaking her thoughts out loud by accident.

Farrah whipped her head around to face Ash, who immediately regretted speaking. "Rude? You think *I'm* being rude? This from the girl who ruined both my farewell ceremony in Rosedale, an event my mother had been planning for months, *and* my welcoming ceremony with the professors!"

The kids all looked at each other nervously. Marni bit her lip and fumed.

"I'm sorry, I didn't mean—"

"Don't apologize to her, Ash," said Marni. "Her mane-and-tail shampoo has clearly been seeping into her brain."

Farrah's dark-haired friend lunged at Marni, but Farrah held her back. "Too easy, Talia. Let her be."

"The door is that way," Marni said through gritted teeth.

Farrah smiled sweetly and turned to leave. "You're right. It's getting late. In fact, I was only up here wondering how anyone was supposed to sleep in preparation for our first day with this tree full of idiots being so loud. But it looks like the ratatoskrs will take care of that for me. Ta-ta!"

With a wave, Farrah and Talia disappeared out the door.

The Academy clock echoed through the valley with a loud *bong*.

"Oh no! The ratatoskrs!" exclaimed Lokey. "Everyone to your dorms, quick!"

In a matter of seconds, all the visiting children had grabbed their animals and raced out the door.

"Ratatoskrs? What are those?" Ash asked.

"Come look," Marni said, motioning for Ash to follow her to the window. "You see those squirrel things?"

It was difficult to see in the dark, but Ash could faintly make out tiny critters with long, pointed ears and bushy tails scurrying up and down the branches.

"Those are ratatoskrs, the little snitches," Marni said. "When the big clock strikes nine, they scamper around for a while to make sure all children are in their dorms. If not, they inform Professor Thorne and we get detention. Dirty spies."

"Maybe they'll catch Farrah on her way back to the stables then!"

Marni threw her head back and let out a sarcastic chortle. "Ha! Like a Loomington could ever get in trouble."

She yawned and headed toward her room, calling Mitzi to join her.

"Hey," Ash called. "Thanks for sticking up for me tonight."

"No problem," she said. "We're friends."

Marni smiled and retired to her room.

Ash curled up in her cozy new bed. She gazed out the window at the night sky and the leaves fluttering in the breeze. Flynn was comfortably nestled in the crook of her right arm. Both nodded off.

While it wasn't a Cascadian Apple Tree, Ash would forever claim that it was the best night of tree-sleep she ever had.

CHAPTER 8

THE FIRST WEEK

Ash woke pleasantly for the first time in six months. No monkeys launching projectiles at her head, no old witch yelling at her, and no bugs crawling in her hair. She did sneeze a small, red feather out of her nose, though.

Flynn circled the room and landed on the windowsill, ecstatic to begin his second day as the world's most handsome baby bird. Even at just two days old, Flynn seemed to have grown slightly bigger and his eyes were even more expressive.

Ash looked out the window at the Academy clock. It was seven. One hour until her first class!

Ash scooped up Flynn in her arms and kissed his head. He fidgeted to get away, so she pulled him down to the bed. Ash forcefully snuggled and tickled him, and they respectively chirped and laughed until both spilled to the floor beneath a pillow avalanche.

"That's how I used to wrestle the older you in my tent when we performed the old switcheroo!" Ash said, as Flynn shook his head and raced back inside his cage. He instinctively began to preen his feathers—a very long process.

Ash stood up, searching for her hairbrush to tame her own messy head, when something caught her eye. On her bed, under where her pillow had rested, was a small piece of ripped parchment. In black ink, it said:

YOU DO NOT BELONG HERE.

"Very funny, Farrah."

Ash crumpled up the paper and tossed it in a wastebasket by the door.

One limb at a time, she changed into her school uniform. It consisted of a tan, long-sleeved undershirt with matching cloth leggings. Then, a sleeveless tunic, which hung to the top of her thighs and had two pockets. It was form-fitting, clean, and comfortable, but the tunic was such an awful shade of brown. It reminded her of the smelly monkey projectiles she had endured at the circus—something she hoped she would never experience again.

After pulling on her second knee-high boot, she paused. She looked at the crumpled paper in the wastebasket.

But wait…Farrah didn't go anywhere near my bed last night, she thought.

Who could have left that note under her pillow? She thought of options while sprinkling birdseed in Flynn's cage.

The other children who had visited last night didn't seem mean or nasty at all. Perhaps the note was there before she ever entered the room? Perhaps it was left there by the dorm's previous student as a prank?

Her thought process was interrupted by a loud knock.

"Ash! Are you awake? What's your first class?" yelled Marni through the door.

Ash checked her syllabus. "Um...orientation in the Skylark Amphitheater with Professor Thorne, then Avian with Professor Talon."

"I have orientation with Thorne, too! Hurry and get dressed—we'll go together!"

With Mitzi on a leash, Flynn fed and happy, and both girls in their uniforms—Marni's tunic was a beautiful amethyst color—the roommates departed the treehouse early for their first day. They quickly discovered that what they considered early might not be early enough.

The entire campus, inside and out, was buzzing with students and their beasts. Dodging and weaving their way through the crowd was made much more difficult by the added obstacles of dragons and other creatures of all sizes.

"Skylark Amphitheater—where's that?" Ash asked Marni, shouting to be heard above the noise.

"This way!"

Marni grabbed her friend's wrist and they ran toward the right side of the Academy building.

"No pushing, no shoving, no horseplay, no practicing magic on your own, no discussing black magic, no taunting beasts that aren't yours, and no touching beasts that aren't yours, no running down the entry steps, no leaving school property, no parties, no plotting, no scheming, no back talking, no—"

Ash and Marni sat in the center of about a hundred first-year students and their antsy beasts in an outdoor amphitheater. The three rows of children vigorously scribbled notes as Professor Thorne rattled off dos and don'ts during orientation—and they were mostly don'ts.

The two girls looked around nervously.

"Were we supposed to bring a notepad?" Ash whispered.

"I thought they would tell us at orientation!" Marni whispered back.

Ash exhaled and hoped for better luck once the actual classes started.

Ash's first week at the Academy was nothing like she'd imagined. Sure, there were classrooms, assignments, and average-tasting sloppy joes served in the commissary, but the learning process was much more involved than she had anticipated. In her Avian class, all birds were required to sit on a perch beside their desks silently unless called upon. In fact, Professor Talon said that after their introductory class, all birds that chirped, cheeped, or squawked out of turn would be required to leave the classroom with their student and sit in the hallway for ten minutes. In addition, any bird that took flight in the classroom when Talon had not properly asked them to would have to wear a muzzle and leash for the remainder of the class.

There was also zero tolerance for rowdy pets in her Beasts of Prey and Herbs and Healing classes. Finding the balance between listening to the teacher's lectures and controlling a baby phoenix proved greatly difficult. It seemed like every other student's bond gave them a basic control over their animal. Sure, the first-year beasts went a little nutty sometimes—Marni's fox, Mitzi, being a perfect example—but the children could still tell their animals to "Come!" and they'd come, or "Stay!" and they'd stay. Flynn wouldn't even do that. It was proving true that not coming from a family of Regal Kin put Ash behind her fellow classmates. She didn't have the luxury of being pre-schooled about magical animals by her parents or siblings. But she tried not to let it get to her. The frustrations of keeping Flynn under control and continuing to get lost in the corridors of the Academy aside, Ash was having a marvelous time.

In just one week, she had already learned so much: Professor Talon taught her the importance of a varied menu for Flynn, such as the nutritional differences between seed and pellets and the benefits of fresh vegetables. Professor Thorne wasted no time jumping into the subject matter in Herbs and Healing. She began the first class by teaching students how to treat cuts and scratches on both themselves and their animals. While a few of Ash's classmates yawned and rolled their eyes at some lessons they considered elementary, Ash found every bit of it fascinating.

Perhaps the best part of the Academy's first week being so chaotic was that Ash didn't have a single run-in with Farrah. With five grades and fifty to a hundred students per grade, the Academy had the population of a small town. Even in the few classes Ash and Farrah shared, they sat far apart and focused only on the lesson. Well, at least Ash focused on the lesson.

"...and many flying beasts can perform spectacular magic attacks with their wings," said an energetic and passionate

Professor Suarez during their first Introduction to Magic and Special Skills class. "Force fields, wind gusts—some can turn their feathers into knives! It's an incredible attack called a Wing Slice. Tell me, has anyone here seen a winged beast perform this ability?"

Farrah shot her hand up. Suarez nodded and she stood, unnecessarily.

"Well, as you know," she began, with folded hands and an affected smile, "my aunt, Regal Kinswoman and Elderess Odetta Loomington, has a pegasus. He's not quite as dazzling as your beast, Professor Suarez, but it has been a great honor and pleasure becoming so intimately familiar with such a sensational creature, when I know so many in this classroom haven't had that wonderful learning opportunity."

Suarez paused. He opened his mouth to speak, but she cut him off.

"Oh, and my older brother, Edmund, has an even rarer breed: a black pegasus. I truly am blessed to be around such company on a regular basis."

"And have you witnessed the Wing Slice attack? As I mentioned?" Suarez asked.

"No," Farrah said confidently, with that same pompous grin across her flawless face.

Professor Suarez pursed his lips. Students shifted their eyes back and forth in the awkward silence. Marni and Ash shared a look, rolling their eyes so hard they nearly saw the back of their skulls. Finally, Suarez spoke.

"All right. Great. Let's move on."

By week two, Ash had a fairly good sense of how to get to each of her classes on time and which foods in the cafeteria to avoid. While many children were already forming cliques, Ash kept to herself whenever Marni wasn't around. Ash didn't mind. She needed to spend time with Flynn anyway, who had already grown another inch in length. She'd only been acquainted with her Bonded Beast for a little over a week, while most children had been with their animals for months, even years. Thankfully, Flynn was a quick learner. He could pick up a command almost instantly and had already learned to perch on anything Ash pointed to when she said, "Perch!" Unfortunately, he was also stubborn, so he only obeyed his master when he felt like it.

While first year students were divided for most classes, they all gathered outside on the athletic field for the one class they took together: Combat. As the course with the most potential to be dangerous, the professors thought it best to introduce it in their second week.

"All right, kiddies. In your positions. Let's form five rows of six."

One of the fourth-year students assisting the class was Apprentice Rebecca Crump. She was a beautiful sixteen-year-old girl who always had her hair tied back away from her face with a ribbon. Her hair was an interesting mixture of golden blonde with red highlights. From the way she walked to the way she rolled up the sleeves of her uniform, it was evident she was a tomboy through and through.

Before the professor arrived, Rebecca's job was to ensure all safety gear was present for the dangerous beasts and arrange the first years in order of where to stand, grouping animals that were the least likely to have a tiff with each other. Her own beast, a Golden-Horned Magma dragon, stood thirteen feet tall at the front, observing the scene with rather intimidating deep green eyes—the same eyes as Rebecca. Ash had to stop Flynn from flying over to play with him several times.

Ash glanced behind her to see Rebecca approach a shaggy-haired boy wearing a scarf and sweater. He stood beside a ten-foot-tall, light-blue and silver dragon that appeared to have icicles on his wings. Rebecca playfully punched the boy in the arm.

"Straighten up, Hammie. Mum's always going on about your poor posture," Rebecca said with a smirk.

"Ouch! That hurts, Becca!" he whined, while rubbing his arm. "And you have to call me *Hammond* at school, not *Hammie*."

"Sure thing, Hammie." Rebecca flung the boy's scarf over his face before walking to the next student.

"I'm so glad I don't have siblings," Marni whispered to Ash.

When Rebecca had worked her way through the lines and gotten to Ash, she glanced down at her feet.

"Are those my old boots?" asked Rebecca.

Ash sheepishly looked down at her toes. "They, um, gave them to me at the lost and found."

"I was wondering where those went!" Rebecca said with a smile. "They look better on you anyway."

"Very good, Crump. I'll take it from here."

Every student head turned toward the booming female voice. Before them stood a six-foot-tall, powerfully built woman wearing black combat boots and a leather-skirted outfit overlaid with armor. Ash recognized this woman from her first day at the Academy.

Standing beside her was a deep-orange and brown Wyvern—a variety of dragon that had two legs, a reptilian body, and a barbed tail. It was a bit smaller than Rebecca's dragon at about eight feet tall, but beefier and more muscular, less lean and elegant. The speckles on the beast's face and throat matched those on the professor's face. Bera's skin matched the light olive color of the creature's belly. They also had matching orange eyes. The woman and beast actually *looked* like each other.

Ash leaned over to whisper to Marni. "The professors actually resemble their beasts!"

"Uh, yeah, of course," Marni replied with a teasing smile. "The stronger your bond, the more traits you take on from your animal. But every bond is unique. Sometimes Regal Kin look like their beasts, sometimes they act like their beasts. One time I saw a unicorn master with a horn of her own!"

Dickon turned toward the gossiping duo to chime in with his own comment. "Who cares about that, this lady is supposed to be our Combat teacher? A *woman*?" The professor whipped her head toward Dickon. She marched over to him and the kids nearby backed away. She grabbed him by the front of his uniform with one hand and raised him up.

"You got a problem with that?" she said.

Dickon shook his head "no" and she dropped him on his bum.

"My name is Bera Jarnskeggadottir," she said with an accent Ash couldn't quite identify. "Not only am I your Combat teacher, but I am the captain of the Beast Army serving King Tiberius. You, sprouts, will refer to me as Captain Bera."

The Wyvern snorted.

"Oh, yes," she continued. "This is my baby, Bertha the Speckle-Throated Wyvern. He has been honored by the king three times for bravery in battle."

"You have a *male* Wyvern named Bertha?" asked Farrah.

Captain Bera snapped her fingers and Bertha roared. The noise was an ear-piercing screech balanced with an earth-rumbling low bass tone. It was the scariest sound that Ash, and by the looks of it, her classmates, had ever heard in their lives. The screech made Maurice's deep howls from the traveling circus sound like mouse squeaks.

"Any other inquiries?" Bera asked.

The field of children was dead silent, save for a nervous gulp from Lokey.

"Good," she continued. "Welcome to your first Combat class. Survive five years with me and you might be ready to serve your king like many before you. You will learn to fight, defend yourself, and, eventually, perform magic attacks utilizing your beast's special powers."

"Special powers?" asked Naomi, her kongamato perched on her arm. Ash was relieved to hear that at least one other person besides herself was curious as to what Bera meant.

"Being bonded to a magical creature does not simply mean they come when they're called. Every year you train with your Bonded Beast, you become more connected. Your minds meld. You know each other intimately—what the other thinks, desires, and fears."

Bera placed a hand on her Wyvern. "That, students, is what makes the pair of you so eminently dangerous."

Ash looked at Flynn on her right shoulder. He hiccupped. The involuntary contraction nearly jolted his tiny body right off his feet.

Oh, yes. Dangerous indeed, she thought.

"Magical beasts possess magical powers," Bera said, motioning for Rebecca to have her dragon face Bertha. "And all of you normal, non-magical humans will learn to both control the various magic attacks of your beasts and, once your connection to them is strong enough, cast spells to complement and intensify their attacks."

She waved for the students to back up. "Rebecca's dragon, Roast, is a Magma dragon. Aside from physical abilities such as flying, biting, and the use of talons, Roast can breathe a long stream of molten lava and rock at enemies. He can also breathe hot air out of his mouth and nostrils that melts anything in its path at five hundred and ninety degrees—in other words, hotter than any hot spring you'll find in Cascadia."

Bera motioned to Rebecca. Rebecca said a command, only audible to Roast, and the beast reared back. Out of his mouth came glowing liquid fire, which hit Bera and Bertha. The children gasped. A few animals squirmed in their harnesses.

The attack ceased and there stood Bera and Bertha, completely unharmed.

"Lucky for me, magma cannot melt dragon scales," Bera said. "And even better that I am bonded closely enough to Bertha to share his method of defense."

Bera's skin, which had turned the texture and color of Bertha's scales, faded back to normal.

"And wearing flame-retardant armor. That helps, too."

The children applauded, awed.

Bera and Rebecca walked the children through simple beginner's exercises. They paired up the students and taught them how to assume a one-on-one defensive position. Ash was thankful to be paired with Marni.

"So, you're about to fight Ash, yeah?" Rebecca said to Marni as she made her rounds. "First, defense position. Knees bent, arms up, protect yourself at all times. Go on, put your hands up! Haven't you ever been in a fight before?"

"I've never even *seen* a fight before," Marni retorted, hands on her hips.

"Sheltered kid. Real shame," Rebecca teased. "Ash, you're scrappy, I bet. What would you do if someone tried to attack you?"

"Well," Ash began, sheepishly. "Someone did attack me, the first day I had Flynn. A man pushed me. Flynn swooped in and set him on fire with some kind of flame attack."

"Awesome!" Marni exclaimed.

"That's a bond for you," Rebecca explained. "Even his first day of being alive, the tiny thing let adrenaline take over and he defended your honor. Isn't that neat? So, what would you do now if you sensed I was about to push you?"

Rebecca took a forceful step toward Ash. Ash bent her knees and put her hands up, ready to keep her away. Flynn immediately saw her defensive stance and rushed to her side, ready to set Rebecca ablaze if necessary.

Rebecca smiled and stepped back. "See that? He recognized your positioning as his time to act. You were ready, so he got ready, and now he's—"

Flynn, a slave to his short attention span, noticed a nearby butterfly and instantly chased after it. Ash winced. Her cheeks turned bright red with embarrassment.

"—chasing bugs," Rebecca said with a laugh. "He'll get it. Practice, practice."

Even after forty long minutes of practice, all of the other animals were still training diligently. Flynn seemed to be the only animal who thought the whole ordeal was silly. He refused to participate. Instead of listening to Ash's commands, he flew from student to student inspecting the other beasts. However friendly he meant to be, his presence jerked most beasts out of their concentration.

Ash beckoned for him and finally chased him around the field, catching him before a boy's kludde dog could trap him in his jaws.

Bera signaled for the rest of the children to continue practicing and approached Ash with hands on hips. Ash straightened up and started rehearsing an apology in her head.

"The girl with the phoenix," Bera said. Surprisingly, her tone wasn't as unpleasant as Ash had expected. "I have only heard stories of its abilities."

Bera uttered a command and Flynn immediately perched on her finger. Ash shook her head with frustration. He wouldn't listen to her, his master, yet he'd sit on a stranger's finger, calmly and quietly?

"Great potential, this one. He is feisty and eager. Stubborn, yes, but stubborn, under strict control, will one day prove invaluable. A stubbornness to learn turns into a stubbornness to retreat."

Ash faked a smile. Invaluable later, a giant headache now.

"It's true, he's young and you've had him only a week now, but for that I cannot simply give you a pass. You have many doubters at this school, girl. You will fail or you will prove them wrong. In order to prove them wrong, you must work doubly hard."

Bera handed Flynn back to Ash. He snapped out of whatever trance Bera had him in and once again showed no interest in associating with Ash. There were far too many odd-looking children to examine and beasts to befriend.

"Rebecca!" Bera called. "Fetch a harness and leash for Flynn. It'll be the smallest size we have in the supply room."

Bera continued observing the children and correcting their form.

"You hear that Flynn?" Ash whispered to her bird as he flew dizzying circles around her head, chirping merrily. "No one at this school thinks I should even be here! And you're not helping my cause!"

Not three minutes after Rebecca headed inside the Academy to retrieve the harness, she jogged back outside holding a note. She handed the note to Bera.

"Everyone!" Bera bellowed after reading the note. "I must tend to something and will be back shortly. Hold your positions and do not move until I return. Is that clear?"

"Yes, Captain Bera," the children responded in unison, like miniature soldiers-in-training. Rebecca and Bera headed swiftly into the Academy.

Everyone remained silent for a few moments, before Farrah opened her big mouth.

"Struggling a bit, are we, Ash?" she sneered, looking picturesque as always in a shimmering fuchsia tunic. "Too advanced for you, I'm sure. Perhaps a kindergarten would be more suitable for the two of you."

Ash refused to look at her. *Just ignore her, Ash. Just ignore her.*

"Let me guess, you and your albino mule are acing the class on the first day?" Marni shot back.

Ash motioned to Marni with a gesture that said *Cut it out.*

"Fiona's talent speaks for itself," Farrah retorted.

"All right, then," Marni said, crossing her arms. "If she's so fabulously gifted, let's see it."

"Marni, Captain Bera said not to move," Ash whispered.

"Farrah's going to move, not us!" Marni whispered back.

Farrah faced Fiona and extended her arms. "Fiona! Rise!"

She flicked her arms in an upward motion, and Fiona slowly began to rear up on her hind legs. As Farrah turned her head to smirk at Marni and Ash, Fiona began to teeter, losing her balance.

The horse stumbled sideways, falling hard on the tail of the kludde. The kludde growled with pain and took off running, dragging the leash out of his child's hand. He sprinted through the crowd of children and they dove out of his way.

Running past Hammond, the kludde's leash whipped the boy's large ice dragon in the face. The provoked dragon roared at the kludde, who turned toward him and snarled. The fun was over. The students were genuinely frightened.

"No, Hermaeus! Stop! Don't fight the dog!" screamed Hammond, yanking on the chain attached to Hermaeus's harness.

At the sound of Hammond's voice, the kludde turned his angry eyes on him. He lunged at the boy, who shrieked.

Ash quickly grabbed a stick on the ground and stepped toward them both. She began singing, the talent her father had taught her that always calmed unruly farm animals.

> *What troubles you meet, oh my darling dear*
> *What evils you face, whatever you fear*
> *Do not be 'fraid for this, too, will pass*
> *We'll lie soon down on green, silky grass*
> *We'll lie soon down on green, silky grass*

At the hypnotizing sound of her voice, both the kludde and the dragon calmed. They returned to a non-threatening stance and stared only at Ash. At the end of her verse, she threw the stick far to the right, into the open field. The kludde ran toward it like a puppy playing fetch. Once again, her father's unique lessons had proven invaluable.

Every student exhaled with relief, especially Hammond. They looked at Ash in surprise.

"How did you learn that, Ash?" Marni asked.

Ash tensed when she noticed so many eyes on her. "My, um, my dad—"

"Congratulations, Ash," scoffed Farrah. "You've bonded to every animal except yours."

Ash scanned the area for Flynn, who was several yards away playing with Lokey's large rabbit, Lucky. Ash groaned.

"Ridley!" called the voice of Captain Bera.

Ash quickly turned around and saw Bera, Rebecca, and Professor Suarez all standing outside the Academy. Ash was convinced she was in trouble for something. Throwing the stick for the kludde? Having no control over Flynn? Singing?

"Ms. Ridley, please come over here at once," commanded Suarez.

Ash walked to the professors, relieved that Flynn actually followed her, landing on her shoulder.

"I'm so sorry, Captain Bera. The kludde was—"

"Not now, Ridley," Bera said.

"Ash," Professor Suarez said, smiling. "Your immediate presence has been requested...by the king."

CHAPTER 9

HIS EXCELLENCY, THE KING OF CASCADIA

"Quickly, Ashtyn. We mustn't keep His Majesty waiting."

Professor Suarez walked swiftly as he led Ash and Flynn through several school corridors she'd never seen before. Ash was certain she'd never find her way out of the Academy's labyrinth of passages and foyers.

Eventually, they reached a spiral staircase that opened up to the roof of the school. There was a large, circular stone platform surrounded by eight chambers facing inward. It was like a small version of a battling arena. Each chamber was four times as tall as Ash and blocked off by a golden gate. Behind several of the gates, Ash noticed movement and heard murmurs, grunts, and the flapping of wings.

"This, young Ashtyn, is where the professors and Elders keep our beasts," said Suarez as he searched his jacket. "Ah! Here's my key."

"All of your beasts are here?" Ash said, peering through one gate that had a green glow deep within.

"Yes. Well, some of us, anyway," he said, unlocking Chamber Five. "Rather difficult to fit a Hydra or a Zmey dragon in a stall like this, wouldn't you say?"

Suarez laughed heartily at his joke. Ash pretended to laugh with him, but secretly hadn't the slightest clue what a Hydra or a Zmey dragon was.

"Why must you keep them locked up?"

"It's more to keep students locked out," he said with a wink. "Animals like their privacy, too."

Flynn flitted over to Suarez as he turned his key in the chamber gate's large lock. He zipped up and down and side to side like a hummingbird trying to see what was inside.

"Curious one, isn't he?" Suarez commented.

"Too curious to stay with me when I want him to," Ash confessed. "Flynn! Come over here! Flynny!"

Flynn ignored her. Suarez paused before opening the gate and turned toward her. "He knows his name by now, yes?"

"Yes. But sometimes he comes and sometimes he doesn't."

"Try it again. This time, lower your voice. Speak from your diaphragm with assertion. As a mother would calmly call a child away from a cliffside, abstaining from panic."

Ash took a deep breath, using her diaphragm instead of lungs, as she did in preparation to sing. In fact, maybe that was the very mindset she needed. When she sang, animals would focus and calm down. Perhaps if she spoke with the same concentration, Flynn would listen.

"Flynn. Come," she ordered firmly and deliberately.

Upon hearing a command with authority behind it, Flynn zipped back to her shoulder. He tilted his head and looked at her, as if to say, *I'm here. What do you need?*

Suarez smiled. "Having a Bonded Beast is a delicate harmony of friendship and leadership. You must establish both trust and dominance, equally. It can be more challenging than it sounds."

Ash, quite satisfied with herself, reached in her pocket and fed Flynn a small piece of carrot. He chirped his appreciation and gave her a love-peck on the ear.

Suarez entered his chamber and disappeared in its depths for several minutes. Ash could hear nothing but the occasional snort and snarl.

When Suarez emerged, he walked beside a beast so magnificent that Ash rubbed her eyes and blinked rapidly to ensure she wasn't daydreaming. The animal was a great lion, bigger than any Ash had seen depicted in paintings. Its backbone was as tall as Suarez's shoulders and its legs as thick as tree trunks. Folded to its sides were enormous wings, dark purple in color, while his shaggy mane was a dark brown, almost burgundy—the same color as Professor Suarez's hair and beard. The beast's shining, sharp talons clicked against the stone floor as it walked, but that wasn't the most intimidating part of him. Curled at his hindquarters was a red scorpion tail with a sharp stinger at the end. Unfolded, it looked like the tail would stretch upwards of twelve feet.

The beast, while calm, still growled softly, showing his dagger-like fangs.

"This is Diego. He is my manticore," said Suarez. "And it is upon him we will ride to the kingdom."

Ash noticed the large saddle on the lion's back, dangerously close to that scorpion tail, and her throat dropped into her stomach.

"Pardon me, did you mean *ride*? Or get pulled by a comfortable sleigh that stretches far beyond the reach of that tail?"

Suarez laughed and patted her on the back. "Funny! You've got a sense of humor. Not many students here do."

If only she were joking.

Before Ash knew it, she was mounted on Diego, holding tight onto Suarez's waist in front of her. Diego unfolded his massive wings and, with a few sprints, sprung into the air. The Academy fell away, smaller and smaller as they rose into the clouds. It was nothing like flying on Odetta's sleigh—it was much more dangerous, much more terrifying, and much, much more exciting.

"Nothing beats a flight on a beast, eh, Ash?" said Suarez with a smile.

Ash nodded and squeezed him tighter as the manticore hit turbulence.

Flynn flew nearby, careful to give plenty of clearance to the stinger-end of his new cat-bird friend.

"He's a good flyer, that one!" Suarez said, watching Flynn's aerial maneuvers through the clouds. "Impressive speed for his age."

"Excuse me, Professor," Ash interrupted. "Why does the king want to meet me?"

"King Tiberius has a great love of beasts. When the Elders informed him that a phoenix had returned to Cascadia after four hundred years, he sent for you without haste."

Ash bit her lip. She had so many questions, but was unsure about etiquette. Tilda yelled at her any time she asked about anything, so would her professors expect her to keep her mouth shut, too?

"People keep saying four hundred years," she blurted. "What does that mean? Where was he for all those years?"

Suarez chuckled, which Ash took as a good sign. "Apparently he was an attraction in a hokey sideshow for several of them."

Ash didn't appreciate the sidestep. She tried again. "Why did he disappear?"

Suarez paused a moment, then took a deep breath. "I wish I had more answers for you, Ashtyn. He's the only one of his kind and he's been a rumor until now. There are many folktales and legends about the bird, but I can't confirm any as truth."

Suarez was holding back, that was obvious. He had to know facts about the phoenix, so did the other professors. Why else would they be so fascinated by him? But if Suarez, the most approachable of all of them, wouldn't tell her, then likely none of them would.

Instead of pressing her luck, Ash changed the subject. "How far is the kingdom?"

"Castle Dragoon is just up ahead, nestled within Fir Forest. Only thirty miles east of the Academy. We'll arrive shortly."

Ash tried to relax and enjoy the rest of the flight on the hairy lion, but not a minute after her nerves had calmed, they abruptly dipped down out of the clouds.

Rising out of a green forest on a rocky crag was a white stone castle with conical spires and blue pointed roofs. It seemed to glisten in the sunlight, and Ash could hardly believe it was real. The elegant fortress had groomed courtyards and parapet walks with merlon walls. The Academy's cracked and aging stones gave it character, yes, but the immaculate castle was in an architectural league of its own—a castle straight out of a fairytale.

From their height, they could see that stretching several miles in front of the stronghold was a city with many streets, buildings, and houses. Surrounding that was nothing but fir trees far into the horizon.

"Dragoon City. Many Regal Kin reside there."

Diego glided earthward and landed gently at the castle entrance. From the ground, the castle looked a hundred times bigger and even more breathtaking. Ash commanded Flynn to return to her shoulder as Suarez had taught her. Sure enough, the bird obeyed without hesitation.

"Good boy," she whispered.

They were met with guards and footmen who assisted Ash's dismount and led Diego away per Suarez's request. Then an older man with white hair and cream-colored robes greeted them with a bow. On his left arm was a white, elegant bird, hardly larger than a dove. Flynn trilled a happy greeting to the fellow fowl, but Ash pinched his beak shut and shushed him.

"Welcome, Suarez," the man said. "The king is expecting you."

"Thank you, Elder Raleigh," Suarez responded, bowing to him.

Raleigh led the two across a footbridge and up a grand staircase to the castle doors.

"Remember, Ash," Suarez whispered. "Be respectful, stand up straight, speak with purpose when spoken to."

"Yes, sir. I mean, Professor," Ash stuttered.

"Oh, and Ash," he added. "Relax."

He gave her a wink and she returned it with a smile. She forced herself to take a deep breath.

The interior of Castle Dragoon was in perfect accordance with its magnificent exterior. Delicate traceries and pendant ornaments adorned the walls of the spacious throne room, accented in dark blue and gold. In the center on a raised platform stood two thrones, side by side. Two smaller thrones flanked those. A royally crowned man and woman occupied the large thrones, while a small boy about Ash's age with pale, sunless skin and dark eyes, sat in one of the smaller thrones.

"Welcome!" said a jolly voice that echoed through the hall.

King Tiberius rose from his royal chair and walked toward them. "Sir Domingo Suarez, I presume. Have you brought your glorious manticore with you today?"

Suarez bowed. Ash did the same.

"Yes, Your Majesty," Suarez said with a smile as the king interrupted his bow with a hearty hug. "Diego would never miss a trip to Dragoon to see his favorite king."

"Wonderful!" said the king. "I will visit him before you depart. Beautiful animal. Almost as imposing as me."

"Perhaps if you had a scorpion tail, my love!" said the queen, joining their circle.

The young boy remained in his throne, frowning at Ash. Ash avoided looking in his direction, and focused on addressing the king with good posture and eye contact. Though, the king was much less intimidating than Ash imagined. He was quite pleasant, actually, and his laugh was infectious.

"Please, Domingo. Introduce me to this young lady and her elusive red bird," said Tiberius, smiling at Flynn.

"Of course, Your Majesty. This is Ashtyn Ridley from Oatsville. She is the daughter of a farmer. Her former employment was as a stablehand with a traveling carnival boasting mythical creatures. There, she witnessed the rebirthing ritual of this phoenix and it bonded to her instantly."

Tiberius glanced occasionally at Suarez to confirm he was listening, but the truth was he was much too busy giggling like a schoolboy at Flynn. Ash nudged Flynn as a go-ahead to leave her shoulder, and he flew around the king's head, pecking at the tassels on his robes and investigating his fluffy beard.

"Ashley, yes, splendid," he said, holding back laughter. "But who is this little flying beastie?"

Ash thought it best not to correct him. She cleared her throat. "That's Flynn. He's just under two weeks old."

"Flynn! What a delightful bird! Verna, my love, are you seeing this?"

Queen Verna had to contain her own laughter as she watched Flynn fly over to her and plink his beak against one of her crown's jewels.

"I apologize," Ash said. "He's a bit meddlesome at times."

Suarez glanced to Ash and gave her a nod, as if to say, *Well done so far.*

"Evan! Come see the phoenix, lad!" the king called to the young boy. The boy responded with an eye roll and nothing more.

Suarez gently placed his hand on the king's arm to get his attention. "Pardon me, Your Grace. May I have a word with you in private? I have some important matters to discuss."

Flynn landed on Tiberius's right shoulder and nestled himself comfortably in the velvet material of the king's robes. Tiberius glanced to Ash. "Would it be all right if Flynn accompanied me?"

"He would be delighted," Ash said with a smile.

Suarez and the king walked into a nearby hallway, out of earshot. Queen Verna walked away to converse with Elder Raleigh, leaving Ash alone.

Ash took the opportunity to admire the castle's décor. From the throw rugs to the chandeliers, everything was picturesque. On the wall hung many paintings of past kings, with plaques. A few that caught Ash's eye were Phineas, Deverus, and Ivarr. The resemblance made it clear that they were Tiberius's grandfathers. Beside a painting of Tiberius was Viktor, his late father.

Captivated by the texture of the intricate brush strokes, Ash reached out to feel the painting.

"Don't. Touch. That."

The calm but stern voice came from Prince Evan, who remained in his throne. The boy wasn't even looking at her. He was slouched down with a small black dragon perched on his left shoulder, about the size of a chameleon. The creature was skinny and spindly, with a long tail that curled around the boy's neck. The sharp edges of the dragon's body matched the blunt cut of the boy's black hair.

"The oils from your fingers corrode the surface and lessen the life expectancy of the art," Evan explained in an annoyed, deliberate tone.

"I'm sorry," she quickly said.

Evan said nothing. He just stared straight ahead.

"That's a neat dragon," Ash said, breaking the awkward silence.

"Is it? He can't do anything," the boy snapped back. "He's nothing but a silly Pygmy Whiptail."

"I think he's adorable," Ash said, walking over and reaching out to touch him. The dragon hissed loudly, and she jumped back.

"Erebus doesn't like to be touched, either," Evan said.

"Life expectancy, huh?" Ash joked. It was not received. "Will he get any bigger?"

"Unlikely."

The boy seemed less than eager to continue chatting. Ash turned to leave.

"So, how did a peasant stumble upon a phoenix?" he asked. "Did you steal it?"

Ash turned back to him. "No, no. I mean, well, I suppose you could say...I rescued him."

"Hm." Evan seemed less than convinced. "Don't you find it odd?"

"Find what odd?"

Evan smirked, making Ash feel even stupider. "That you have the most sought-after creature in the world. You, amongst the hundreds more qualified."

Ash didn't know what to say. His callously honest words stung.

"It's a shame. I'm sure you're tremendously further behind than your peers. You'll be lucky if you ever utilize the bird to even half of its potential."

Ash glanced to the hallway where Suarez and the king stood. They kept motioning toward Flynn, clearly talking about him. Were they discussing the same matter? Did everyone agree that Flynn was in the wrong hands? Evan had just mentioned that there were hundreds of people more qualified to own a phoenix...were they planning to take him away from her?

"It's ironic, really," Evan said with a laugh. "I'm a prince, yet I have a useless pygmy dragon. Basically a cat with wings. While you have a phoenix. And you're—well, you're nothing special at all."

Before Ash could even think of a rebuttal, the entrance doors were flung open. Inside soared a man on a peryton.

"Whoa, Vicky! Whoa!" yelled the man.

The creature bucked its head and whinnied as it slowly lowered itself to the ground, struggling to regain its balance as its hooves touched the slippery marble floor. The creature was almost a clone of Perry, and Ash smiled at the memory of her old uppity friend.

Flynn rushed back into the hall to Ash's shoulder to investigate the source of the noise.

"What have we told you about bringing Vicky inside?" said Queen Verna with a sigh.

"Sorry, Mum!" said the rider, dismounting with a lively hop and rubbing the beast's head. He grabbed Vicky's ears and the two wrestled for a moment—anyone could see they were best friends.

"A peryton!" Ash said, not intending the exclamation to be out loud.

"A peryton, indeed," the man said with a smile, walking toward Ash. "You like perytons?"

"Love them! I used to know one. I named him Perry," Ash said, fondly remembering the good times at the circus. "Perhaps it wasn't the most creative name I could have come up with."

He laughed heartily and kneeled down to her level. Ash nearly forgot how to breathe when she looked at him. He was strikingly handsome, with dark, moppy hair and warm brown eyes, like toffee swirled with cinnamon. He had the most inviting smile and an infectious laugh, like his father. She guessed he was a bit older than twenty.

"You must be the girl everyone's talking about," he said, kissing her hand like a gentleman. "How very nice to meet you, fair lass, and your bird, Sir..."

"Flynn," she said with a smile.

"His majesty Sir Flynn, mighty warrior and loyal friend."

He bowed his head to both. Ash giggled and Flynn chirped at him until he raised his head back up.

"My name is Victor and that's Vicky, back there," he said, motioning toward the peryton, who was very much resisting the footman's attempt to catch her. "She's my only love. Though, our love is quite hopeless, as she's more stubborn than even a human female."

"Flynn's stubborn, too."

"The best ones always are." He leaned in close to whisper. "My fuddy-duddy father insists she's not allowed to fight.

Some boring nonsense about how I'm needed for diplomacy, not combat."

He rolled his eyes in an exaggerated manner and Ash giggled.

"But I've been teaching her moves here and there. Don't tell."

Ash nodded and pretended to seal her lips.

"Victor, my boy. You finally join us," said the king as he and Suarez reentered the room. "Now that you've met our honored guests, I expect you will go put that horrid beast in the stables."

"Ah, come on, Dad. Vicky loves you."

Victor motioned his head toward Tiberius. Vicky ran up and began licking the king's face.

"Enough, enough!" he cried.

Victor laughed and led Vicky away. He turned once more to smile and seal his lips at Ash. Ash grinned from ear to ear.

Suarez bowed to Elder Raleigh and the king and queen. "I thank you greatly for your time today, Lord and Lady. We'd best be off before it gets too late."

"One more thing, if it's all right," Ash said, bravely speaking out of turn. "Your Majesty, regarding my father. I was wondering if your men had gathered any information."

Suarez grew visibly uncomfortable at her impertinence, but remained silent. The king squinted his eyes, as if to rack his memory. "Father? I'm sorry, dear. I'm afraid I don't know what you're talking about."

"My father? He's missing. Odetta mentioned that she would talk to you—"

"What is she going on about, Domingo?" interrupted the king.

"Elderess Odetta is quite busy, Ashtyn. It's only the second week of school, after all," Suarez said. He turned to the king and bowed his head. "Pay her no heed, Your Majesty. We at the Academy are addressing the situation."

Ash bit her lip, knowing she should have refrained. She bowed and said nothing more.

They bid goodbye to the royal family and returned to the skies on Diego's back. The ride home was quiet, though Suarez assured her she wasn't in trouble. What he didn't do, however, was assure her that the Academy was, in fact, looking into her father's disappearance. Why didn't it seem like they were treating the matter with seriousness? Were they downplaying the situation on purpose?

They landed at the Academy just before dusk and Ash walked to the beech tree, with a tired Flynn in her front pocket. Ash noted that he seemed like a bigger lump in her pocket than before. The bird was definitely growing.

Upon returning to her dorm, Ash saw a boy sitting on her front stoop reading a textbook. His scarf and mittens lay beside him.

"Hi?"

"Oh!" the boy jumped and scrambled to his feet, dropping his book and nearly kicking his scarf off the tree. "Hello! Hi! Yes, my name is Hammond Crump and I met you—well, sort of met you today in Combat."

Ash recognized him as the boy with the ice-blue dragon. "Oh, yes. You were nearly kludde food today!"

"You're telling me," he said with an exhale. "That's why I'm here. The Crump family takes rescuing very seriously. You

LISA FOILES

saved my life today, and I am forever in your debt until I repay
the favor."

"How are you going to do that?"

The boy's nobility faded and he resumed the speech patterns of an awkward twelve-year-old. "I dunno. I figured I'd
know when the time comes. Isn't that how it works?"

Ash laughed and shrugged her shoulders. "I suppose. How
long have you been sitting here?"

Hammond glanced through the leaves to the Academy
clock. "About an hour."

"An hour!"

"I knocked and Marni said you weren't home yet, so
I waited."

Ash glanced to Marni's window and saw Mitzi staring at
them, panting and fogging up the glass.

"Well, I'd better get going," said the boy, grabbing
his belongings.

"That's it then? You waited an hour just to say that and
then leave?"

"I guess so," he said. "I really have to get back to Hermaeus.
He gets nervous when I'm gone too long."

Hammond took a few steps, then turned back around.
"Hey! Do you and Marni want to come over? Just for a bit.
We'd love the company."

Ash peeked through the window to see Marni desperately
trying to pull Mitzi away from the window. She paused to wave
happily at Ash.

Ash turned back to Hammond. "It would be our pleasure."

The three children and two animals departed the beech
tree. They began climbing the stairs and paths cut into the

mountain that led to various cave dorms. Mitzi led the group despite not knowing the way, delighted to be outside. This resulted in a lot of backtracking. There was also a lot of sniffing. Flynn followed Mitzi, though he didn't quite understand what the fuss was about all the sniffing. That is, until Mitzi found a bug. Then Flynn was glad to take it off her paws for a quick snack.

Halfway up the mountain, they arrived at Hammond's place. There was a small house with one room and a bed, similar to Ash's room, and beside it, a very large cave that went a quarter of a mile deep.

As the girls stepped into the cave, they immediately got shivers. Mitzi slipped onto her belly. The entire cave was lined with a thick sheet of ice.

"Goodness, it's freezing!" said Ash.

"I can s-s-see my breath!" said Marni.

Hammond, bundled up in a coat, scarf, and mittens, tossed them warm clothing and blankets he'd snagged from his room.

"Mum sent me with extras," he said, his cheeks and nose turning cherry red. "There's a little bench behind you I made out of packed snow. With a rug over it, it's not that bad."

"Not that bad?" Marni whispered to Ash. "The kid lives in an igloo!"

The girls sat down on the snowy bench and shared a big, fuzzy blanket. Flynn, having no problem with the cold, sat comfortably on Ash's lap. His heat was so intense, it kept both Marni and her warm.

"He really c-c-comes in handy," said Marni.

Toward the back of the cave, they heard a low, rumbling growl.

"Oh, boy. He heard us," said Hammond.

Sure enough, the sound of running feet got louder and louder, almost shaking the whole mountain. Then they saw him—Hermaeus the ice dragon sprinting full speed at Hammond.

"No, no. Slow down, Hermie. Calm—"

The dragon nearly tackled Hammond off the side of the cliff. He made an affectionate sound, almost a purr, and wrapped his large wing around his very small master, curling up beside him. The girls burst out laughing.

"N-n-nice little puppy you've got there!" said Marni. Mitzi, busy eating snow, barked loudly at the word puppy.

"He really likes you!" said Ash.

"Yeah, sometimes too much," said Hammond.

The boy stroked the triangular nose of the ice dragon. Though enormous and covered with pointed spinal ridges and a thick, destructive tail, the beast really didn't seem frightening. He shimmered with about twenty different shades of blue and his mouth was turned up, almost in a smile.

"He has a hard time being away from me. In fact, I have to keep the door open to my dorm room so he can rest his head in there while I'm sleeping. He chills the place up with his cold breath all night! I have to tunnel under a heap of blankets like some kind of ground squirrel!"

The girls laughed again. Hammond couldn't help but laugh, as well.

"I guess it is pretty funny," he said.

"It's hilarious!" blurted Marni. "Now I understand why you wear sweaters all the time. You're not unfashionable, you're just eternally freezing!"

Hermaeus sniffed at Hammond's hair, followed by a long exhale that nearly froze his face off. "Hey, every boy wants a d-d-dragon, right?"

"So, Ash, tell us about the king!" said Marni.

"Oh yes, how was that?" asked Hammond. "Normally students don't get to meet him until their fourth year, when they become an Apprentice. He sent for you!"

Ash reflected on the trip, trying to forget about opening her big mouth at the end.

"King Tiberius was very pleasant," she said. "But...he didn't really seem interested in me, just Flynn. Not surprising, I guess."

"What do you mean by that?" asked Hammond.

"Just something Prince Evan said," she answered, lowering her head and staring at the frost on her boots. "He said that, perhaps, it would've been better if Flynn had bonded to someone more...worthy."

Marni frowned. "Are you sure you weren't talking to Farrah in disguise?"

"She is rather awful, isn't she?" said Hammond.

"The worst," said Marni.

"No, you don't understand," Ash interrupted. "From a young age, your parents have prepared you to bond to a beast and attend the Academy. You've been groomed for it. You're special. I just sort of lucked into it."

"No, Ash," said Hammond. "My mother always taught me and Rebecca—"

"Rebecca *and me*," corrected Marni.

"—Rebecca and me that it's fate to bond to an animal, never coincidence. You are Flynn's master for a reason."

"Don't forget you saved Hammond's life today! I thought he was dog meat for sure."

Mitzi barked again upon hearing the word dog.

Ash sighed and looked down at Flynn, curled up sleeping on her lap. Maybe it worked for Hammond's family, but it was hard for Ash to believe in anything like "fate" when so many things seemed to be going wrong in her life.

"If it is for a reason, I sure wish that reason would hurry up and get here."

The girls waved goodbye to Hammond and Hermaeus with just enough time to return to their dorms before the clock struck nine. As they walked, neither of them said anything. Ash was lost in thought. Today she had been singled out to meet the king of Cascadia and his charming son, Victor, and she got to ride on a manticore and receive valuable advice from Professor Suarez. So, then, why did she feel so unwanted? Her friends were encouraging, but not enough to drown out Prince Evan's words. Maybe she was just the thorn attached to the rose, the undesirable tagalong of the chosen one. She had never felt this way with her father.

Her father. If only she could speak to him and vent her worries to him. Imaginary monsters no longer haunted her closet and the underside of her bed. She had real fears now.

Ash and Marni retired to their respective dorm rooms with a wave goodnight. Ash flopped on the bed and pressed her face into the pillow until she felt little feet walking on her head. She giggled and sat up. Flynn circled her head twice, then hid behind her neck in her hair. He cooed and purred, rubbing his tiny noggin against hers.

"You're quite lovable tonight, aren't you?" Ash said. She snagged a bag of berries from the desk and fed him a few. "You were such a good boy today, Flynny. Everyone loves you."

He looked up and cheeped at her for another berry. She supplied it.

"I love you most of all, Flynn. You and my father, wherever he may be," she said with a glance out the window at the night sky. She sighed. Her eyes returned to her bird. "I hope you approve of me."

Berries were Flynn's favorite and made him hop around the bed merrily afterward, even pecking at Ash's fingers. She laughed and played with him for several minutes before catching a glimpse at the Academy clock. The hour was late.

She changed into her sleeping shirt and brushed her hair. She rubbed a bit of oil on Flynn's wings and filled up the food dish inside his cage with seed. He flew immediately inside.

A few seconds later, Ash heard Flynn scratching at something. She walked over to investigate. There, in the bottom of his cage, was a small piece of ripped parchment with writing, similar to the one under her pillow. She reached in to grab it. The message was different than the last:

DO NOT TRUST THEM.

CHAPTER 10

THE BEAST GAMES TRYOUTS

Two weeks passed. Cascadia was well into autumn and the trees on campus clung desperately to the last of their golden leaves. Flynn had grown twice the size he was on the day of his rebirth. His tail was just shy of two feet in length and the tips of his wings were beginning to spark when he took off quickly. He grew feathers in even more brilliant shades of red and his eyes seemed more expressive. Despite his enhanced beauty, he still hadn't quite grown into his big beak.

Flynn had finally mastered one magical attack. Most other students had mastered two or three, but for Flynn, just one was a big deal. Ash could now say, "Flamethrow!" and Flynn would shoot a short stream of fire from his beak. The first time he actually did it on command, the flame had hit the rump of Dickon's bildad and sent it hopping wildly around the field, but it was worth it. Flynn had done something right, for a change—and was rewarded with about a hundred walnuts that evening.

Unfortunately, it was still two steps forward, one step back with the bird. With his growth, he was also developing odd behavior. He seemed even less interested in paying attention to Ash during any class that wasn't Combat, he was more vocal, and he was now getting chronic hiccup attacks. The hiccups were uncontrollable once they started and with each hiccup came either a spark, or worse, a small ball of fire that shot out of Flynn's mouth. Nearly all of Ash's clothes, textbooks, and belongings had gotten singed as a result, and she had to carry a spray bottle filled with water everywhere she went in case of accidents. Needless to say, it was embarrassing.

She did, however, excel in her book work. She studied hard and aced every quiz. Not only was it her way of balancing out her poor performance in animal handling, it was a perfect distraction.

The two mysterious notes began to eat at her. Was someone sneaking in her room and leaving them as a funny prank? If so, it was less than humorous. If not, then perhaps it was something more sinister. She pondered alerting the professors, but if they weren't treating her missing father as a priority, then why would they care about this? Strange little messages? They wouldn't take it as a serious problem. Plus, if it did end up being the work of a fellow student, she'd forever be labeled a tattletale.

Most of all, Ash wondered about the second note. "Do not trust them." *Them* who?

"And that, children, is why birds, all birds—your birds, my birds, all birds—have strong senses of sight to see, yes, and hearing t-t-to hear above all other senses."

The flighty Professor Talon, in his floppy, velvet hat with a feather and matching velvet cape, stumbled over his words in Avian class as usual. His brain always seemed to move too fast for his lips to keep up with and he jumped from subject to subject almost erratically. With his large, pointed nose, sharp fingernails, and twitchy mannerisms, Ash was convinced he was some sort of bird himself.

"One of the greatest, what's the word—yes, benefits! That's it, benefits of bonding to a bird is that, in time, in much time, you yourselves, children, will also experience these heightened senses," continued the professor. "Your sight will be noticeably keener and you will hear sounds in high pitches, sometimes very far away, yes, that-that-that your human ears would never hear. Normally, that is."

His staccato speech made it especially hard to take notes, but still the room full of students scribbled away furiously. It was a small class, only about twelve children at desks next to wooden perches. Naomi with her large kongamato sat in the back, a boy with a terrifying owl sat to Ash's left, and near the front were two maroon-haired twin girls with identical multicolored birds.

"But moving on! Yes, let us move on," said Talon. "Let's see how you're doing with the flight patterns we learned last week. Well, not you, but your bird. You and your bird. Yes, quite right."

Great, flight patterns, Ash thought, rolling her eyes and exhaling her frustration. *Might as well ask Flynn to cook dinner and recite a sonnet while you're at it, Talon.*

"Uri and Nuri! Step up and we'll begin with your adarna birds."

The twins, in matching periwinkle uniforms, came forward with their adarnas, Uli and Nuli. They were gorgeous songbirds the size of pheasants, and their feathers were different metallic colors every time Ash saw them. This time, they were bright green with red throats.

The girls instructed their birds to fly in a circle around the large room with its remarkably high ceilings. At least Avian class wasn't outdoors—there were enough distractions for Flynn without adding in butterflies and squirrels.

Hic!

A flame shot out of Flynn's mouth and onto Ash's notes. They were instantly set ablaze, but she patted it out.

Hic!

"Something the matter, Ms. Ridley?" asked Talon.

"Nope. No, sir," she said, scrambling to find her spray bottle. "Flynn's just got a slight, manageable case of the hiccups. Again."

Hic!

Another spark shot out of his beak and onto the girl's back that sat in front of Ash. It burned a hole in her tunic before Ash could spray her.

"Hey!" the girl screeched. "Watch it!"

"Sorry about that," Ash apologized. "Just put a little ice on that burn. It'll heal right up."

"Not to worry, Ashtyn! Flynn's body is growing, changing, evolving. Thus, his fire-breathing organs are also developing. A hiccupper now, yes, but a controlled fire warrior he will become!"

Hic!

Talon motioned for the twins to continue. In unison, Uli and Nuli flew perfectly to the top of the tall ceiling in a figure eight pattern and back down to the twins' elevated forearms. But as the birds landed, their bodies tensed. With a *plop*, the birds defecated on the twins' sleeves, which dripped down to their boots.

The students laughed at the girls' disgusted faces, but Ash was just happy to have everyone's attention diverted to something other than her nuisance.

"No, no, children! The droppings from an adarna are a wonderful thing, yes!" said Professor Talon, scooping up the droppings into a glass jar with his bare hands. "You see, with magic, they can be transformed into special stones for healing. And look at the birds now!"

Everyone looked at Uli and Nuli. Gradually, they faded from bright green to a stunning yellow.

"They turn colors after relieving themselves! Remarkable! Splendid!"

While Talon continued to be weirdly excited about bird poop, Ash fed Flynn berries and carrot pieces in hopes of finding a hiccup cure. Nothing helped, but he hiccupped only a few more times and settled down.

As Ash leaned over to set her spray bottle on the floor, she noticed something sticking out of the pages of her textbook, *A History of Aviary Animals*. Talon called on another student to demonstrate, so Ash used the opportunity to subtly draw the book to her desk. She opened it, and bookmarking the chapter on firebirds was another ripped piece of parchment paper with a message:

THEY WILL TAKE THE BIRD FROM YOU.

Ash's heart rate increased to the pace of a frightened wasp. She could feel her stomach drop and her breathing quicken. No one had touched the book but her, and the note was not in the pages when she left her dorm that morning.

She looked around the room to see if anyone had noticed. Perhaps someone in the class had slipped it in while she was fussing with Flynn, and they were waiting for her to see it. No one was looking anywhere but at Talon.

Her thoughts raced. The second note had instructed her not to trust "them"—whomever that was supposed be. And now, "they" were going to take the bird from her. Could Evan have been right? Could the professors be planning to take Flynn away from her?

It would make sense in a distressing situation like this to alert the professors, but they could be the very people plotting against her. If that were true, then who could she tell?

Whatever the next step, she was certain now that someone—someone at the Academy—was deliberately targeting her.

Suddenly, Ash was startled out of her mental turmoil by a white ball crashing through a high window of the classroom. Glass shattered and the children shielded their faces. The quick-thinking Professor Talon grabbed his cape with each hand and flapped it toward the falling glass like a bird wing. A magical gust of wind pushed the dangerous shards far from the heads of the students and the glass landed safely in the back of the classroom. Ash was amazed.

The ball bounced on three desks before landing near the door. Every bird in the classroom squawked and flapped their wings with fright, except Flynn—who immediately flew to the peculiar round bouncy thing to investigate.

Jeffrey soared through the window on his beautiful hippogriff and landed near the front of the class. He wore a helmet and grasped a long-handled mallet in his right hand. Another boy on a black pegasus hovered by the window with a mallet of his own.

"Sorry, Talon!" Jeffrey shouted. "Don't mean to interrupt, but the ball is still in play!"

The excited classroom murmured with curiosity.

"Oh, don't tell me—"

"That's right, Professor. Tryouts for the spring Beast Games are today! We have to train before the snow comes!"

The professor sighed and tossed Jeffrey the ball. "There's no bringing this class back to a state of learning now. Yes, everyone, yes! Outside for the tryouts!"

Jeffrey rocketed back through the window as the students cheered and raced out of the classroom, nearly knocking Talon over.

Students of all grades poured out of the Academy doors and onto the athletic fields like milk from a punctured carton. Tryouts for participants of enrollment years two and above were already underway, spreading across the valley and even into the sea.

Ash held Flynn tight to her chest and took in the chaos. A crowd watching some event to the left cheered, another group to the right booed, and several students even walked about selling popcorn for three silver. A girl holding the leash of a massive saddled-up spider nearly ran Ash over, while a snake with three heads and a painted number seven on his back tripped her up.

"Watch it, firstie!" the snake's owner snapped. "Slith's a three-time champion!"

Ash waved an apology then ducked to a quieter spot.

"Ash! Ash, there you are!"

Ash was thrilled to see Mitzi dragging Marni in her direction.

"Goodness, no one told me about Beast Games!"

"That's because first-year students can't try out. Boo," Marni said, then blew a raspberry. "But hey, we can still watch the events."

The girls stopped abruptly to let a group of celebrating students pass by. They were jumping and chanting, while a boy and his water monkey—both in matching red uniforms—were propped up on their shoulders.

"This is nuts!" Ash said.

"You haven't seen anything yet," Marni said, grabbing Ash's wrist. "Come on! The wing polo match is tied!"

Weaving through children, animals, teachers, and school personnel, they met up with Hammond at the polo field. He stood in the back with Hermie by his side, hopping up and down to see over the crowd.

"What's the score, Hammond?" Marni shouted.

"I don't know. You can't see a thing back here. Unless, you want to climb up on Hermie?"

"No way, I'm cold just standing next to the big guy," Marni said, swatting Mitzi's nose away from a passerby's rear end.

"I suppose I should take Hermie home," said Hammond. "All this noise will likely give him indigestion."

"You do that. We're going to the front."

Marni gave Ash a sly smile and yanked her into the thick crowd. After a bit of pushing, shoving, and some "Excuse me, Pardon me"s the girls reached the sidelines.

"Wow" was the only thing Ash could utter.

Before her was a field of polo players, four to each team— only this wasn't any kind of polo Ash had ever seen. There were mallets and a ball, yes, but six out of the eight players spent the game in the air. The red team had one ground player, a student on a beautiful white Kirin, and three players on flying mounts, consisting of a peryton, a manticore, and Jeffrey on his hippogriff. The blue team had a mngwa cat on the ground with a cockatrice, griffin, and black pegasus in the air.

"See that pegasus?" Marni pointed. "That's Edmund, Farrah's big brother. So, based solely on that fact, I want the blue team to lose. As miserably and humiliatingly as possible."

Just as Marni finished, Edmund, pale with short, midnight-black hair, whacked the ball away from the red team and straight into the air. The crowd cheered, including Farrah, who was watching from across the way.

"Darn it! He's so good every year—it drives me crazy!"

"You've seen him play before?" Ash asked.

"My parents take me to the Beast Games every spring," she replied. "Edmund's made Professor Atlas's wing polo team every year since his second. He'll likely play on a Regal Kin team once he graduates. The Kin are twice as exhilarating to watch, as you can imagine."

Jeffrey on his hippogriff, Jareth, flew up to meet Edmund in the air and whapped the ball away toward the blue team's goal. The crowd cheered again, especially Marni. Flynn chirped merrily at seeing Jareth again.

"If anyone can keep Edmund from winning, it's Jeffrey, on Captain Bera's team. Isn't he just the dreamiest?" Marni waved to Jeffrey as he flew by.

Ash blushed. Yes, he really was the dreamiest.

The game finished with a score of 19-18, blue team.

Marni looked at Ash and shrugged. "Not a huge loss. There are still three more matches to determine which students will play for Atlas and Bera in the spring. Come on, let's go watch more events!"

For the next hour, Ash, Marni, and Hammond, now sans Hermie, explored the grounds viewing various sporting events. They watched a diving competition that took place in the bay by the treehouse with aquatic animals, then they headed to the field behind the Academy for a dressage event for horses and horse-like beasts. There were agility courses for small critters, a rhythmic dance performance by girls with mid-size beasts—one girl performed with a kitsune, which greatly intrigued Marni— and they even saw the finish of the bird trek, a long-distance event where birds were released hundreds of miles away and had to return home.

When the other events had concluded, nearly everyone congregated to the center field.

"What's going on now?" Ash asked, wishing she could find a place to sit and rest. The combination of walking all day and keeping Flynn from interfering with the events had exhausted her. The bird had an endless supply of energy.

"The final and best event of the day: the track and flight relay," Marni said, clapping with excitement.

"Actually, I thought the bird trek was the most interesting," Hammond added.

"You would," Marni replied, rolling her eyes. "Totally boring."

In the center of the gathered crowd were Professor Suarez and Professor Thorne, standing by a white line drawn in the grass. About a quarter mile from the white line was a black and white checkered finish line.

Professor Suarez mounted Diego and lifted off into the sky. At his master's command, the manticore stung his scorpion tail at cloud bundles and formed them into huge yellow rings, suspended in mid-air. Some were high up, some low. They circled around in a U-shape and the last one ended above the white line in the grass.

"What is he doing?" Ash asked.

"You really don't know anything about anything, do you, Ash?" Marni said. "He's using magic to place markers in the sky."

"That's no magic I've ever seen," Ash said, gawking at the flying lion.

"The competitors have to fly through each ring or they're automatically out."

"They can't drop the baton, either," Hammond added. "Or hit the markers out of sequence."

"You'll understand once you watch," Marni assured her. "It's brilliant."

Nearby, seven participants were prepping their beasts: one had a purple tri-horned dragon, one had a kongamato, one had a chimera, and one had a strix, a frightening red-eyed owl. Ash had determined the chimera was her least favorite beast. The combination of a winged lion's body with the snake and goat heads was the creepiest thing she'd ever seen.

The fifth participant was Rebecca Crump with her Magma dragon, and the last two were Edmund and Jeffrey.

"Edmund and Jeffrey again?"

"Yep. And it'll be stiff competition to qualify, even for those three. Bunch of overachievers, if you ask me."

"Sounds like someone's just jealous they have a hyperactive, smelly mutt instead of a flying creature," said a familiar, cringe-worthy voice.

Farrah and Talia pushed past the three friends for a spot in the front row.

"Hello, Farrah," said Marni. "Have you enjoyed the try-outs? Or have you been too busy yanking Fiona's horn out of plumbing pipes again?"

Farrah whipped her head to Marni and burned with anger.

"That was one time and it wasn't her fault," she said through gritted teeth. "It was that stupid maintenance dwarf's fault, leaving a pipe just open like that! The incompetence of this school is completely unacceptable. Just wait until Aunt Odetta hears—"

"Uh-huh. Save it, honey," Marni replied.

Farrah's stare drifted to Hammond, who was trying—and failing—to hide behind Ash.

LISA FOILES

"That your sister up there, Crump?" she said with an evil smile.

"Y-y-yes," he replied. Ash couldn't tell if he was uncontrollably nervous or just chilly, as usual.

"If I recall correctly, she didn't even qualify last year. Or the year before that. In fact, my brother has edged her out every time. Isn't that right, *Hammie?*"

Ash pressed her lips together, but couldn't stop her tongue.

"So what if it is?" she said, puffing up her chest and standing in front of Hammond.

Farrah faced Ash and narrowed her gaze. "Why don't you stay out of it, Ridley? Not like your family has ever done anything of worth."

"Not true at all."

"What did you say your father did again? A farmer, was it?"

"Stop it."

"So philanthropic of the Elders, really. Never thought they would allow tuition to be paid in oats."

Before Ash could decide whether to respond articulately or deck her in the mouth, a loud whistle blow from Professor Thorne commanded the attention of the crowd. The competitors were lined up on the white line with batons in hand. Their flying creatures stood nearby.

"Let us commence qualifying round one of three for the track and flight relay team," announced Thorne. "Our seven competitors must toss their baton to their beasts. The beasts will then fly through each of the eight markers. The beasts will then release their baton to be caught by their humans, and the humans will race to the checkered finish line. Any missed

154

markers or dropped batons will result in immediate disqualification. Are we clear on the rules, players?"

The competitors nodded. The crowd silenced as the seven players crouched in a ready position.

"Don't worry, Hammond," Ash whispered. "Rebecca's going to kick Edmund's—"

Thorne blew the whistle. The players threw their batons high into the sky, and their flying creatures shot from the ground, catching them in mid-air. The race was on. The seven flyers battled for the lead as they entered through the first ring. The rings turned from yellow to white once every animal had passed through. The crowd cheered wildly watching the aerial race, as each competitor readied himself or herself to catch the baton once their beast had hit every marker.

Ash couldn't believe the speed of the smaller creatures— and the violence of the bigger ones. Rebecca's Magma chomped at the strix in an attempt to knock him off course, while the purple dragon body-slammed into Jareth. Edmund's pegasus sharply cut off the kongamato as they met the first turn, and the frazzled bird's baton fell from its talons.

"Kongamato is out!" Thorne announced.

The creature flew back to its human and the two walked off the field, disappointed.

"Didn't I tell you, Ash?" Marni said. "The most exciting event of the day!"

The race continued through the second ring. Edmund's pegasus was in the lead with Rebecca's Magma at his heels. Jeffrey's hippogriff had been knocked back to last, but was maneuvering swiftly to gain position.

The third ring was lower than the first two, and the animals gained even more speed as they pinned back their wings to sail downward.

Ash was so enthralled with the scene that she momentarily forgot about Flynn—and the fact that he was twice as captivated as she was.

Taking advantage of Ash's loosened grip, Flynn rocketed from her shoulder as if released from a slingshot.

"Flynn!" she shrieked. "No! Flynn! Come back!"

The crowd gasped and murmured. Thorne blew her whistle at the sight of him, but it was too late. Flynn was flying at full speed—but not toward the competitors. Much to the intrigue of the onlookers, Flynn's target was the first ring, which he sailed through. Then the second. Flynn was following the flight pattern of the competing animals—and was gaining on them.

Like a blazing red shooting star, Flynn whizzed through the third ring and by ring six, he had caught up with the competitors.

Impossible!

A phoenix is that fast?

What incredible speed!

Students buzzed with disbelief while Thorne continued to blow her whistle. She motioned harshly for Ash to get ahold of her bird, but Flynn ignored her.

The race continued, now with Flynn in the ranks. At ring seven, the Magma dragon, pegasus, and hippogriff were battling for first, but the other dragon head-butted the Magma back to last. The eighth and final marker approached. The animals dodged and weaved, but none could pass the two leads: the purple dragon and Flynn.

Ash had never felt so nauseated. Her phoenix was ruining the event that everyone had gathered to see. Her inability to control her beast was on display, like a giant sign reading *Ash Ridley: Worst Student Ever*. She held her stomach and prepared for the worst.

Flynn pinned back his wings and zoomed forward like a dart, right through the final marker—in first place.

Whoever finished next in the race, no one saw or even cared. The entire crowd of students erupted in cheers. Half the professors looked shocked, while the other half were smiling and shaking their heads. Flynn circled above the cheering students who began chanting "Phoe-nix! Phoe-nix! Phoe-nix!" He finally landed back on Ash's forearm.

Thorne blew her whistle a few times more.

"The rematch will take place in one hour!" she announced. "Students and beasts who are *actually competing*, please rest and return at that time."

With that, the crowd dispersed. Ash inhaled deeply and readied herself for the aftermath.

Thorne marched over to her. "Get that bird of yours under control, Ridley," she reprimanded. "And I suggest skipping the rest of the events."

Ash nodded and Thorne left with an exhale.

Despite Thorne's tone and look of annoyance, that was the extent of Ash's punishment. She wasn't sure why she had been granted such mercy, but she wasn't going to stand around to find out.

Ash hurried home to the treehouse for the rest of the day so Flynn would refrain from entering himself into any more tryouts. As she walked through the grass, students called out things like "Good one, Ash!" and "Flynn smoked them all!" She responded with a sheepish smile and a wave.

"Ashtyn!" called a familiar voice as she passed the stables. It was Jeffrey.

"That bird of yours was quite the flyer today," he said.

"I—I know, I'm so sorry he interfered with your race," she replied.

"Sorry? Ash, I've never seen a bird so fast in my life!" he said with a laugh. "You ever thought about training him for the games?"

Ash shrugged and shook her head. It was hard enough training him not to cough fireballs on her classmates.

"Say, why don't you and Flynn meet me in the field on Monday during lunch?" he said with a smile. "I'd like to see what else he can do."

CHAPTER 11

THE SPECTER

The second set of exams for Academy students loomed in the near future, instilling chills that were perfectly timed with the plummeting outside temperature. Ash and Marni hardly saw any of each other in the three days following the tryouts. Their first set of exams had been described as "mind-numbingly simple" by a self-assured third-year student, yet Ash and Marni still found themselves drawing blanks when it came to the Herbs and Healing questions. Wanting to be prepared, the girls kept their noses in books and their fingers hugging pencils. Ash stayed after school on Wednesday to work on three flight patterns with Professor Talon that Flynn couldn't quite master, and Marni stayed late on Thursday running math drills with the hopelessly dull Mrs. Brown.

Mrs. Brown was an interesting choice for school personnel. She had no Bonded Beast, practiced no magic, and was
void of all personality. She wore a permanent frown and hardly
opened her eyes past slits, peering icily through half-moon
spectacles. Her gray hair was always pulled back into a bun,
her chocolate-brown dress was always perfectly ironed, and her
hooked nose always drew in oxygen with a slight whistle. Being
as "exasperatingly boring" and "endlessly normal" as Marni
described her, she stuck out at the abnormal Academy like a
stubbed toe. This didn't seem to faze the old teacher. She simply arrived every day to teach Arithmetic and Grammar, then
returned home to Mr. Brown to eat supper and go promptly to
bed, probably.

Marni had been going out of her mind unable to vent and
complain about Mrs. Brown, math, Farrah, Mitzi's drooling,
Professor Thorne's lectures, and the awful nettles popping up
in the grass by the treehouse—so much so that she and Ash
decided to spend Friday evening together. After class, they
accompanied each other to the Helena Crump Library, so
named due to the boundless amount of monetary donations
from the Crumps for several generations, chatting and gossiping the whole way. Marni couldn't wait to tell Ash about Jeffrey
and Rebecca, supposedly seen canoodling on the beach behind
the Academy Wednesday night. And rumor had it that Farrah
was acing all of her classes except Equine, which she was failing miserably. Ash listened intently to Marni's hearsay, taking
each story with a grain of salt. But true or untrue, Ash would
have liked to skip the bit about Jeffrey and Rebecca. Even if he
was much older and certainly out of her reach, it was selfishly
comforting to think of him as single.

The girls gathered as many books as they could stack from the tips of their fingers to the bottoms of their chins and precariously walked from the Academy to the treehouse. Farrah, noticing the opportunity, bumped them with her shoulder just enough to make them trip over Mitzi and spill their books all over the grass. But to Farrah's dissatisfaction, the two simply erupted in laughter as they sat amidst the aftermath of their textbook avalanche. Ash couldn't recall the last time she'd laughed so hard.

The two roommates spent the next few hours quizzing each other on challenging subjects, peppered with the occasional snippet of gossip that popped into Marni's head. By nightfall, their neat stack of books was scattered all over Ash's room while Marni lounged upside down on Ash's bed with Mitzi lounging beside her, also upside down. Flynn preened his wings while perched on the curtain rod. Ash labored away cleaning Flynn's cage while Marni lobbed her questions from a book called *Healing Beasts: Remedies, Revives, and Resuscitations.*

"All right, next question," Marni said, her uncombed hair dangling off the side of the bed. "What are the four most common sources of magical healing?"

"Um...let's see," Ash said, biting her lip in thought as she scrubbed the cage's bottom tray. "Saliva, blood, tears, and, with some birds, their songs or droppings. Ick."

"Correct!" Marni said, rubbing Mitzi's ears. "Say, does Flynn have a song? Is he a healing beast?"

"Talon and Thorne said it's too early to tell," Ash said, working on a stubborn smudge on the cage's swing. "But from what little they know of the phoenix, he's more of an attack bird and less of a healing one. Guess we'll know more when he's older."

"That's too bad. I got an awful paper cut on my finger the other day. Mitzi licked it and the wound was healed not three days later! She's my little miracle worker, aren't you? Aren't you, girl?"

Marni scratched Mitzi's fuzzy belly and the fox kicked her legs in the air merrily. Ash chuckled at Marni calling her goofy pooch a "miracle worker" for supposedly healing a small cut that would have healed itself in three days anyway. Ash recalled the many times she had cut, scraped, and bruised herself on the farm without ever bandaging herself up. Only when an injury was particularly bad would her father step in as "Doctor Landon" and patch things up. His usual prescription of "eat this piece of candy and contact me in the morning" was always a perfect cure.

Ash figured Marni's parents had just taken her to pricey doctors who prescribed the best medication money could buy. It seemed the two girls had had very different childhoods.

"Okay, where were we. Next question," Marni said, returning to the textbook, much to the sadness of her kitsune. "Dragons are the only healing beasts that—"

"—heal their humans by contracting their human's illness onto themselves."

"Including—"

"—diseases, fatal internal wounds, and broken bones."

Marni slammed the book closed and threw up her hands. "Correct again! You're some kind of brainiac freak, I swear. You haven't missed one all night."

"I guess I'm just fascinated by it all," Ash said with a shrug, finishing up Flynn's cage.

"It's totally not fair. Most days I feel like I can't commit anything to memory. Yesterday, Mrs. Brown asked me to define an isosceles triangle. I blanked! I told her it was the name of an ancient math scholar who invented triangles."

Ash giggled. "Good one."

"I thought so, too," Marni said smugly.

"Well, I may be good at the book work, but Flynn's really far behind the rest of the class when it comes to the actual training."

"I'm the opposite! Mitzi's doing incredibly well. See, watch."

Marni proceeded to have Mitzi sit, roll over, shake, shake with both paws, balance on her back feet, finally saying, "Speak!" Mitzi barked loudly. Ash applauded and turned to Flynn.

"Hey, Flynn! Speak!" she commanded. Flynn simply looked at her and tilted his head, as if to say, *Sorry, were you talking to me?*

"I don't know how we'll ever advance to real combat and more advanced magical attacks if Flynn can't even get the basics down. Being book smart won't help me there."

Marni's face lit up with an idea. "If only we could splice ourselves up and combine our better halves! We'd create a super-student! Great at tests, great at training."

"Plus one dumb student from the other halves who can't do anything right. It would probably wander around the school drooling and running head-first into walls."

"We'd send it to drool on Farrah's homework."

The girls giggled at the thought, until they were interrupted by the gong of nine o'clock and the scratching on their window from a nosey ratatoskr.

"Little pests," Marni said, throwing her sock at the window to scare off the critter.

Marni and Mitzi yawned, almost simultaneously. Marni waved goodnight to Ash and Flynn and headed to bed.

Ash sprinkled fresh seed in the bottom of the clean cage and Flynn zipped inside to scarf it up. Ash caressed his head. Even while munching his supper, his body purred at her touch. It was hard to be upset at such an adorable bird, even if he was the reason she was failing her classes. Flynn was obnoxious and stubborn, yes, but it never seemed to be on purpose. His happiness was contagious and his excitement was understandable, being such a tiny bird in such a big, curious world. To that, Ash could relate.

Ash was so exhausted from the long week that she turned out her lamp and collapsed on her bed, fully clothed in her uniform, boots and all. In an instant, she was fast asleep.

The wind had a particularly soothing melody that night as it swept through rock crevices and rustled the crispy autumn leaves. Its whisper was the only sound, save for the occasional howl and snarl from the nocturnal beasts on campus. Flynn dozed peacefully in his cage, balanced on his swing. But the slightest scratch of a claw, scurrying of an insect, or creak from a wooden floorboard could wake him, and that night, it did.

Ash could usually sleep through bumps in the night, but the bumps that night were loud and unusual. She stirred awake to the sound of her furniture somehow bumping into each other, her lamp teetering, and Flynn spitting fireballs at nothing.

"Flynn!" Ash shrieked, springing out of bed to calm her tiny bird.

He ignored her and kept attacking. Ash ducked as the fireballs barely missed her hair. She patted out two fires on her blanket before they spread. She grabbed for Flynn, but he was too quick, zipping back and forth like a crazed hummingbird. His bright eyes had turned from yellow to deep red, indicating his anger. She puffed up her chest in preparation to scold him when she noticed what he was after. Floating in the air on its own was a small piece of parchment paper. It looked identical to the three that had already been left for her.

Ash lunged at the paper. Her arms felt instantly cold, like she'd stuck them both in an ice chest. Flynn shot another flame, and this time there was an audible *"Ouch!"*

The two cornered the floating paper.

"Reveal yourself!" Ash commanded. She assumed an attack position with Flynn next to her.

The cold mass of air before them shimmered, like ripples in a disturbed pond. A man appeared, but not a whole man—a skeleton, dressed in floppy robes much too big for his skinny bones. He had a grin that stretched to each side of his head, filled with more teeth than seemed natural. Bits of black, rotting flesh remained on his arms and neck, and the cavernous holes where his eyes used to be seemed to still look directly at her.

"W-who are you?" Ash said, her voice shaking with fear, but holding her position steady.

"Who am I? Me? It's a riddle, it be! The more you have of it, the less you see. What is it?"

The maniacal skeleton flew into the air, flipping over the top of them and landing in the center of the room on one toe. "Such grace have I, wouldn't you say, girl and bird?"

He laughed to himself and spun on his toe, like a macabre ballerina from a jewelry box.

"Stop! Who are you? Why are you here?"

He stopped mid-spin. "Wrong! The answer was: darkness. Because the more you have, the less you see! You see?"

He pranced around the room, dizzying Flynn to the point of running into a shelf.

"I don't want to answer riddles—"

"I know a word of letters three, add two, and fewer there will be!"

Ash grunted in frustration, watching this ghostly being bounce around her room like a bumblebee. She decided to play his game. She had plenty of experience with riddles—her father asked them all the time. This one seemed easy enough. A three-letter word...add two...

"Few! The word is few!"

"Ding ding ding!" The skeleton nodded his head and marched around the room like a one-man parade. "Yo ho ho and a bottle of rum!"

"All right, now settle down—"

"You heard me before, yet you hear me again, then I die, 'til you call me again."

Ash squinted her eyes, racking her brain for another answer. What does one call? A child? A lover? And why would it go and come back again?

"An echo!"

The skeleton pretended to play a trumpet, then drums, then stood on his hands.

Ash was certain ghosts only existed in the pages of spooky stories, but here was one right in front of her. If any of those tales were true, then this ghost could be cunning, volatile, and surprisingly dangerous. So far, he was just nuts.

"Ghost! I command you disclose your identity!"

"Ghost, *pffh*. I am no ghost," he said, highly offended.

"Then what are you?"

"I am a specter."

Ash rolled her eyes. "Same thing!"

The specter giggled wildly and blew a kiss to Flynn. Flynn shook his head from the rush of cold air and sped to Ash's shoulder.

"What is your name?" she asked.

The specter turned into a puff of smoke and disappeared under Ash's bed. "I don't want to tell you. You can't make me!"

Ash leaned down to find him. "Maybe I'll guess it. Can you give me a hint?"

The specter paused a moment, then posed yet another riddle.

"To learn my name, you must be deserving. You need that word minus half a serving."

Ash sat on the ground, picking the sentence apart in her brain.

"That word...meaning *deserving*...half a serving, would be half the word...Irving? Your name is Irving!"

The specter appeared on top of the bed now, peeking his head over the side to look down at her.

"You are a mean girl. I wanted it secret. You've gone and told the whole world."

Ash rose to her feet as Irving sobbed into her pillow.

"You haven't even got eyes to cry with," she said.

"Rub it in, why don't you," he said, muffled by the pillow.

"Specter Irving, you've got some explaining to do. You're behind the mysterious notes. The one in my book, in the cage, and right there under my pillow!"

Irving seemed to turn to liquid, melting off the side of the bed and into a puddle on the floor. "It's not my fault. You're the one who won't listen."

"Listen to what? The notes?"

In his puddle appeared an image of the three notes, each with their messages. They quickly dissolved, showing only Ash's reflection once more.

"When one is delivered a note, does one not respond accordingly and promptly?" said Irving's voice in a thick, proper accent. "Or perhaps etiquette has fluttered away with the summer wind after the days of His Majesty King Ivarr."

"King Ivarr?" Ash said, recognizing the name. "I remember his painting in the halls of Castle Dragoon. Did you know him when you were alive?"

"Know him? Know him *indeed*!" With a slurp, Irving's puddle returned back to his previous shape. "Show some respect! I'll have you know I was a confidant of King Ivarr."

"You worked in the castle?"

"I was a Mage. His trusted Mage. I performed charms and conjured enchantments! I hexed his awful little son and boggled the queen with card tricks!"

As he spoke, playing cards whirred around the room, along with toys and small fireworks. Flynn flew wildly around the room chasing and chomping at them.

"So what happened? How did you die?"

The charms disappeared. The skeleton threw a hood over his head. "Depends who you ask."

Shackles appeared around his wrists and a rope around his neck. Ash gasped as he hung himself from the ceiling.

"No one appreciates me," he said with a choking voice. "I was innocent and they killed me. Over a simple misunderstanding of starting a silly war."

Flames engulfed him and he disappeared. Ash looked right and left, and finally spotted him, now three inches tall, swinging on Flynn's hanging perch in his cage. She leaned down to speak to him.

"Well, did you?"

"Start a war?" he said in a squeaky high-pitched voice. "Hard to say. Probably yes. But again—it depends who you ask."

Growing increasingly frustrated, Ash slammed her fist on the desk, shaking Irving off the perch.

"Enough of this! I don't care how you died or what war you started! Tell me why you're in my room and why you've been leaving these notes or—or I'll call for the professors!"

Irving reappeared before her in his full-size form. "They can't help you."

Ash narrowed her gaze.

"The Academy is but a rook in our existential chess game. Its Elders are bishops and its Kinsmen are knights. All easily conquerable in a few strategic moves." The chess pieces appeared one by one in the air. "And what are you, lowly pawn?"

The pawn piece circled her head. She swatted it away.

"You haven't listened to your warnings."

"I don't know what they mean!"

"We told you that you shouldn't be at this school. We told you not to trust your nasty professors, yet you remain." Irving's voice had a creepy edge to it. "Oh, I just hate taking drastic measures..."

"We? Who is *we*? What are you talking about?" Ash shouted.

"Or, do I love taking drastic measures? I can't remember..."

Ash stomped her foot. "I'm not leaving this school until you tell me why!"

"Feed me and I live...give me drink and I die."

Irving struck a match.

"Perhaps we'll expel you...if you won't comply?"

With a giggle, he dropped the match and disappeared. The fire caught the floor rug and exploded into an enormous flame. Ash grabbed for her spray bottle and doused the fire with water, but it was too little, too late. The flame latched onto the pages of the piled library books and grew three times its size. Ash screamed for Marni to wake up.

Flynn squawked frantically as the flames took hold of the curtains. Ash shook with panic and dripped with sweat from the intense heat. She rushed to the window, but it refused to budge. With a mighty heave, Ash threw her desk chair through the glass and it shattered. Quickly she tossed Flynn's cage out the window. She reached for her second uniform and other belongings, but the fire had already gotten to them.

"Flynn! You have to warn everyone! Go!" Ash shrieked, pointing toward the window.

Flynn zoomed outside. Ash could see it was too far to jump. She'd have to get through the flames to the door. Her books, blankets, clothes, journals—all of it was ablaze. She gritted her teeth and jumped through the flames to the door. She opened it to see Marni and Mitzi standing in the entryway.

"Go! Run! Get the others and get out of the tree!"

Marni and Mitzi hurried out of the dorm as the flames licked at Ash's back and began to spread to Marni's room.

Ash took two steps to follow them, then quickly turned back.

Her father's flute. It was the only fragment of him that remained in her life. It wasn't just a set of musical pipes—it was her past, it was his love. It was hope that he was still out there, somewhere.

She leapt back through the flames into her room, now unrecognizable. Boards snapped beneath her feet and embers singed her cheeks. She lunged for her burning desk and opened its bottom drawer. The flute. It was still there in its velvet bag, untouched. She snatched it and turned back toward the door, but reaching it was impossible now.

With a haunting crack, the wooden dorm room began to collapse, tilting out of the tree. Ash screamed and grabbed for a tree branch that appeared through the charcoal. As the boards fell away, she saw students fleeing from the tree, assisted by Marni. More boards disintegrated and Ash found herself hanging from the branch with no support beneath her.

In the distance, she saw an older student arrive on an ice dragon, twice the size of Hermaeus. The dragon spit ice chunks on the tree. Ash had no idea if it was helping, but at the moment, the flames weren't her biggest concern—it was the thirty-foot drop below her. Her support branch cracked. She screamed. With another crack, Ash felt it give way.

Before she hit the ground, she caught a glimpse of wings—dragon wings. She looked up into the stoic face of Captain Bera atop her Wyvern, swooping in to catch her mid-fall. Bera set Ash on the grass and returned to the scene. Students from all over campus had gathered to the flaming tree, which was almost fully engulfed. They held their beasts close. Ash coughed and she collapsed on the ground. Marni rushed to her side.

Nearby, the Aquatic teacher, Professor Laguna, raised her enormous sea serpent out of the bay. The beast opened its jaws and breathed a large stream of water onto the tree. The flames slowly decreased. The fire seemed to be under control for now.

Ash burst into tears. Flynn zipped to her side, using his head to dry her cheeks. She rubbed her eyes and stood up.

"Did everyone get out?" she asked.

"Everyone's safe, Ash," Marni said. "It's okay."

Professor Thorne was the last to arrive on the scene. She covered her mouth at the sight of the burning tree. "How—How did this happen?"

"Hmm, I wonder," came the unmistakable drawl of Farrah, causing Ash's heart to plummet. "Couldn't possibly have been the girl with the uncontrollable firebird."

CHAPTER 12

THE FLAMER AND FLYER

"detta, surely you understand better than anyone that the families of the Academy will not tolerate a dangerous child in the midst of their own."

Ash stood motionless in the center of a circular chamber with Flynn on her shoulder. The bird, for once, remained silent and still, as if even he could sense the tension.

The round room was furnished with dark marble, which swallowed whatever light its two small windows provided. A hanging candelabrum compensated for the darkness, but the flickering yellow glow of its twenty candles failed to make the environment more comforting. The chamber was known as the

High Council Room, where the four Elders of the Academy gathered when important matters pertaining to the school required discussion. The professors made Ash nervous enough, but the Elders were the ones with the real jurisdiction. They decided who attended, who graduated, who joined the king's army—and who didn't belong.

This particular morning, they were there to discuss the previous night's fire.

"*Tuition-paying* families, mind you," Elder Raleigh added to Elder Pyrrus's statement.

Ash recognized Raleigh from her day at Castle Dragoon, when she met King Tiberius. She closed her eyes for a moment, hoping that just an ounce of the thrill from that day—the thrill of meeting the king and visiting his lavish castle—would relieve some of the stress of this one. She couldn't keep her fingers and knees from trembling, despite her deep breaths.

"Precisely my point," replied Elder Pyrrus, a man slightly older than Raleigh with a dark-brown beard and red, velvet robes. His narrowed gaze framed by thick, unruly eyebrows gave him the look of an alert, yet patient attack dog. "These are tuition-paying students! There is enough inherent danger at this school with the beasts. If the parents got wind that a girl, attending the Academy on essentially a scholarship, was recklessly adding to that danger—"

"You mustn't misdirect your anger, Pyrrus," said Odetta. "The decision to allow Ash to attend the Academy as a grant recipient was just as much yours as it was any of ours. If that is where your contempt lies, then it is our error, not hers."

Her melodic voice in response to Pyrrus's irritated tone felt to Ash like her only saving grace. She'd forgotten that attending the school normally cost money—likely lots of money. And now it appeared she was a waste of their charity.

"The child set an entire section of dormitories on fire! Your bias blinds you, Odetta. Are you saying that the Loomingtons would not be outraged to find their kin harmed or injured by a girl we took in off the street?"

"That has not happened. Let us deal in existing matters, not hypothetical ones," she responded calmly.

"It is true, however, that the girl has no family history to vouch for her," said Raleigh.

Ash winced at the comment, a point she could never argue. Her parents weren't well-known aristocrats or socialites. They didn't donate handsomely to the Academy like Hammond's family, or travel the world like Marni's. She had no mother, and a father who worked backbreaking hours to barely make ends meet. She loved her father, but there was no denying they were the lowest of the low in society.

It seemed two out of the four Elders were against her and only one was for her, so far. The oldest man and fourth member of the council, Elder Mortimer, still had not spoken. He sat quietly with his hands folded on his long white beard that rested on his lap. For such an old man, he surprisingly wore no glasses and used no cane. His expression portrayed either deep thought or frozen sleep. Either way, he said nothing. He simply stared at Ash with turquoise eyes perched above a long, sloping nose.

"You both should be well aware that the demands and concerns of our students' families have a tendency to be less than rational," continued Odetta. "Let us not forget this is still our university."

Pyrrus leaned back in his chair with an exhale, signaling he was finished arguing with Odetta. He cleared his throat and reached for a piece of parchment.

"Ms. Ridley, prior to the tree fire, there have been several student complaints about your phoenix and his inability to control his flame capabilities."

Ash swallowed loudly. She knew Flynn had coughed fireballs on a few of her classmates, but was it really enough to file a formal complaint?

Pyrrus continued. "Melany Grindle claims Flynn singed a one-inch section of her hair, requiring a full haircut."

Ash remembered the incident. It wasn't Flynn's fault that Melany flipped her hair whenever a good-looking boy passed by. It especially wasn't his fault when she had flipped her hair during combat practice, the only time Flynn was allowed to spit fire whenever he wanted. It had been a simple accident. *Some girls just don't realize how long their hair is.*

"And Talia Vontaine says Flynn attacked her in the hallway and burned a hole clean through a jacket that she describes as being very expensive."

Flynn was just being playful! And he had barely singed the hemming on the back; he certainly hadn't burned an actual hole through it...had he?

"They were accidents, sir," Ash said, barely more than a whisper. She knew Flynn had upset some people, but she hadn't thought it would be a serious issue. Angry students, a fire on school property, Elders who distrusted her—perhaps she *should* be expelled, to save everyone the trouble.

"We let most accidents slide for first-year students," Pyrrus said, "but if you plan on advancing at this school, you must get your animal under control."

"For the safety of yourself and especially your classmates," added Raleigh.

Ash nodded.

"This is your first warning, Ash. We will discuss additional tutoring with Professor Talon and deliver you an updated syllabus. Should you continue to violate basic school safety rules, we will be forced to remove you from this school. You are dismissed."

As Ash turned to leave, she quickly glanced to Odetta, hoping the look would translate as one of gratitude.

Her thin arms struggled to push open the thick, wooden doors, carved with symbols and pictures. She closed it loudly behind her and, when it latched, immediately exhaled in relief. She shook off her built-up tension and wiped the sweat from her forehead. Never before had she felt such anxiety. Even Flynn ruffled his feathers and shook his head.

Ash quieted her breathing for a moment. Faintly, she heard voices—the voices of the Elders. *Impossible*, she thought. *These doors are two feet thick.*

She pressed an ear against the wood, and sure enough, she could hear the Elders speaking through the massive, soundproof door. As it was, she cared less about her suddenly increased hearing and more about eavesdropping.

It sounded like Odetta and Pyrrus were still arguing.

"The girl is wielding a beast far more rare than anything we've seen in this school, or in all of Cascadia, for hundreds of years," Odetta said with passion. "Is it not understandable that there is no guidebook for raising such a creature?"

"If she cannot control the phoenix then perhaps it shouldn't have bonded to her at all," Pyrrus rebutted. "It wouldn't be the first time a beast was in the wrong hands."

Ash gasped and backed away from the door.

In the wrong hands?

Ash sprinted out of the corridor and down a hallway. She didn't care where she was going as long as it was away. Flynn sped after her as she ran, catching tears that leapt from her cheeks.

She came to an outdoor bridge that connected to the next tower and collapsed her head into her hands on the thick, stone railing. The clouds were gray and rumbled with thunder, threatening a storm that Ash welcomed. Perhaps the rain would melt her into a puddle, and she could drain into the inlet and flow out to the ocean forever. Maybe she could find somewhere at the bottom of the sea that wanted her. Maybe she belonged far away from the Academy, from Flynn—from everyone.

As she cried, Flynn landed on the railing beside her. He tilted his head at the sound of her sobs and cooed softly. He hopped toward her and nuzzled his beak against her forehead.

"Now you choose to be sweet," Ash said, stroking his head. "That awful ghost was right. They want to take you away from me, Flynn. I just know they do."

Ash glanced up. The bridge overlooked the valley—including the treehouse. It was an awful sight. The old beech tree, once a sentinel that watched over the Academy, tall and inviting with ages of wisdom in its flourishing branches, now haunted the grounds like a black claw emerging from the underworld to prey on the innocent. Its charcoal limbs seemed to taunt the green shrubbery around it, as if to warn that they were next.

Several professors and dwarves were clearing debris and gathering the crispy belongings of treehouse inhabitants amidst the blackened lumber. About twenty students, all previously housed in the tree, began to set up cloth tents for temporary housing. The tents were flimsy and wouldn't stand up well to rain—which had just begun to fall.

"Oh, Flynn," Ash said, tears welling up again. "I know you didn't set that fire. But who will believe us?"

"We fear what we do not understand," said a kind, familiar voice.

Ash turned to see Odetta's elegant frame in her snow-white robes standing beside her.

"It is human nature," she said with a soft smile. "It makes us no better than the animals."

"I don't belong here," Ash said. "I'm just a poor girl who happens to be packaged with some bird everyone wants."

Odetta kneeled to her. "On the contrary. Flynn is just a wild creature in need of a master to show him the way. A master with passion, with heart, with a fire of her own."

Flynn chirped at Odetta, and hopped onto her finger.

"He's just a child," she added. "As are you, Ash. Give each other time."

Ash and Flynn collected raindrops on their heads as they left the Academy and headed toward the beech tree. By this time, nearly all the students formerly of the treehouse dorms had set up their tents and were proceeding to make them comfortable before the rain picked up. As Ash walked, she couldn't help but notice the looks and whispers from those she passed. One student even bumped hard into her shoulder, practically knocking her over. It wasn't an accident.

There was a line of students waiting to look inside a large barrel, as Dennis the dwarf carried a second barrel over.

"Here's the last barrel full o' salvaged belongin's," he said, setting down the barrel with a grunt. "Have a look and take what's yers. And don't take stuff that ain't yers!"

Half the line of children flocked to the new barrel, so Ash got in line herself. The two children ahead of her frowned when they noticed her and immediately began whispering. No one was speaking to her, only about her.

"Treehouse dorm students!" called Professor Thorne, approaching with Dottie and Donnie. They carried bags full of clothes. "For those who lost uniforms in the fire, we've gathered replacements from the lost and found. Please see Dottie and she'll provide you with the closest size."

"Great, now we can all look like Ash," said Dickon to Lokey.

Though he was fifty feet away, Ash still heard him—another instance of her hearing being increased. It had to be because of her bond with Flynn. Unfortunately, it was hard to be excited about a heightened sense of hearing when the only words she heard made her feel utterly gutted.

She sighed and held back her emotions. Crying in front of students who already hated her wouldn't help her reputation.

"Ash! There you are!" Marni yelled, dragging what looked like a two-hundred-pound trunk behind her. Mitzi excitedly pranced alongside.

She dropped the trunk. It thudded, even in the grass. The trunk appeared to be half burnt and completely soaked in water.

"Your trunk survived?" Ash asked.

"Survived? This thing is a Bellington traveler's trunk. Very expensive. My parents bought it while traveling in Argania. Lyle fetched it out of the bay for me. Must have tumbled out of the tree and plunged in there when our dorm collapsed."

Marni kicked off the crispy latch and opened the lid. It was filled to the brim with water.

"All right, so it's not airtight," she said defensively, responding to a comment Ash hadn't made.

Marni kicked the trunk over and drained the water onto the grass. All of her trunk belongings—clothes, shoes, hair ribbons, necklaces—spilled out in a sloppy, wet pile. Marni picked up a sweater that looked expensive. She wrung it out and held it up, ignoring the several strands of seaweed caught in the stitches.

"Good as new!" she said.

Ash hung her head. "I'm sorry about our dorms, Marni, and all your lovely things. I'm just glad you got out all right."

"Me? I got down the steps and out of that burning bush before things got dicey—it was you I was concerned about. You really waited until the last second, huh?"

Marni gave her best friend a playful wink. Ash, who had never felt more depressed in all her life, couldn't help but smile at Marni's optimism.

"You sure seem a lot happier than everyone else," Ash said.

"You should have seen her earlier, when she thought her trunk was gone," said Hammond, approaching in his usual scarf-and-gloves combo with Hermie trailing behind.

"Shh! Don't tell her that," Marni whispered.

"She was wailing and falling over herself as if the world ended."

"Shh! I just said *don't* tell her that!"

Ash's half smile turned into a full one. "I'm sure glad you two are still talking to me."

"Of course," Marni said. "Why wouldn't I talk to you? We're roommates!"

They awkwardly glanced up at what was left of the beech tree. Another crispy branch snapped off.

"*Were* roommates," Ash corrected.

"Hmm. For now, we'll push our tents together and be tentmates."

The sky rumbled loudly and now it really started to rain. Mitzi, being from a thunder clan of kitsunes, howled at the sky. Her three bushy tails sparked with electricity. She was clearly at home in a storm.

"You guys could always stay in the cave with me and Hermaeus if you'd like," Hammond said, seeming delighted at the idea of company.

The girls exchanged a glance, remembering the freezing-cold ice prison that was Hammond's cave. "No, thanks," they said in unison.

"And it's Hermaeus *and me*," Marni corrected. "Honestly, Hammond. Mrs. Brown may be as boring as a sponge, but you still need to pay attention in grammar."

As the line moved forward, two second-year students with snakes shoved ahead of Ash, knocking her back. Flynn assumed an attack position, but Ash quickly snatched him out of the air and pinched his beak shut.

"The firebirdie wants to fight me, does he?" said one boy, his snake hissing at Flynn.

Ash backed away and shook her head.

"He's already burned all our things. Might as well burn the clothes off our backs as well," said the other boy.

They laughed to each other and their snakes slithered around their necks and arms.

"Never met a snake charmer I liked," sneered Marni. "Ignore them, Ash. They don't know what really happened."

Hammond bit his bottom lip and grabbed nervously at his shirt. "If you don't mind my asking, Ash—and please tell me if you do, in fact, mind—but what *did* happen?"

"Oh, yes, I meant to ask as well. Goodness, Ash, what happened?" asked Marni.

Ash sighed. Her instincts pressured her to say it was an accident and leave the topic alone. Tilda had always punished her for telling outlandish tales, even if Ash swore they were true. Years of being conditioned to keep her mouth shut caused Ash to fear telling even her most trustworthy friends a farfetched story.

"I—I'm not sure I should tell you."

"Why on earth not?" Marni said, eager for the scoop.

"You can tell us, Ash," Hammond encouraged. "We'll believe you. Promise."

Ash swallowed her apprehension and told her two friends everything—the first note, the second note, the third note, and Irving the insane specter. She recounted his incessant riddles and, finally, the dropping of the match that started the fire.

Unfortunately, the gratification of spilling her secret was met with blank faces. Even Marni, who salivated over every bit of gossip, was speechless.

"You don't believe me, do you?" Ash said, unsurprised.

"No, no! It's just—"

"It's not that we don't believe you," Hammond interrupted. "It's just that—"

"Ghosts don't exist, Ash," Marni blurted.

"Are you sure you didn't dream this ghost?" Hammond asked. "And Flynn really just had an accident and set the fire?"

"I've had lifelike dreams before, too, Ash," Marni added in a reassuring tone. "Just two nights ago I dreamt I was eating a giant marshmallow—"

Ash sighed. "That still doesn't explain the notes!"

Ash reached the front of the line and was finally able to step up to the barrel of burnt items. There was almost nothing left but some lumps of charcoal that sort of looked like they could have once been someone's belongings. She wondered how these were considered salvaged.

"I don't know, Ash. Farrah has it out for you. Maybe she's trying to scare you away from school," said Marni.

"Maybe it's Dickon, or Lokey, or—"

Ash pulled two items from the bottom of the barrel: her birdcage, now fried and warped, and a small box. The box was so damaged from the fire that it was nearly unidentifiable—but Ash recognized it as the jewelry box her father had given her. While it was blackened, looking as though it had barely survived being completely destroyed, the inscribed letters of her name could still be made out. The corners crumbled and the top fell off as she opened it. It had been empty before, but now held something.

"Or maybe I'm telling you the truth."

Inside the damaged box was a perfectly unharmed piece of parchment paper, exactly like the others. Unfolded, it read:

FOLLOW THE MUSIC.

Her two friends gawked at the note.

"I believed you from the start," Marni finally blurted. "It was Hammond who didn't."

The rain had begun to fall so hard that everyone on campus, including Marni and Hammond, returned to the warm corridors of the Academy to study in the library or socialize in the commons. Ash remained outside to finish erecting her tent, cursing the clouds. Why had they chosen *now* for a monsoon instead of last night, when it would have actually been welcome? It seemed even the weather was against her. At least the aquatic animals of the Academy were enjoying themselves. Ash saw several sea serpents breaching and diving in the bay, as well as two water monkeys splashing around by the beach.

She spent the rest of the day in the commissary studying arithmetic and sipping hot mint tea. The other students avoided her completely and threw nasty looks. She was thankful that Flynn gave off such heat, since the children sitting near all the fireplaces made it clear she was not welcome to join them.

By nightfall, the rain had downgraded from deluge to sprinkle and everyone returned to their dorms, stables, caves, and tents. Ash was less than delighted to find that someone had ripped a hole in the roof of her tent with a knife, and her bed of blankets was now sopping wet. She heard a few snickers behind her, but didn't bother to turn around. Perhaps if she ignored the tormenting, it would stop.

Ash squeezed the excess water from her blankets and curled up into a ball, shivering from the wind and the rain droplets that invaded her shelter. Flynn opted for cuddling with Ash over his bent birdcage, wriggling his way under the blankets. He purred once he got comfortable. She welcomed his warmth in such chilly conditions.

"Tents aren't so bad, are they Flynn?" she whispered. "We've had worse."

She stared through the gaping hole in her cloth roof. She was thankful at least for the few stars that peeked through the clouds, rebellious little balls of light that refused to be concealed by the gray masses.

When she fidgeted, she felt the pan flute in her pocket. She removed it and ran her fingers along the soft wooden pipes. Visions of the day it was given to her flashed in her mind. The hide-and-seek chase. The Random Gift holiday. Her father's smile when she gave him that silly yellow egg. His reassurance that things would be all right. That together, they would be all right.

She blew a puff of air into the smallest pipe to hear the high-pitched toot.

Flynn cooed, muffled by the blankets.

She wondered if he remembered the flute from his last life, how she had played it for the animals to relax them. Tilda was the only one out of the group who hated the sound, so eventually, she had simply sung to them.

Softly, she sang:

> *The road is long, for my darling dear*
> *The wind is cold, the sun's disappeared*
> *But don't be 'fraid, for this, too, will pass*
> *We'll lie soon down on green, silky grass*
> *We'll lie soon down on green, silky grass*

As she sang, Flynn popped his head up and began whistling the simple tune along with her, just like her father used to whistle. It sent chills down her spine. She couldn't believe how much she missed him.

He had once told her that humans were the only animals that could fool themselves. Perhaps if Ash imagined that everything were all right, she just might believe it.

The following week, the weather cleared up and returned to sunshine with a slight autumn breeze. The professors could be seen out by the beech tree in their spare time, casting magic spells on the bark and branches. The tree already looked significantly better than the spindly black eyesore of the previous Friday. The charcoal was fading, the branches were growing and thickening, and even the trunk looked broader than before. Perhaps the old tree wasn't dead after all. Perhaps it could be reborn from the flames, like Flynn.

Ash, still unpopular with her peers, kept herself busy with classes, studying, and training exercises in preparation for exams now just two days away. She'd discovered in her academic time that she enjoyed tests like she enjoyed stubbing her toes, even though she was good at them, but she was thankful that everyone had something to focus their attention on that didn't involve her. Maybe they'd resume their ridiculing once the week was over, but for now, she was content with being invisible.

The combination of seeing so little of her best friends, sleeping on an uneven patch of ground, and studying so much her brain felt like it might explode was exhausting. One day, Ash was in the commissary, fighting the urge to lay her head down on the sticky table that smelled like cheese and feet and nap for perhaps a thousand years. It wasn't until a student passed through, blaring an awful trumpet, that Ash jolted back awake. He continued to play a horrid tune that could be heard echoing through the halls of the school, no matter how far away he walked. Ash concluded that bad music was actually worse than no music at all.

Music.

She reached in her pocket and pulled out the fourth note. "Follow the music," it said. What music? Just the thought of that wretched ghost stalking her and planting notes in her jewelry box that no one aside from her even knew she had made her furious. The nerve.

She crumpled it up and set it on the table next to Flynn.

"It's all yours," she said, pointing toward it.

Flynn opened his mouth and spit a flame that burned the note until it disappeared into ashes that floated away.

"No fireballs in the commissary!" she heard the cafeteria lady yell from the kitchen in her shrill, raspy voice.

Ash felt surprisingly satisfied burning the note and gave Flynn a carrot from her pocket as a reward—but she was still not entirely at ease. If this Irving character were willing to burn down the oldest landmark on Academy property, putting her and other children's lives at stake in order to get her expelled, he wouldn't be pleased to learn that his plan failed. She hadn't gotten expelled, she hadn't left, and she'd ignored his warnings. The ghost was a lunatic, but he was a lunatic who meant business. Who knew what he would do next?

Ash glanced at a clock on the wall. It was six forty-five, fifteen minutes before the library closed.

"Come on, Flynn!"

She grabbed her belongings and ran to the room's exit.

"No running in the commissary!" she heard the cafeteria lady yell again.

Dodging and weaving her way down halls and across walkways, she arrived at the library with ten minutes to spare. Frantically, she searched the sections for any sort of history of Cascadia, specifically the history of King Ivarr.

She located a large section filled with books about the royal families.

"King Phineas, King Deverus...King Ivarr!"

On her tiptoes, she pulled down a book: *The Reign of King Ivarr, MLII–MCL.*

"Five minutes 'til close!" called the librarian, Vilhelm.

"All right, Flynny," she said, scanning the index. "Let's see if this Irving really is who he says he is."

She flipped to page 756, to a section titled "The Execution of Irving the Mage."

She skimmed the paragraphs quickly as she heard Vilhelm order two children near the front of the library to finish up and get out.

"A-ha! Flynn, listen to this: 'On March the third of MCII, the Mage Irving was found guilty of selling military secrets, which brought upon the Human and Minotaur War and the death of Queen Lita...He was sentenced to hanging, but survived due to what was believed to be black magic. He was subsequently burned at the stake.' No wonder he's got a thing for fire."

"Time you must go now! Out, child! Take bird!" demanded Vilhelm in his thick accent. He shooed Flynn off the back of a chair and snatched the book away from Ash.

"May I check that book out?" she asked.

"Too late to check book. You go now. And no bird next time!"

Ash returned to her tent, heart pumping with adrenaline. She spent her last moments before passing out asleep thinking about Irving. He had been telling the truth about who he was, and he was certainly dangerous. Ash knew one thing was for sure: she had to figure out what his last note meant. She had to find the music.

The next day—the last one before exams—Flynn performed well in Combat prep and adequately in Avian. He had begun to comprehend that obeying Ash's commands actually allowed him to practice his fire attacks more often. When he disobeyed, he had to sit out of class. By now, Flynn knew three attack positions, five defensive maneuvers, and three attacks: Flamethrow (the first attack he'd mastered), Fireball, and a swooping, diving attack called a Wing Strike. For the most part, he struck when commanded, but occasionally he improvised. Combat classes were without a doubt his favorite parts of the week.

Avian, however, was more of a struggle. Ash was all set for the test portion, but Flynn was wholly uninterested in flight patterns and resisted participation. Whenever she guided him through figure eights, she got the sense that he was saying, *What is the point of this? Let's just fight instead.*

At lunchtime, she sat alone on the front steps of the Academy. She shared a tuna fish sandwich with Flynn, who was now slightly bigger than a common blue jay and had a significantly increased appetite. Her thoughts were divided. How could she possibly focus on tomorrow's exams when she couldn't stop thinking about the mysterious music? Every time she heard a melody, whether it was someone whistling or a lark singing, she was distracted from whatever she was doing and thought, *could it be?*

Flynn caught sandwich pieces out of the air as Ash tossed them. He never missed, no matter how poor her aim.

"You been avoiding me?"

The voice startled Ash into dropping her sandwich—an accident that Flynn very much approved of. The voice belonged to Jeffrey, who plopped down on the steps beside her. Ash swallowed her last bite and hoped desperately that there was nothing stuck in her teeth.

"Sorry?" she said.

"You were supposed to meet me last Monday on the playing field, remember?"

Jeffrey had wanted to see more of Flynn's flying abilities. She'd completely forgotten.

"I suppose I didn't think anyone wanted to be around me after the fire. Honestly, I'm just happy not to be expelled."

"Expelled? Did those crusty old Elders give you that 'first warning' blather?"

He laughed when she nodded. "Oh, blimey," he continued. "Ash, do you have any idea the amount of damage beasts have done to this school? You see Zachary over there? With his Zmey dragon? It's the one with three heads."

Near the stables was a dark-skinned boy playing catch with a huge, thirty-foot-tall three-headed dragon. Despite his size, the Zmey was prancing around with the boy like a puppy.

"Each one of those heads breathes fire, ice, and wind, respectively. In our first year, that thing lit the stables on fire, froze the entire inlet, and blew all the professors into a tornado that destroyed the Academy's center spire. We still laugh about it! That's what magic is for, silly. They can repair just about anything in a week or two."

Ash's gaze wandered to the beech tree. She hadn't checked its progress in a while, and what she saw now was astounding. Thanks to the magic of the professors, the tree looked nearly back to normal. Its bark appeared healthy, its branches looked sturdy—it was as if the fire had never happened at all, save for the lack of the treehouses.

"And look right now," he said, pointing to the Academy campus entrance near The Shoppes. "They're bringing in the carpenter elves."

In single file, fourteen-inch-tall elves marched to the beech tree with tools in hand. They had pointy ears, pointed hats, and very small tool belts around their very small hips. Dennis and his fellow dwarves stood nearby with fresh lumber as the tiny elves got to work rebuilding the treehouses.

Ash smiled, not just at her first sight of elves, but at the thought that things might turn out all right, after all.

"Well, come on, then," Jeffrey said, standing up and whistling for Jareth. The hippogriff trotted over and whinnied at his master. "Let's have a bit of fun on your lunch break. Flynn looks antsy to do some flying."

Ash went against her better instincts, which told her to study for the next day's exams and instead joined Jeffrey on the athletic field. The area was still marked for the track and flight relay, although the lines had significantly worn off since the tryouts and were in desperate need of repainting.

Jeffrey mounted his hippogriff and took to the sky. Not quite as advanced in magic as Professor Suarez, his eight floating markers were simply clouds that he formed into fluffy circles with the help of Jareth's wings. They weren't as shiny and perfect as Diego's golden rings, but they'd do for practice.

Back at the starting line, Jeffrey tossed her a baton.

"You remember how the relay is played, yes?" he asked.

"Um, the animals race through the rings, right?"

Jeffrey laughed. "Seems that way, doesn't it? But you, young lady, are just as important to this race as Flynn. You have to participate, too."

He explained the rules to Ash. She would toss the baton to Flynn, he would catch it and race through the eight markers, then drop the baton back down to her. She would then run it a quarter mile to the finish line.

"All right then," Jeffrey said after she understood the sequence of events. "Let's see a toss."

Ash put her hand out, motioning for Flynn to settle. She took a deep breath and flung the baton into the air. Flynn shot from the ground and caught it, despite it not exactly being thrown straight up.

"No, no. Let me show you," Jeffrey said. "You're tossing the baton like a stick you'd throw to a dog. Notice how it flipped end over end in the air?"

Ash nodded.

"That makes it quite hard for your animal to grab it. He could lose valuable time trying to compensate for a whirly, wobbly baton."

Jeffrey grabbed her wrist and flattened her palm. He set the baton on top of her hand and curled her fingers around it.

"Just like this," he said. "Throw it straight up and let it roll off your fingers."

She did, and this time, the baton stayed horizontal in the air, as opposed to flipping wildly.

"Perfect," he said. "Get it as high as you can throw it. The key is to give Flynn the easiest start possible."

Ash nodded and felt her cheeks blush. She hoped it wasn't too noticeable.

"Let's try a race then, shall we? Jareth wasn't too happy with his defeat against Flynn last time. He's the one demanding a rematch, not me."

Jareth whinnied and pranced happily, eager to begin.

"You want to race? Right now?" Ash said.

"What better way to learn than to jump right in?"

Ash motioned for Flynn to return to the starting line.

By this time, Ash noticed a small group of students had gathered—a couple of fourth years who were giggling, most likely at Jeffrey associating with a first year. Rebecca strolled up and elbowed one of them in the stomach to knock it off.

"Ready?" Jeffrey said, in position. "Three, two, one...go!"

They both launched their batons into the air, with Jeffrey's sailing at least ten feet above Ash's. Jareth and Flynn lurched after them, catching both perfectly in their talons. The race was on.

Jareth and Flynn weaved back and forth, neck in neck from the first marker to the second. At marker three, Jareth swooped toward Flynn, knocking him off course and causing him to drop his baton. Ash gasped.

"He can still grab it if he's quick," said Jeffrey.

Flynn chased the falling baton and snatched it in his claws right before it hit the ground.

"He got it!" Jeffrey said with a smile. His fellow fourth years cheered on the little bird.

Flynn had some catching up to do now. He sped through the fourth ring as Jareth sped through the fifth. Flynn tucked his head and picked up speed, meeting his opponent at ring six. He didn't even stop to greet the hippogriff—instead, he whizzed passed him through ring seven and had an enormous advantage by ring eight.

"Incredible, that bird!" yelled Jeffrey. "Get ready to catch the baton!"

Ash opened and closed her hand quickly, signaling to Flynn to drop the baton. He released the stick from his talons. Ash stepped right, then left, then right, then barely caught it in her left hand.

The onlooking crowd cheered, "Run! Run!" She grasped the baton tightly and ran toward the finish line. She was in the lead and didn't look back. This event was simple—perhaps she and Flynn had found their calling.

Like a whizzing dart, Jeffrey suddenly sprinted up beside her at an incredible speed. He easily overtook her and gained a lead of ten yards before crossing the finish line. His fellow classmates booed him playfully before losing interest and leaving the field.

"What did—how did you do that?" Ash exclaimed, doubling over out of breath. "I had an impossible lead on you! Am I really that slow?"

Jeffrey laughed and walked over to her, not out of breath at all. He patted Jareth on the neck, who beckoned for another go.

"Don't you know? Years of bonding with a swift animal increases your own speed. I'm twice as fast now as I was before I bonded to Jareth. And thus, you understand why the relay is for both beasts and their humans."

Flynn returned to her, pecking at her pocket for his well-deserved reward. She retrieved a carrot for him.

"Sure, you haven't gained running speed from your phoenix yet—and goodness help us when you do—but you still have a faster beast than anyone competing. If Flynn gains enough of a head start on your opponents, you could merrily skip to the finish line and still win."

Flynn gave her a natural edge in the sport, and Jeffrey had recognized it. Even better, it was a heck of a fun time.

The clock chimed one o'clock—both of them needed to head to class. In the distance, Rebecca motioned for Jeffrey to join her.

"Remember, Ash," he said before he left. "School is hard. The professors can be unreasonable, the Elders can threaten to kick you out. But things like the relay will help you remember why you're here in the first place: to bond with Flynn. Just imagine it. You and Flynn as a magical, powerful team, leading an army of Regal Kin into battle to protect the royal family and the innocent people of Cascadia. There's nothing in this world more honorable."

Ash did picture it. Could a peasant girl and a scrawny red bird really be heroes someday? It was a marvelous dream. And it was worth striving for.

Jeffrey continued. "Flynn's your buddy, your comrade. Having a bit of fun will bring you closer. With a strong enough connection, you two can do awesome things."

He jogged off to meet Rebecca, shouting to Ash that he'd contact her for another practice soon. She watched the two stroll off to class.

Flynn landed on Ash's shoulder and rubbed his head against hers. In all the chaos of exams and the messages and the tree fire, had she been ignoring him?

She recalled the night she had first met him, just an elderly bird in a traveling sideshow act. She would make up stories in her head of his past adventures, traveling to ancient worlds and being marveled at by all who had the chance to lay eyes on his glittering feathers. Then, she remembered the night he died, and how she had felt dead herself, watching him burn to ashes right in front of her. But the old had turned to new, and she had met her friend all over again, as a baby.

From tiny chick to beautiful flyer, with bright eyes and fiery spirit, Flynn had picked her to be his master. No one else.

"I suppose I haven't been the greatest friend lately, have I?"

Flynn cooed at the sound of her voice. Whether he knew what she was saying or not, he always responded when she spoke to him.

Ash reached in her pocket and retrieved another chunk of carrot. "Come on. Let's get to class."

C H A P T E R   1 3

THE MUSIC

he examinations went as Ash expected. She aced the written tests and Flynn performed passably in the physical portion. Instead of becoming frustrated with the firebird, she strove to maintain patience. She decided that from then on, she would seek to understand the reasons why Flynn ignored her commands instead of simply punishing him. She even switched his rewarding treat from walnuts to black-berries, which he seemed to love. However, the blackberries created a purple stain on his golden beak that Ash found very stupid looking. She was constantly using her shirt to wipe off his beak, like a tireless mother with a messy child.

After the strenuous day of testing, she promised Flynn a picnic. She swiped two handfuls of granola from the commissary and stuffed them in her pockets before the cafeteria lady could shout objections and angrily shake a ladle at her.

Ash, fowl on shoulder, trotted through the brisk air to the beach behind the Academy, crunching leaves with every step. Ash spent an hour hunting for pretty shells and munching on granola while Flynn attempted to dive-bomb for shallow ocean fish. He swooped and dove and swooped some more, occasionally letting the strong wind lift him up and carry him like a kite. He caught only one fish—a blenny, but ended up much more interested in a blue crab that hobbled sideways along the shoreline. Ash giggled as he provoked the shelled creature, dodging his pinchers and snapping his beak at it. He even pecked at the crustacean's noggin.

Let's play! He seemed to be saying to the grumpy crab.

They finished the day with a game of catch. Ash found pieces of driftwood similar in size to the relay batons and practiced her tosses, over and over. Flynn enjoyed the added challenge of the wind and water, though one wave smacked him so hard that he tumbled onto the beach, which covered him in sand like a piece of taffy rolled in sugar. Ash laughed heartily and scooped him up in her arms. She wiped the sand from his eyes and he sneezed some granules out of his nose. Swaddling the wet bird in her shirt, they returned to their tent.

The next morning, students in classrooms with a view of the beech tree could hardly pay attention to their teachers. It was the final day of construction for the carpenter elves, and by sundown they had packed up their tools and marched single file away from the Academy grounds. Dottie, Donnie, and Dennis had finished painting and furnishing the new dorm rooms and the tent-dwelling students were allowed to move back in.

"Wow!" Marni exclaimed, yanking her trunk through the entry door of their renovated dorm. "These rooms are much nicer than before!"

Ash examined the new room. Her roommate was right—it was much, much nicer.

Marni hopped up and down. "And less creaky. And look at this furniture—brand new! Ash, you should've burned down those rickety old dorms a long time ago."

"I didn't burn them down, Marni," Ash corrected with an eyeroll. She set Flynn's dented birdcage on her brand-new desk.

"You know what I mean," Marni said, pushing her trunk through the door to her side of the dorm. Mitzi's nose worked overtime as the fox curiously sniffed every last inch of the place. "You smell that fresh lumber, Mitz? Mmm...I love that scent. I'm going to sleep like a baby tonight, I'm sure of it."

The blankets on Ash's bed were thicker, her desk chair was freshly polished—even her window opened, whereas before it had been stuck shut. She slid it open for a bit of fresh air and Flynn immediately perched on the sill. She really hoped she'd never have to throw a chair through it again.

The downside of the new room, of course, was that it was missing her belongings. Everything she had brought from home, and all of the supplies Odetta had purchased her from Flanagan's Feathers—nothing had survived, except her damaged birdcage, pan flute, and the crumbling remains of her jewelry box. She retrieved the flute in its velvet bag from her pocket and placed it in her desk's bottom drawer.

She paused. For some reason, the flute didn't feel safe in the desk. She returned it to her pocket.

Dudley, Dickon's hyper little bildad, hopped into Ash's room. The wily creature left dirty, webbed footprints on her rug and bed as he chased after Flynn.

"Honestly, now!" Ash whined, shooing the critter out before he left any more dirt. "Out!"

"Don't be so uptight, Ash. Dud's just being friendly," said Dickon, leaning against her door. "Not like he's burnin' your house down or anything."

"Very funny," she remarked, wiping the dirt off her bed.

"Naomi said she saw you on the athletic field training with Jeffrey."

Ash shrugged, waiting for him to make his point.

"None of us have gotten to play any sports yet. Is he going to put you on the team?"

"He can't," came the cold voice of Farrah. She stepped inside with crossed arms. "I told Professor Thorne that Jeffrey was letting Ash train with the older kids. She said Ash can't even try out for the Games until next year. It's policy."

"Funny how you can't keep your nose out of her business *or* her dorm room," retorted Marni, entering from her room.

"I wasn't training with anyone," Ash said in defense. "I met with Jeffrey one time to see how Flynn would do in track and flight relay, nothing more."

"And he did spectacularly!" Marni announced.

"Marni, you didn't even see it," Ash whispered.

"I can assume," she whispered back with confidence.

Farrah pressed her lips together tightly and examined the room. "So, let me see if I'm understanding this correctly: Ash burns down school property and gets rewarded with better dorms?"

Ash bit her cheek. She had a point.

"Why do you care, Farrah?" Marni said, stepping toward her. "Stables getting a bit drafty these days?"

Marni and Farrah began bickering, stepping on each other's words and shouting until even Mitzi started barking in frustration. The dog rumbled like thunder and her eyes sparked, but it did nothing to stop the catfight.

Ash tried and failed to interject. Dickon, on the other hand, took a front-row seat in Ash's desk chair and watched the quarrel with an interested smile. She sighed loudly and covered her eyes with her hands.

Suddenly, the chaos around her seemed to fade away. She heard a different sound. It started off faint, but when she focused, it grew louder. She removed her hands from her eyes and stepped toward the open window. In the distance was a high-pitched sound—a lovely, haunting voice. It was singing.

Ash stared through the window in a trance. The melody was beautiful, but how could she hear it? It had to have been coming from miles away.

The music. It had to be.

"Ash? Ash!"

Ash snapped out of her hypnotized state.

"What on earth are you staring at?" Farrah said sharply.

Everyone in the room was looking at her. "You...you don't hear anything?"

They listened and looked out the window.

"No," said Farrah and Dickon.

"Was it the sound of Farrah's gums flapping as she spewed out lies?"

"Watch it, Mayberry."

"Bring it, blondie."

"All right, out! Both of you, out," Ash said, gently pushing her unwelcome guests toward the doorway of her room.

As Farrah marched out the door with her nose in the air, she turned toward Dickon.

"Come on, Dickon," she said sweetly.

Marni narrowed her gaze. "Running with a bossier crowd these days, are we, Dickon?"

"I said. Come. *On.*"

Dickon shrugged at Marni and left with Farrah.

Ash hardly slept that night. She decided she couldn't keep it to herself—she'd speak to Marni the next day. Unfortunately, her earliest opportunity came during Mrs. Brown's Arithmetic class. It was long division day, made no more interesting by Mrs. Brown's nasally droning and elongated words.

"...and then the above operation is multiplied by the divisor, which is placed under the last number divided into..."

"Marni. Psst, Marni," Ash whispered to her friend, who sat to her left. "I figured it out."

"Figured what out? How not to fall asleep whenever Mrs. Brown opens her mouth?"

A student three seats away gave them a hearty "*Shh!*" Marni responded by sticking her tongue out.

"No," Ash continued. "The music. My last note from Irving said to follow the music, and last night, I heard it. When you guys were in my room, remember? There was this beautiful voice—a woman's voice, singing a melody. It was coming from...I'm not sure, but I think near the ocean."

"Maybe it's a singing fish!"

"*SHH!*" the student hissed again.

"*SHH* yourself!" Marni replied, quietly of course.

Mrs. Brown turned slowly from her chalkboard. She scanned the classroom for do-badders. With her same, dull expression, she returned to her long division.

"The whole number result is placed at the top and any remainders are ignored..."

"What are you going to do?" Marni whispered.

"I suppose I should go find it," Ash responded.

"Are you sure that's a good idea?" Marni asked.

"Of course not," Ash said. "But what choice do I have? That silly ghost doesn't want me at this school for a reason, and things haven't exactly been going well for me here. He warned me that certain people might not be trustworthy and I'd be lying if I said I didn't have my suspicions. Doesn't this seem worth investigating?"

Marni shrugged. Her eyes showed neither agreement nor denial.

"I'm sneaking out after dark tonight. Will you keep anyone from sniffing around my room?"

"No way!" Marni whispered back, a little louder than intended. "I'm going with you."

"Never," Ash said, shaking her head. "I don't know what's waiting for me and I'd never want to put you in danger."

"Don't care. I'm going with you."

"No, you're not," Ash said.

"Yes, I am."

"No, Marni. You're not."

"Yes. I—"

"SHHHHH!"

Mrs. Brown turned around and zeroed in on the shush-ing child. "You. Come up to the front and complete the next long division problem."

The kid glared at Marni, who mouthed "sorry" with a wave. Ash rolled her eyes and gave her friend a disapproving look. Marni shrugged and Ash chuckled to herself. Perhaps she could use some of Marni's luck.

That night, the girls waited for the sun to go down and the Academy clock to chime nine o'clock. They put out their lamps and lay motionless in bed until the scurrying of the ratatoskrs ceased. After an hour or so, the furry little sentinels would hopefully be off duty.

Ash whipped off her blankets, dressed and ready to go with Flynn. Marni and Mitzi met her in her room and the four of them sneaked out the door, as quietly as could be.

They had just about reached the wooden steps that led down the trunk of the tree before they heard a squeak. Both of the girls looked down to see that one sentry remained: a curious ratatoskr sat on a thick branch in front of them. The critter tilted his head to the right, then tilted his head to the left. He readied himself to cause a ruckus, his little body looking like an over-filled balloon ready to explode. Marni and Ash exchanged a look.

They swiped the nosy squirrel and stuck him in Flynn's cage back upstairs. They covered it in a thick blanket to muffle his angry squeals. They'd deal with him tomorrow.

Swiftly and quietly, the girls, the bird, and the fox trotted through the grass toward the mountain on the far side. They crossed a wooden bridge with a plaque reading *Nadyne's Crossing* that led over the Steelhead River. Marni, already nervous, shrieked at a steelhead salmon leaping up out of the water. Ash placed a comforting hand on Marni's shoulder and they continued.

They spotted the path that lead up the side of the cliffs and carefully ascended. The previous weeks of rainfall had made the Underspring Falls flow down the mountainside much more violently than usual, and several smaller waterfalls had sprung up, as well. The path mostly allowed for them, with portions of rock carved out so travelers could walk beneath the plunging water, but very soon, the girls came to one that completely covered the way forward.

Flynn, of course, flew right around and even tried to get a little drink of it along the way. Mitzi also saw no problem. The fox loved water and pranced right through, happily getting drenched. From the other side, she barked at the girls to hurry up and follow. Ash winced and hurried through the waterfall. She wiped the drips from her forehead and wrung out her wet shirt.

"Come on, M-M-Marni," she called with a smile, loud enough to be heard over the sound of the rushing water. "Just a warning though, it's p-p-pretty cold."

Marni was frozen stiff, staring at the roadblock with disgust as if it were a gushing stream of cockroaches. Mitzi trotted back through the water and nudged her master forward. Marni backed away from the dog with an even more repulsed expression.

"What are you waiting for?" Ash asked.

"I hate being wet."

"What?"

"I hate being wet," Marni said again, shooing her sopping kitsune away.

Ash gave her a *You've got to be kidding me* expression.

"It's fine when I'm bathing or out for a swim," Marni continued. "But I hate being wet when it's not appropriate to be wet. If I jump through this waterfall, I'm going to be wet and cold for the rest of the night! Do you know how unpleasant that's going to be?"

"No, Marni, I have no idea," Ash said with an eyeroll, motioning to the water dripping off her own clothes. "You're just going to stay here, then?"

Marni examined the situation.

"Here, look! I'll just step around it," she finally said. "I'll jump from this boulder to that boulder and hop right to the other side, easy-peasy."

"Marni, do you see how those boulders are shining in the moonlight? They're covered in water and probably algae—you'll slip and fall a hundred feet down!"

"No, no," she argued. "Mitzi is as sure-footed as a mountain goat, so therefore, as her bonded human, I, too, have developed sure-footedness. That's what having a Bonded Beast is all about, remember?"

Marni's persuasive tone was still unconvincing. Ash bit her lip as Marni readied herself to leap. Tucking a few wayward strands of hair behind her ears, Marni carefully stepped onto the first boulder, which jetted out past the falls.

As Marni hopped across the gap, she tripped. Ash lunged forward to grab her wrist. Marni's foot slipped on the second boulder, and there she hung, clinging to Ash's outstretched arm to keep from falling to her most certain death. Flynn got a hold of Marni's shirt with his beak.

"Sure-footedness, huh?" Ash said with a grunt as she yanked Marni safely back up onto the path.

"It's possible I haven't quite adopted all of Mitzi's skills yet," Marni said, out of breath.

With that, Mitzi ran through the waterfall once more and shook her wet coat right beside the girls. Marni looked down at her dripping clothes.

"I hate being wet."

An hour passed. The duo reached the corner of their narrow road that turned them away from the Academy and toward the ocean. With the sea to their left, they continued on the path—though every step seemed less and less groomed. Whoever had kept the path maintained hadn't intended on anyone traversing it this far. Their clear, even route turned rough and overgrown, with loose stones to traverse and pokey plants to dodge. Before long, the girls were precariously walking along a cliff side, with loud waves crashing onto pointy-looking rocks below. Ash wasn't hearing any music, but she was confident they were headed the right way.

Marni's mood had improved only slightly, thanks to the ocean winds drying her wet clothes. Still, she was clearly unprepared for the journey. It had turned out to be less of a nature walk and more like some kind of absurd hiking trip that rich children certainly did not undertake without expensive supplies.

"Ugh, it's freezing. I cannot believe I didn't bring my Arganian coat."

"Eighteen," whispered Ash to herself.

"Why does the air taste so salty? How does salt even float in the air? It's disgusting."

"Nineteen."

"Ouch! My finger!" Marni whined. "Stubbing your fingers on hard rock hurts so much more when they're cold."

"Twenty."

Marni narrowed her brow. "What are you muttering up there?" she asked Ash, who was about ten feet ahead of her.

"I've been counting the number of complaints you've had since we left."

Marni stopped. "How many?"

"Twenty, so far," Ash responded, matter-of-factly.

"Don't you think that's a bit rude?" Marni retorted, struggling to squeeze through two boulders. "You don't see me counting how many times you—you—talk about—music, or ghosts, or whatever."

Ash grinned at the winning comeback. "I'm passing the time, that's all."

Marni let out a *hrmph* of annoyance. Mitzi squeezed by her on the narrow walkway and Marni braced against a rock for balance. A few stones crumbled into the ocean below. "Lest we forget, Ashtyn, *you* are the reason I'm out here on this dangerous cliff, like, a billion feet above a freezing-cold ocean, surrounded by—*ouch!*—pokey rocks. And bugs!"

Marni swatted at a mosquito investigating her face.

"Lest we forget, Marni, *you* didn't have to come," Ash said. "And twenty-one, twenty-two, and twenty-three."

"That should only count as one!" Marni argued. "Plus, we've been walking for hours and I haven't heard any music. Have you heard any music? No. Hey, Mitz? You heard any music? Nope. Because maybe—and I know this is an *outlandish statement*—but just maybe, *there is no*—"

Ash shushed her. "Up ahead!"

Sure enough, Ash could hear voices in the near distance between crashes of waves.

"Am I missing something? I don't hear a thing," Marni whispered.

"It's got to be right around that bend! Come on!"

Ash, with an alert Flynn following closely, hurried forward. Mitzi sprinted after them, panting with canine anxiety. Marni groaned.

"We could have at least brought snacks."

"Twenty-four!"

The singing voices grew louder. The girls crept around a bend in the cliff that opened to a large cove. There, they saw them: three mermaids—beautiful women with the upper bodies of a human and the lower bodies of a fish—were lounging on rocks far below. They had vibrant, flowing hair with scaly tailfins that shimmered green in the moonlight, and they were singing the most beautiful and haunting song Ash and Marni had ever heard.

The two girls peeked out from behind a large boulder, keeping their animals out of sight.

"Would you look at that," Ash said, hardly believing her eyes.

"Sirens!" Marni said, with eyes like saucers. "They're gorgeous."

The sirens seemed frisky, tossing shells back and forth and giggling in between the verses of their songs. One mermaid in particular had hair the color of sea foam, and a voice that was enticing, yet severe, like a dagger wrapped in silk. The creature basked in the moon and starlight, relishing every wave that washed over her. She combed her hair with her fingers and tied it up with a string of seaweed. Watching them was mesmerizing.

"So, when I said it was a singing fish...I was half right," Marni whispered.

Ash rolled her eyes.

Mitzi yelped at something and Marni clamped the dog's jaws shut. Ash glanced in the direction Mitzi was looking.

"Marni, a boat!"

The stiff winds billowed the sails of an incoming ship. It was tossed to and fro by the waves on its way into the harbor. The sails were black and red and the men aboard wore unmistakable garb. Ash had visited enough seaside towns with Tilda to know what that ship meant.

"Pirates," Ash whispered. "They're sailing toward the voices."

With flirty smiles, the sirens giggled and waved to the pirates, beckoning them closer with their melodies. The ship's captain commanded his crew to row faster, extending a rose toward the siren with sea-foam hair. Closer and closer they sailed, until she could reach out and grasp the captain's long-stemmed flower. The pirates leaned over the sides of the boat for a closer look at the beautiful women, catcalling and whistling as they waved to them.

The Siren reached forward past the rose and instead grabbed ahold of the captain's neck. Even from their distance, Ash and Marni saw the mermaid's expression morph from seductive to malicious. She screeched, her open mouth revealing yellow fangs.

Out of nowhere, a hundred more mermaids leapt out of the ocean and attacked the ship. Some soared onto the deck and fed on the crew. They plunged razor teeth into their flesh and dragged them into the drink. Others slammed against the hull and clawed at the siding until the entire ship began to smash apart. Their lovely songs had turned to terrifying shrieks.

The sea-foam-haired siren tightened her grip and pulled the captain off the bow into the ocean. The girls never saw him or any other crew member return to the surface. The water was scattered with debris, as the mermaids continued their rampage.

Ash and Marni looked on in horror, too petrified to even comprehend the disaster happening below. Before they could think of how to escape unseen, Ash heard a loud, frightened squawk from Flynn.

She turned her head to look, and everything went dark.

CHAPTER 14

THE HALF-BEASTS

he rough burlap scratched hard against Ash's cheeks as the sack was removed. The last several minutes had been a blur—nothing but muffled voices, the clip-clop of hooves, and the tight grip from large, calloused hands around her ankles and wrists as she was carried to...well, wherever it was she was. And wherever she was, Flynn was nowhere nearby.

She blinked open her eyes and found that she needn't adjust to light. She was no longer outside, but in a spacious cave.

"Holy Hydra..." she heard Marni whisper.

Ash exhaled with relief when she saw Marni sitting beside her against a rock, with Mitzi excitedly licking her face. At least she wasn't alone.

The girls' jaws nearly anchored themselves on the hard floor as they beheld the sight before them. Over two dozen men inhabited the cave—except they weren't men, exactly. Four of them, three stuffing their faces with bread and ale and one playing a lively tune on a fiddle, had the torso of a man and the legs of a goat. Several men with horse bodies sparred with swords and clubs. An enormous serpent was coiled in the corner. When a club was thrown and landed near it, the snake popped up and revealed the upper body of a beautiful woman. She hissed. The men laughed heartily and took swigs from their mugs.

Ash had only begun to mentally process the scene in order to determine whether she should be frightened or *extremely* frightened when the ghostly outline of Irving rose up out of the ground, nose-to-nose with her.

"You came! You came! You missed me, yes? Oh, my heart, it melts with joy," he said with an eerie, sing-song inflection. "Though, having been burned alive, I suppose my heart has already been permanently melted."

Irving chuckled giddily to himself and spun around at a dizzying speed. Marni shot Ash a look that conveyed confusion, concern, a bit of panic, and an obvious inquiry of *"Are we supposed to laugh, too?"*

"Oh! I've got a splendid, splendiferous, splendiful idea! Won't you play? I've got a riddle: It walks on four legs in the morning, two legs at noon—"

"Enough of your riddles, ghost!" said a deep, gruff voice.

The roaring fire across the room cast an ominous shadow on Ash and Marni. Towering over them was a creature from a nightmare: a man, easily ten feet tall, with the head of a long-horned bull and black hooves for feet. Both his human upper body and his fur-covered animal legs bulged with muscles. Ash thought his massive hands could crush her skull like a peanut shell.

Ash hadn't heard these creatures ever mentioned within the walls of the Academy, and she wasn't sure what many of them were, but the beast before her was a different story. She had listened to enough folklore in her travels to recognize him as a minotaur.

"Welcome, young friends! We've been expecting you for quite some time, Ash," he said, placing his hands on his hips where two hatchets and a knife hung from a red kilt.

"You're—you're—you're—" Marni stuttered, staring wide-eyed at the barbarian.

Ash elbowed her in the stomach to keep quiet.

"You're Half-Beasts!" she finally spat out.

The word triggered several nearby beast people to pause in their tracks and grimace in Marni's direction.

"We...prefer not to be called that," said the minotaur, motioning for his fellow beasts to carry on. "We've begun instead to call ourselves Dissidents. The term Half-Beast has developed...somewhat negative connotations as of late."

"*Connotations*, eh? Look who's a'talkin' all fancy-like with the frilly words!" shouted one of the little half-goat men with a mouthful of tomato, spitting chunks as he spoke.

"Satyrs," the minotaur said to the girls with an annoyed grunt.

"So those are satyrs!" Marni said in realization, staring at the half-goats. "And look, Ash! The ones with the swords are centaurs and that snake-lady is a naga!"

The naga uncoiled from the corner and slithered across the floor. She weaved through catcalling satyrs without paying them as much as a glance.

"I've only ever read about them," Marni said. "Though my mother swears she saw a nest of them in the marshlands during her and my father's travels."

A skinny, regular-looking human man casually walked out of one of the many nearby tunnels, licking on a chicken bone.

"Um...what about that guy?" Ash whispered to Marni. "He looks pretty normal to me."

A centaur called in the man's direction while polishing a shield. "Hey, Joe—isn't it a full moon tonight?"

The man dropped his chicken bone and examined a small crack in the rock wall, which let in the tiniest sliver of light from the outside world.

"Oh, blast."

As soon as his skin came into contact with the small beam of moonlight, the man's arms and legs violently began jolting and seizing. His plain face morphed into a long snout and his feet and hands sprouted sharp, rounded claws. He bulged to nearly twice his body size, ripping his clothes to shreds. Finally, his pale skin became coarse with dark hair as a tail snaked out from his coccyx. In his new werewolf state, he ran one lap around the perimeter on all fours before sprinting out of the cave down a long tunnel. The echoes of his howls could be heard for several seconds after.

Ash and Marni seemed to be the only ones who found the ordeal mind-numbingly terrifying.

"That...was...wicked," Marni finally said, her horror turning to awe. Mitzi was panting with so much excitement that she began wheezing.

Ash, however, was less interested in the transformation of wolf-people and more concerned with her bird. Was Flynn being held captive? Had he escaped? Did these beasts even see him at all?

"Excuse me, mister—"

"Gunnar," answered the minotaur. "My name is Gunnar. I'm the general of this army of brutes."

"Speak for yourself, *brute*," said a second naga, popping up out of a hole in the ground. She had silky onyx hair and yellow eyes.

"At least *we* don't leave hoof prints everywhere," said the original naga, coiling back into her corner.

"To hooves!" bellowed a centaur with his drink in the air.

"TO HOOVES!" cheered the room, raising their mugs.

Another log was thrown in the fire and it roared as the beasts drank sloppily and danced arm in arm.

A mug of foaming ale was pushed into Marni's hands from another minotaur, wobbling on his hooves and clearly drunk.

"Ew," Marni said with a wince. The brown ale spilled over the top of the cup and trickled down her fingers.

"General Gunnar, please sir—tell us where we are. Why are we your prisoners? And where is my red bird?" Ash yelled over the boisterous cheers, singing, and music.

Gunnar threw back his bull head and laughed. "You hear that, fellahs? They think they're our prisoners!"

Some nearby minotaurs and satyrs laughed along with him, slapping their knees and spilling their beers.

Ash was getting nowhere with them. She exhaled her frustration and scanned the vicinity for anything that would clue her in on their whereabouts.

Her eyes fell on the only quiet person in the room. A man, quite normal looking, sat beside the fire reading a book. He seemed unbothered by the chaos around him, as if he didn't notice it at all. He was muscular with shoulder-length sandy hair and showed no signs of being half-anything. Ash thought perhaps he was another werewolf, pre-transformation, but there was something different about him. The other werewolf man had been scrawny and twitchy, while this man seemed perfectly calm and collected.

Another cheer from the wild room disrupted Ash's thoughts. A centaur, cantering by, clinked his mug against Marni's. Marni began to drink.

"Marni!" Ash barked, startling her to the point of spilling liquid on herself.

"I wasn't gonna!"

Gunnar had finally finished laughing and joking with his fellow minotaurs when he decided to return to Ash's question. "Lass, if you two were our prisoners, you'd be fending off flesh-eating spiders in our dungeon right now."

Ash gulped as a half-woman, half-spider known as an arachne lowered from the ceiling beside Gunnar. She hung upside down from a thick web. She had two extra eyes and smaller spiders crawling up and down her arms.

"We'd only take nibbles at first...promise," said the spider-woman, venom in her voice.

A small black widow dropped onto Marni's shoulder. She shrieked and swiped it away. The arachne hissed in her direction, but a nearby naga hissed even more wickedly at the arachne.

"Leave the little ones alone, six-legs," threatened the naga.

"Make me, you overgrown worm!"

The naga lunged at the arachne and the two wrestled on the ground. A satyr rushed over and cheered on the fight before getting tail-whipped into a stone gargoyle.

The gargoyle came to life as a horned beast with wings. It roared at the satyr, who ran into a centaur, who punched the gargoyle, and before Ash could even keep straight what was happening, half the room was brawling.

A cold chill crept up Ash's spine as she felt something materialize behind her. Whipping around, she met a bored-looking vampire face-to-face, hanging inverted with a half-filled wine glass—right side up—in one hand.

"Where is the *decency*? Honestly, it's *embarrassing*," moaned the vampire with a yawn.

"That's just Alexandru. Don't mind him," said Gunnar in Ash's ear.

Alexandru disappeared with a *poof* into the form of a bat, his wine glass shattering on the stone floor. The bat flew quickly out of the cavern down the same tunnel Joe the werewolf had exited.

"Back to your inquiries," said Gunnar, his articulation seeming forced and uncharacteristic for a talking bull. "Where are you, you ask? Why, you're inside the mountain! This is our encampment—one of our many secret hideouts. Sorry about the bags on your heads. Can't risk you finding your way back here."

"I beg your pardon, Gunnar, sir," Ash interrupted, "but I also asked you about Flynn. Where is he? I'd like him back, please."

"Flynn?" Gunnar said, confused. "Oh! The bird. Max! Fetch the red bird!"

Max, a satyr, hurriedly trotted out of a nearby corridor holding a brown bag. The bag pulsed with an orange glow.

"Here, sir!" said Max, nervously trying to hand off the bag before his fingers got scorched.

"Release him," commanded Gunnar.

"Are-are you sure?" said Max. "He seems upset."

"Out with him!" yelled Ash.

Max opened the bag. Flynn soared out like a lit firework, sparks trailing from his wings. He zeroed in on Max and zapped him on the backside with a small fireball. Max yelped and ran off, holding his roasted rump.

Flynn swooped down to Ash, and his eyes switched from red to yellow. He hovered eye-to-eye with her and erupted in a chirping frenzy. While Ash was equally excited to see him, his silly chirps were making him appear rather unthreatening at a time she was hoping for a bit of leverage.

"Shh, shh, Flynny. You're safe now...I think."

Flynn nuzzled her nose once before perching on her shoulder. He dug in his talons just enough to say, *Don't ever leave me again!*

"GRUB'S ON!"

The loud shout came from a minotaur, who stood beside the big wooden table in the center of the room. The table was now piled high with meats and vegetables. All dancing, fighting, and drinking ceased as the room of beasts lunged for the food. Gargoyles came alive from all parts of the room, nagas slithered out of holes, arachnes dropped from the ceiling. The creatures dug in.

"Uck, they eat like animals, too," Marni said quietly to Ash with a wince. "What a bunch of disgusting—"

A dead fish flew over her head. She ducked just in time. It landed with a *splat* against the rock wall behind her. A terrifying, winged woman with a hunched spine and a permanently bitter face swooped down and snatched the fish with a cackle. She flew to a high perch and swallowed it whole. Ash identified the creature as a harpy. Its wrinkled, hag-like features made her instantly think of Tilda. Seeing the creature made Ash's stomach the most uneasy it had felt all night.

"We eat a lot of fish. Don't tell the sirens," Gunnar said with a wink.

Ash returned a half-hearted chuckle as the room of clomping hooves and flying fur carried on with their merriment.

She'd never seen such boorish behavior, even in the poorest slums of Cascadia. Juices and beers dripped down their fronts; bread on the dirt floor was quickly recovered and eaten. Fish bones rained down like confetti. They devoured meat like a pack of wild dogs—which Mitzi happily participated in once she finally escaped Marni's grip. Ash was no princess, but even she thought the display was downright nauseating.

Flynn cooed in Ash's ear and hopped into her lap. His eye contact sent the clear message of *Can we leave this place already? I want to go home.*

"Pardon me—"

She snatched Flynn out of the way as a sprouted potato was thrown in her lap.

"Eat, little one!" encouraged Gunnar.

Ash picked up the potato with two fingers as if it were a large dung beetle and set it aside.

"No, thank you," she said politely. "You said you call yourselves Dissidents. What is a Dissident exactly?"

"A Dissident is anyone who opposes the king and desires to be treated as an equal!" said a nearby gargoyle, animated from his stone state and spitting corn with every syllable.

"Down with the king!" cried a centaur as he reared up onto his hind legs.

The room cheered in agreement, clinking mugs and throwing arms around each other's shoulders. In Ash's peripheral vision, she saw Marni take a swig from her mug.

"Marni!"

"I'm not doing anything!" Marni lied as Mitzi rushed over to lick foam off her top lip.

A particularly obnoxious satyr jumped onto the food table and led the room in a song:

> *Cast aside like a bum while he drinks his rum*
> *Fresh bread in his hold while we eat the mold*
> *Down with the crown! Down with the crown!*
>
> *He wears all his riches with gold in the stitches*
> *Scarfs apple butters while we're in the gutters*
> *Down with the crown! Down with the crown!*
>
> *Our hooves and our fins, our leathery skins*
> *Unworthy of castles and red velvet tassels*
> *Down with the crown! Down with the crown!*

We tear down the wall, his Beast Riders will fall
If it's us or them, we'll fight to their end!
Down with the crown! Down with the crown!

"Come on, Ash!" Marni encouraged as a centaur pulled her into the dancing circle.

"I'd rather not."

Down with the king? King Tiberius? The man who had been so nice to her? This was wrong. In fact, all of it was wrong—the whole ordeal. First, they had been taken against their will with scratchy bags over their heads, then forced to sit in a dirty cave with horrid beast-men, and now they had to endure a celebration about the king of Cascadia's downfall? It was the last straw.

Ash rose from her sitting position and marched to Gunnar. She tapped him harshly on the shoulder—or as close as she could get to his shoulder on her tippy toes.

"You dragged Marni and I here blindfolded! I do believe that earns us an explanation of why we're here!"

"He wishes to speak with you, Ashtyn Ridley," Gunnar replied. "You are Ashtyn Ridley, aren't you?"

Ash's anger faded. "He? He *who?*"

The party became suddenly disrupted when three women stepped into the room. They entered through the same tunnel where the werewolf and vampire had departed.

That must be the exit, Ash mentally noted.

The three women had a commanding presence for being so slender and fair. They wore battle armor with knee-height boots, forearm bands, and a chest plate. Their hair was pulled away from their pale faces, with braided strands that looked to be woven with stardust. Folded to their sides were glittering, colorful wings, which originated from their lower backs and hugged their hips like a skirt. Most commanding of all, they held spears topped with large diamond-shaped crystals. They looked no older than a human thirty-year-old, with the thinnest one perhaps as young as twenty.

Ash hadn't the slightest clue what species they were, but from where she stood, they looked like angels.

The girl in front, obviously the leader, marched the trio forward through the belching, snarling crowd toward the biggest tunnel opening in the back of the cavern.

Gunnar stomped a foot in front of them.

"Going somewhere, Adrastea?"

"Out of the way, Gunnar," she said. "My sisters and I need to speak with Draven. We have important news from our mother."

"Draven is busy," he said politely, but sternly. "Any message from your queen can be delivered to me."

The sister to Adrastea's left stood her ground and gripped her spear tightly. The sister to the right, the youngest one, paid less attention to the argument and more to examining the room, curiously. Her eyes met Ash's, only for a moment.

"She said the message is to be relayed to Draven himself," said Adrastea, her patience waning.

Adrastea glanced at Ash and Flynn. The glance felt heavy, peppered with disapproval and doubt.

"What exactly is occupying Draven's time at the moment?" she said suspiciously.

"Ay, why'a ssso forlorn, loverly girl?" slurred a drunken satyr, cozying up to Adrastea. "I'm sure you an' me could figur' out'a way to keep each otha' warm whiles you wait!"

Before the sisters could punch the small goatman twenty feet across the room, a soothing voice interrupted.

"Enough, Fulop. Is that any way to speak to a lady?"

It was the quiet man, who read by the fire. He set down his book and rose to his feet. He still displayed no signs of being a Half-Beast. *Could he be human?* The thought actually comforted Ash.

The man walked toward the trio of sisters and circled them. He seemed to pay extra attention to the youngest before his gaze landed on Adrastea.

"One must treat a Valkyrie princess with respect."

They're Valkyries! And princesses! Ash thought. *Magnificent!*

"Funny, coming from you," Adrastea shot back, her words dripping with disdain.

The man chuckled and shook his head. "The war between Berserkers and Valkyries is over."

"Some of us aren't so sure."

A Berserker? I think I've heard of that species before, Ash wondered. *But he looks so calm...and normal...*

The only thing Ash knew about Berserkers was that they were insane with rage. Their anger would morph them into ferocious monsters and their strength would triple. But this soft-spoken man? Ash couldn't imagine him angry—but wasn't about to set him off, either.

Gunnar returned from Draven's quarters.

"Gunnar, we need to see Draven now," Adrastea commanded. "It isn't wise to keep us waiting."

"Sorry, Your Highness. He says he would like to speak... with Ash."

CHAPTER 15

THE SORCERER

"Isn't this just the cat's *meeeeeoowwww*?"

Irving floated in mid-air, legs crossed on an imaginary stool, as he led Ash down the narrow tunnel toward Draven's chamber. The reverberation of his eerie voice on the rock walls somehow made him even more annoying.

"Oop! Suppose I shouldn't mention cats in front of a bird!" he slurred through his transparent teeth, jittering as he held back his usual riotous laughter.

His skeletal frame turned instantly into a ghostly cat. He hissed at Flynn and playfully took a swipe. Flynn squawked and took off after Irving, chasing him in circles as Ash continued to march forward. Irving's inevitable giggles erupted.

Ash ignored the imbecile and fixed her eyes on the approaching light, shining through cracks in a makeshift wooden door.

The tunnel was more suffocating with every step—especially knowing that the glow at the end of it might be worse than the trek toward it. Irving grew bored of tormenting poor Flynn. He returned to floating beside Ash.

"You're not *spooked,* are you, little girl?"

"No, I'm not spooked," Ash replied, louder than intended.

"You look spooked!" Irving shouted in her ear. "Sweaty brow, sweaty palms, pale cheeks—the signs are all there! You're spooked! Spooked, spooked!"

Ash arrived at the door.

"Well, what are you waiting for? Let yourself in. Nothing to be spooked by," assured Irving as he leaned against the door. "He's only...a sorcerer."

With a giggle, the specter disappeared.

Ash placed her hand on the door handle and took a deep breath.

"Stay beside me, all right, Flynn? Always."

Flynn cooed agreement, but fidgeted on her shoulder.

The room was circular with a high ceiling, well lit by several lamps. A round, green rug lay in the center of the floor. There were bookshelves housing liquid-filled jars and glass vases, a rack of swords, a dresser, a small fire heating a kettle, and a writing desk. Opposite the door, purple robes hung on a hook near a tapestry that displayed an embroidered map of Cascadia.

"Would you like to see what the sky looks like tonight?"

A man in a long black coat stood facing the map. His voice was neither soothing nor frightening. Ash knew this must be the mysterious Draven.

"Pardon me?" she replied.

With a muddled whisper and a swirl of his hand, the candles in the lamps blew out. The room went dim. One by one, tiny pinpricks of light appeared all over, from roof to floor. Wispy cirrus clouds materialized and a Milky Way flowed by. Overhead, a miniature full moon hovered amongst the twinkling stars.

"That's—that's incredible," Ash uttered, mesmerized by the façade as a shooting star caught her eye.

"Just a bit of magic," Draven said. "It's nothing compared to what accompanies you."

Draven drew his hand down. The sky vanished and the lamps relit themselves.

He turned toward Ash and Flynn. His face seemed somehow familiar, with strong bone structure and thin cheeks. His eyes looked sunken in from lack of sleep, though his russet-brown hair was flawlessly brushed from his face. It was difficult to pinpoint his age. Ash guessed he was older than her father, but he had a spark in his eyes that made him seem youthful.

"Ashtyn Ridley. The girl who bridled the elusive phoenix," he said with wonderment. "How old is he, almost two months now?"

Ash nodded.

"Still so small, like a delicate dove," he continued, his voice growing softer as he stepped toward the bird. "I bet his plumage is still soft, clad in down. Can you imagine what he'll look like when he is fully grown? Magnificent."

Ash felt her muscles stiffen and Flynn's talons tense up as Draven reached a hand forward to touch him.

"Only one other has known this creature before you. Wouldn't it be nice to get some tips from his former master?"

Flynn screeched when Draven's hand came within an inch of his beak. The man willingly withdrew it.

Former master? Ash thought. *Flynn had…another master? Before me?*

Ash was still for a moment, letting the information sink in. *This man must know about Flynn's past, about how "powerful" he supposedly is. If everyone else in my life refuses to tell me the truth, maybe I can get some answers from him.*

"I don't believe I've ever met you, yet you seem to know Flynn and me," Ash finally said.

Draven walked to his writing desk and picked up a small wooden stick about a foot long. As soon as his fingers wrapped around it, it thickened and grew to five feet. The surface transformed from woody and brown to a smooth, scaly green, and it glimmered in the dim light like polished leather. As he stood it upright, the staff seemed to come alive as it curled into a spiral at the top.

"You're twelve years old, almost thirteen. Right-handed, worked at a traveling circus, and you live on a farm in Oatsville with your father, Landon Ridley."

As he spoke, perfect images of what he described emerged from the staff in screens of smoke. She saw it all—the circus traveling down a dirt road with Tilda at the reins, all the animals who lived on her farm, her father's smiling face.

"How—how are you making these pictures appear? How do you know what my father looks like?"

"What makes you think I'm creating the images instead of simply provoking your mind to project forth memories of your own?" he suggested.

Ash stood dumbstruck. Draven returned his staff to his desk and it instantly shrank back to its foot-long size. As the smoke images disseminated, he casually removed his kettle from the fire and changed the subject.

"I apologize for Irving's antics," he said, pouring the liquid into a teacup. "I simply asked him to invite you to a meeting. He tends to go about things a bit...dramatically."

"Dramatically!" Ash blurted. "I was lured out here by ridiculous, threatening notes! I would hardly call that an *invitation*."

"And yet, here you are. You didn't alert your teachers; you didn't run away in fear. Curious girl, aren't you?"

He was right. She hadn't told the professors or Elders. She didn't trust that they would help her. Ash shook the thought away.

"Irving nearly got me expelled!" she argued. "People could have been severely hurt in the fire he caused!"

Draven's spoon clinked as he stirred herbs into his teacup. "Unfortunately, pain isn't a rational concept for ghosts, physical nor emotional. But he's the only one who could get to you. Sadly, we're all banned from Academy grounds...and royal grounds. Tea?"

"No, thank you," Ash said sharply. "And I should hope you're banned from the kingdom, allowing such a shameful display from your men out there. Cheering and singing about taking down King Tiberius!"

"I agree with you, Ash. I would like to put a stop to it," Draven said with a calm sigh. He sipped his tea. "After all, he is my little brother."

"You're...the king's brother?"

Draven paced and nursed his drink. "It was never supposed to be this way. I cared about him very much growing up. He was athletic and showed such strength and fortitude—our father beamed with pride. He clearly favored him. I was never much of an athlete. More of a thinker. I spent my days learning charms and honing my magic skills."

Draven danced his fingertips along his small staff. The stick twitched, as if ready and eager to grow in size at his command. "My studies gave me such appreciation for the beautiful world around us. I considered myself open-minded, in contrast to my father and brother, who were cemented in archaic thinking."

Ash could hear his words grow heavy.

"Did...something happen?" she asked.

Draven set down his teacup. He walked to a shelf of books and ran his fingers across the spines.

"Years ago, creatures that were half-human, half-beast roamed throughout Cascadia freely. It was a strained co-existence, yes, but nothing worth destroying. My father and brother wouldn't listen."

His fingers stopped at a red book. He removed it and Ash could see the title: *The Rare and Mighty Sphinx*. He opened it to show Ash an illustration of the beast.

"During the Beast Games one year, Tiberius took a sphinx onto the field, a very rare creature with the body of a lion and a face resembling a human man. He murdered it. In front of everyone."

Ash gasped and placed a hand on Flynn. "That's horrible."

Draven clapped the book shut and returned it to the shelf. "It was a message: Anything not fully human or fully animal was not welcome in Cascadia. So, the Half-Beasts went into hiding."

Ash knew that Half-Beasts were hated across the land, but never knew why. She always figured it was because they were dangerous and hated humans, but Draven made it sound like the opposite was true. That the humans had driven them away. Specifically, the king.

Draven continued. "I was exiled by my father for disagreeing with such prejudice. Tiberius took the crown and...here I am."

Ash paused a moment to process the story. Something didn't make sense.

"I don't understand," she said. "Tiberius doesn't seem... hateful...at all. Flynn befriended him almost immediately. He was very kind."

"You're a child, Ash! Don't be naïve!" Draven snapped. "You students, sheltered and isolated in your Academy, know nothing! Tiberius cares only for his Regal Kin army and Cascadia's wealthiest. You should know that better than anyone, Ashtyn. Your family has never had money, not like your classmates. Am I wrong?"

Ash clenched her jaw and stepped away from the man. Just the mention of her family in his harsh voice made her feel uneasy. But his words held truth.

"The king has been raising taxes every month—wringing out citizens for all they're worth like wet dishrags," he explained. His tone quieted but his intensity remained. "When they can't pay, they're arrested, thrown in prison...like your father."

Ash's heart skipped a beat. Her skin felt boiling hot.

"My father! In prison? How—how do you know about him? Where is he?"

Draven once again used his staff to conjure images in plumes of smoke. This time, the images showed Landon. There he was, with his same messy brown hair and aging eyes, but his skin was covered in cuts and bruises. He had rusty shackles around his wrists. He was in a line of chained prisoners who were being whipped by a guard to march forward down a bleak road lined with dead trees.

Ash gasped when the whip hit his back.

"Dad," she whispered to herself.

Another image in the smoke showed the guard thrusting him into a dirty prison cell and slamming the gate. Landon didn't have the energy to resist. He just sunk to the cold ground and shut his eyes.

Ash was on the edge of tears, but she blinked them back. Maybe the images weren't real. Maybe Draven was fooling with her mind.

She remembered that day in the kingdom meeting King Tiberius. Professor Suarez was quick to shy away from the subject of her father. That would make sense if he really was in prison. Perhaps his prison cell was right there in the depths of the castle! She could have gone to him, she could have seen him!

"Of course the Academy scooped you up," said Draven. "You're just a child wielding a weapon beyond your comprehension. But for what? For the king, who oppresses people like your father, and murders innocent creatures?"

Another image in the smoke. It was Tiberius, plunging a dagger into the sphinx.

ASH RIDLEY AND THE PHOENIX

"Or how about for the Elders and your precious professors, who are plotting even now to take away your precious Flynn?"

Yet another smoke image materialized in front of her—but in this one, she saw herself. She was with Flynn. Professor Suarez grabbed her arms and held her still as Elder Pyrrus threw a net over Flynn. Ash screamed, but Suarez restrained her. She cried as Pyrrus walked away with her bird until he was out of sight.

Ash clapped her hands over her mouth. The scene was so realistic and absolutely possible, given all that had happened with Flynn's misbehavior this school year. Draven knew so much—maybe he knew the future. This would confirm all of her most heartbreaking suspicions.

The smoke images dissolved, and Draven stood in their place.

"Put an end to it, Ash. Stand beside others like you. The poor, abused, and unaccepted."

The words hung heavily in the air. Ash had been whisked off to the Academy in a whirlwind, but until now, she had considered it a blessing. If Draven spoke truth, they really did only want her for her bird, and would maybe even go so far as to steal him from her. She had no business parading herself around a school of rich children—she needed to find her father. He was the only person in the world who meant anything to her.

"Please—please tell me where my father is!"

"Yes, I can help you, Ash. I can tell you where your father is, and help you set him free...but first, I need your assistance. Proof of your loyalty, we'll call it."

"M-my assistance?"

235

"I wish to discuss my peace treaty with Tiberius and bring him to understand...but I can't get an audience with him."

"Your own brother won't see you?" Ash asked, suddenly feeling sympathy for this stranger.

"Sure, my comrades would rather just storm the castle, but that exemplifies the very brutality I wish to end. We are prepared to fight only if we must," assured Draven, making deliberate eye contact with Ash. He smiled softly. "I just need to talk to him. I know he'll see things my way. *Our* way."

Ash felt helpless. "What can I do? He'd never listen to a little girl."

Draven quickly retrieved two glass vials of liquid from his pockets and held each in one hand. One was bright purple, the other murky green.

"These were created by a close friend of mine, an alchemist who lives in the mountains," said Draven, his voice now focused and unemotional. "The vial on the left is an Infizzible Potion. Drink this and it will make you invisible to the human eye for precisely one hour, not a second more."

Ash examined the purple liquid. "Infizzible?"

"My friend said she named it that because of its concentration of bubbles that develop when uncorked. Cheeky, isn't she? You'll need to be invisible in order to enter Castle Dragoon unseen and deliver this second vial to Tiberius."

"What's in the second vial?" Ash asked with leery eyes.

"The vial on the right is Imitation Poison. When consumed, the formula will take effect in the target's body and cause him to feel as though he is dying."

"Dying?" Ash exclaimed.

"He won't really be dying, Ash," Draven reassured her, chuckling. "Think of it almost like a placebo. Everyone will think he is growing weak and ill, but the effects should wear off in twenty hours."

Ash bit her lips. Flynn leaned toward the vials, tilting his head with curiosity. Ash could feel his long tail whipping back and forth on her back.

"Surely a dying man would not refuse a visit from his concerned brother," Draven added.

Ash reached out and grasped the vials. She instantly felt shivers down her spine.

Is this something I should even be considering? she thought.

"Why do you need me for this?" Ash asked, looking for a loophole. "Couldn't you do it? Or Irving, or one of your men?"

Draven apparently found that idea hysterical and let out a hearty laugh. "Have you seen those clumsy, loud brutes out there? And the utter insanity of Irving? I would never trust them with so sensitive a task. And I certainly can't risk going near the castle myself."

Ash supposed he was right. The pieces were in place. The deal was on the table. All she had to do was say yes.

"If I help you, you'll tell me where my father is and set him free?"

Draven took her by the shoulders and smiled. "Ashtyn, if you help me, we will set everyone free."

His touch sent an unnaturally cold chill surging through her body. She backed away.

"This must stay between us. I can trust you, can't I?" he said.

Ash slipped the vials into her pocket.

"I'll...I'll think about it, if that's all right."

"Yes, yes, think it over," he said. "Word spreads quickly around Cascadia. When I hear of the king's illness, I'll know you are on our side and have made the right decision. But move quickly. For your father's sake."

In her side vision, the room looked as though it were moving, like the floor was spinning.

"You aren't alone in helping the Half-Beasts, Ash. While you and I are not beasts ourselves...we both have one by our side."

Ash realized why the room was spinning. Where the walls met the floor, encircling the room, was a camouflaged serpent. It faded from stone colored to bright green and brown, revealing scales with marvelous, intricate markings. It was massive—fifty feet in length, a foot in diameter. Its body slithered around the perimeter before heading for Draven.

Flynn squirmed and flapped his wings at the sight of the creature's head. It was pointed, with sharp fangs peeking out from its thick jaw. Its eyes were red and almond-shaped with black slits. The scales at the base of its head were spiked, like sharpened daggers.

The creature rose up like a viper ready to strike, and green liquid dripped from its elongated fangs. It towered over them and stared Flynn down like he was nothing but easy prey.

"Diabolos, my scitalis serpent. I share your joy of having a Bonded Beast," said Draven, suddenly speaking in a tone that was terrifyingly calm.

Ash backed up toward the door, heart beating out of her chest. She'd never heard of this species before. It looked like it had slithered out of her most horrifying dream.

The small staff on the desk shot to Draven's left hand and grew to its larger size, curling and slithering like the scitalis itself. It cast an unearthly green glow on Draven's face. The sorcerer's eyes turned blood red to match those of Diabolos, and he smiled wide enough to show his matching fangs.

"After all...when a human bonds with an animal, do they not also become half beast?"

Ash backed hard into the door. She searched frantically for the handle. She swung it open and sprinted down the tunnel, away from the room. Flynn kept pace.

"Remember, Ashtyn! Your father needs you!"

Ash burst into the room with the Half-Beasts, who were still merrily drinking and eating. She grabbed Marni by the shirtsleeve.

"We've got to get out of here!" Ash yelled over the noise. "This way!"

The girls and Flynn, with Mitzi catching up, ran toward the tunnel that Ash had determined was the exit. A large, inebriated minotaur stepped in front of them.

"Where do you girlss think yous are going?" he slurred.

The girls slipped through his legs and all four were gone. Echoes of the room's laughter faded with every step. It was dark—the red glow of Flynn was their only light.

They halted, out of breath at a forked passage. Three tunnels: left, right, and middle.

"Which way?" screamed Ash.

"This way!" said Marni, confidently.

They took a left.

Down a long passage they ran, kicking up small rocks and slipping on several frigid puddles. Their throats were tight and painful from heavy breathing. Finally, the tunnel opened to a large cavern. It was eerily quiet and the darkness was all consuming. The absence of light even seemed to swallow Flynn's red glimmer, now faint.

"Ash," Marni whispered. "Where are you?"

"I'm right next to you."

"I can't even see my own hand in front of my face."

"Well, I think we lost them.... Now where's the exit?"

The girls wobbled about with stiff, outstretched arms as they marched forward to find the wall. It was over thirty steps before they felt something solid.

"Ash," Marni whispered again. "This wall is fuzzy."

"Is this grass? Or moss? Why would moss grow inside a—"

The wall rumbled with a long, low growl.

"Um. Ash?"

A huge, orange harvest moon materialized high over their heads. But they weren't outside yet. The orange sphere was an eye.

The girls screamed, and the sound's reverberation revealed just how enormous the cave was.

The eye was attached to a head, a massive head that hinged open to expose the only other thing that could be seen in the blackness: white fangs, nearly as tall as their treehouse and sharper than spears.

The four sprinted back the way they had come.

"Flynn! Flamethrow!"

Flynn spit out a short stream of flames. It was only for a moment, but it was enough light for them to see the exit...and catch a glimpse of the mammoth wolf creature behind them.

Just as the girls reached the exit, the wolf roared. The wind from its lungs blew all four of them down the tunnel, tossed in the gust like helpless leaves in a cyclone. They slammed hard into the first rock wall that crossed their path.

Before they could take off again, their thud awakened a cluster of harpies. The wretched, winged hags flooded out of a small hole above their heads like a colony of bats. They cackled and screeched as they flew.

Only one seemed to notice them. She swooped down and began picking at Marni's clothes with her talons. Mitzi lunged forward and bit the harpy's leg, sending an electric shock through the horrid creature's body. The harpy let out an ear-piercing shriek before Marni followed up the bite with a kick to the face—a lucky shot, considering she was practically blind. The harpy wailed and flew off.

The girls ducked out from under the stream of flying harpies and ran further down the cave. They stopped when the light from Flynn revealed the same fork in the road as before.

"To the right!" Marni said confidently.

"You said left last time and we almost got eaten by a wolf twenty times bigger than my house!"

"That was a fluke. I'm telling you, I have Mitzi's sense of direction!"

"Then I'm following Mitzi!"

Mitzi ran past them down the middle passage, tongue flapping in the wind. The girls and Flynn followed suit. Once they saw moonlight, they increased their pace—so much so that by the time they realized they'd run out of ground, it was too late. The tunnel had no lip and spit them out into the air over the ocean. The two girls and fox plunged into the cold, salty water.

Mitzi's head bobbed up first. Ash was next and finally, Marni. Flynn hovered nearby. Both girls grabbed hold of Mitzi to keep the waves from separating them. Luckily, Mitzi was a fabulous swimmer and gave them a helpful boost toward shore. Marni spit a piece of seaweed out of her mouth and looked dolefully at her friend.

"I really hate being wet."

CHAPTER 16

A DELICIOUS DETOUR

Ash's eyelids sprung apart in panic.

The details were hazy in her tired mind, but she still felt on edge from the previous night. She'd been in danger. She could still be in danger. The last thing she remembered was reaching the shore, clawing at the sand, and pulling herself out of the frigid waves with her last ounce of strength, and now...

...the distinct smell of buttercream frosting?

Ash sat up and braced herself against the surface she'd been resting on. It was cushy—a soft, cloth couch with seven throw pillows, two of which had toppled onto the floor. She was wrapped loosely in a multi-colored quilt.

"Ash! You're awake!"

Marni's chipper voice came from the kitchen—the central area of the cottage they'd found themselves in.

Well, apparently Marni's not panicked, Ash said to herself.

The house was something out of a storybook. Old, but homey, decorated with antique plates, spoons, and dolls. It was furnished with carved oak armchairs displaying decades of wear. Seashells on strings hung like ornaments anywhere it was possible for them to hang. Bookending the couch were two dusty, pink-tasseled lamps, and sitting atop a nicked wooden coffee table was a sweating jar filled to the brim with iced pink lemonade.

"Well, aren't your pretty blue eyes the size of saucers!" said a warm, comforting voice.

A plump, silver-haired old woman bustled in from another room to join Marni in the kitchen. Ash gasped when she saw her—the woman had four arms!

"Come have some cherry scones, dear," said the spry woman as she peeked inside a wood-fired oven with one arm and held plates of baked goods with the other three. "My lemon loaf will be ready in three minutes and that blushberry lemonade isn't going to drink itself!"

"Honestly, Ash. Don't be rude," said Marni, shoving the entirety of a creampuff in her cheeks.

Marni was sitting, napkin around her neck, at a round table piled with plates, platters, and pans of the most delicious-looking desserts Ash had ever laid eyes on: fruit-speckled scones, miniature pies with lattice tops, frosting-smothered cupcakes, gooey chocolate cookies, and cinnamon sticky buns drizzled with a pecan caramel sauce. Ash had to blink her eyes three times to be extra certain this wasn't some kind of sugary dream.

It was clear how the woman was able to cook so many treats. Watching her in the kitchen could only be described as limb-flailing pandemonium. Two arms on one side would be rolling dough into a pie pan while the two on the other side would whisk a bowl of mousse and butter a roll, respectively. Then, the four arms would finish their jobs and, like a well-oiled machine, switch to the next task.

The roly-poly grandmother borrowed one of her hands to adjust her purple-checkered apron, then spun around with a giddy squeal.

"Oh, I just love having house guests! Especially ones with hearty appetites," she said, patting Marni's tummy.

"Keep 'em coming, Mrs. Butterscotch!" she replied, her lips stained purple from a blueberry jelly tart.

Mrs. Butterscotch?

Ash reconsidered that sugary dream theory.

"Sorry if this seems rude but...how did we get here exactly?" Ash asked.

"Francis found you on the beach this morning during our daily sunrise stroll," the woman explained with a friendly smile. Ash wondered who this Francis was. "We thought the worst! Face down in the sand passed out, you were. Like a couple of washed-up flounders. So exhausted we could barely get you to move! Francis scooped you up and carried you all here. Certainly a more valuable treasure than the clamshells we usually find."

"The ocean!" said Ash.

"Well, of course, dear. Where else would we find clamshells?"

"No, no. I completely forgot!"

Ash ran to look out the kitchen window. The cottage was perched high atop a cliff, overlooking the tumultuous ocean below. Waves clawed fiercely at a tan beach.

"The wind has picked up this morning. Good thing we found you when we did," Fran said as an alarm dinged. "My lemon loaf!"

The visions of the previous night flashed in her mind. The cave. The Half-Beasts. Draven. Their escape into the sea. Her eyes glazed over as she wandered back into the living room, mentally fitting the puzzle pieces together. Now, a strange cottage? With a multi-limbed woman they'd never met? Marni the optimist seemed fine with it, but Ash found it hard to trust anyone. Who was this lady?

A painting caught Ash's eye. She snapped out of her thoughts. It depicted a young, strong warrior woman with flowing black hair, wielding a spiked club and riding on the back of an enormous gorilla. Not a normal gorilla, however— aside from its sharp fangs and size, the beast had four arms.

"Admiring the portrait done of me?" Mrs. Butterscotch said with a humble grin.

"That's you?" Ash asked, looking closely at the woman in the picture. That would explain Mrs. Butterscotch's arms.

"Oh, yes! That was painted only days before I sprung my two bottom arms. Funny things Bonded Beasts can do to your body. Other girls grew longer hair or got tanner skin, but I had to sprout these things."

"Gives a whole new meaning to the phrase 'people start to look like their pets,' doesn't it, Ash?" Marni added, licking her fingers.

Mrs. Butterscotch sighed. "I would have much preferred freckles or feathers growing in my hair, like those with avian beasts. You know, birds and such."

"Flynn!" Ash shrieked, mortified that she hadn't realized her bird's absence sooner.

"Flynn?" asked Mrs. Butterscotch.

"Her bird," Marni informed with a mouthful of scone.

"Yes, the red bird! Such a sweet little thing. He's right out that door to your left, playing with Francis and the pooch, Misty."

"Mitzi," Marni corrected with an even fuller mouth.

"Yes. Mindy."

"No, Mitzi," she mumbled.

An alarm dinged.

"The muffins!"

Ash walked to the house's back door. She swept the blue, plaid curtain aside and peered out the window.

In a gated-off grassy yard overgrown with wild roses and black-eyed Susans frolicked three unlikely friends: a phoenix, a kitsune, and a massive gorilla with two extra arms and graying fur.

So that's Francis, Ash thought. She couldn't help but grin at the sight of such a big, goofy animal.

The beasts chased one another, sniffed things, and dug holes. The gorilla even threw sticks for the bird and dog to fight over and picked bugs from Mitzi's fur.

"You're glued to that window like you've never seen a girallon before."

"I—I haven't. He's huge!"

"Francis is just an old softy," Mrs. Butterscotch assured. "A bit grumpy when he first met your two animals, but he secretly likes the company. That big goon. Lemon loaf?"

"Please!" Marni said, snatching a slice. "Ash, you've got to try this stuff. Mrs. Butterscotch's desserts are the best I've ever had, even compared to the treats my parents have brought me from all over Cascadia."

"Oh, please, dear. You can call me Fran."

Ash was too exhausted to be suspicious any longer. If these treats were filled with sleep-inducing dormanberries and she and Marni were next on the menu to be slid into an oven and devoured, so be it.

Finally succumbing to the sensational mix of fruity and savory scents in the air, Ash snagged her blushberry lemonade, took a refreshing sip, and walked into the kitchen to plop down beside Marni.

Fran had already set a plateful of pastries on Ash's placemat before she could even voice a request.

"Aren't they heavenly, Ash? I wish this were my breakfast every day. No more bland cafeteria food that smells like feet."

"Thank you very much for the treats, Mrs. Butterscotch."

"It's Fran, sweetheart," she corrected. "And it's my pleasure! I'm just delighted to see you two are alive and healthy."

While Fran was preoccupied popping muffins out of a pan, Ash leaned over and whispered to her friend. "Marni, about the...you-know-whats last night. Let's keep it between you and—"

"Oh, right! I was going to ask you what that guy talked to you about," Marni blurted loudly, wiping her mouth. "D-something. Draken...Dralen...Draven..."

"Marni—"

"Draven?" asked Fran, suddenly very interested.

"No, no. It was that second one...um, Dralen," corrected Ash. She cringed—it was an awful substitution. She just really didn't feel like discussing the situation with a stranger.

"It's okay, Ash. I told Fran all about the 'you-know-whats' we met last night. Minotaurs, satyrs, centaurs—even those harpies and that spider-woman! Yuck!"

"Very dangerous, those Half-Beasts are," informed Fran, her tone deepening. "Not very bright of you youngins to be consorting with them."

"Consorting wasn't exactly our choice. And Marni—"

"And the wolf! Ash, do you remember that giant, enormous, massive, colossal, mammoth, gargantuan—"

"Fenris wolf, dear," Fran said, shuddering at the word.

"—enormous Fenris wolf! Did I say enormous?"

"Marni, listen to me—"

"But this Dralen guy, Fran—"

"Yes, who did you say—"

"He was no one!" Ash barked, more forcefully than intended. "Just...some man."

Instead of prying, Fran shrugged and poured batter into a cake pan while her remaining limbs scrubbed some dirty dishes.

"You can talk to Mrs. B, Ash," Marni said casually, buttering a muffin. "She's one of us. She graduated from the Academy and served in King Viktor's army."

"Thirty years, until I hurt my back," Fran explained with a longing sigh. "Tweaked it during a melee with a drunken basilisk. Not a bottle left unbroken in that liquor store."

Fran and Marni went on gossiping and storytelling about the comings and goings of Academy people while Ash mentally recalled the previous night's events. Subtly, she slipped her hand into the pocket of her tunic.

The vials. They were still there, unbroken from the night's escape.

Perhaps picking Fran's brain held an advantage. Ash would likely get more information from a lonely woman entertaining company than from her strict, by-the-book teachers.

"Mrs. Butterscotch," Ash interrupted. "I mean, Fran. This man...Dralen...he did mention something strange. He said that Flynn had a former master."

Fran pursed her lips. "Very peculiar.... Bonded Beasts only have one master their full existence. Though I never did learn too much about the phoenix bird. If so, my aging brain surely can't remember."

"But last night the man talked about this mystery master as if he were still alive. I've been told that no one has seen Flynn in something like four hundred years.... He couldn't still be alive, could he?"

"Well, since he bonded to an immortal animal, he also likely became immortal," Fran explained matter-of-factly while drying the dishes and stacking them in the cupboard. "And that bonding power can potentially endure even when either the beast or the master passes. Amazing thing, immortality. You can withstand illnesses and it stunts the aging process—simply look at Odetta Loomington. Odetta bonded to an immortal pegasus. She's eighty-six years old—three years younger than me! She and I went to school together. You'd never guess it."

"Flynn is *immortal*??" Ash cried.

"Odetta is *eighty-six*??" Marni cried.

Ash and Marni clearly had different priorities.

A clay mug slid from Fran's fingers and cracked into several pieces on the hardwood floor.

"Oh, bother. Goodness me," she said in a fluster. "No, no. Don't be going and telling folks I told you anything you weren't supposed to know! Look at this mess. Oh, gracious. Goodness. Where's that old broom of mine..."

Fran bustled away in a dither as Ash sat there, bewildered.

Immortal?

Her thoughts whirled like butterflies caught in a tornado—a twister of realizations, all of them uncatchable.

How is that possible?

She supposed it could, perhaps, make sense. Flynn had died, yes, but he was instantly reborn in flame. If that ritual occurred endlessly, maybe he was immortal. He could continue to exist forever. And if Flynn was immortal, that meant...

"I can't believe it. Odetta looks so young. I would have pegged her at forty, tops."

"Don't you understand, Marni? Odetta is immortal because her pegasus is immortal," she said. "And I bonded to Flynn!"

"You mean...you could be immortal, too?" Marni paused for a moment to grasp the concept. "Wow...you're going to age so well."

Fran scurried back in carrying two different brooms, a mop, and one dustpan. "Girls, you listen to me! If there's something you don't know, there's likely a good reason for you not knowing. I'm not one to meddle, but you should talk to your professors immediately about this 'Dralen' fellow. It's not wise to keep secrets in a place that already has too many secrets. Talk with Bera. Or Thorne! Or Suarez—oh, I remember the day the Elders made him a professor. So young and bright-eyed. Is he still teaching?"

"Mm-hmm," responded Marni.

"I find him so handsome," Fran divulged. "If I were thirty years younger..."

"Gross, Fran! He's our teacher, yuck!"

The grandfather clock beside the front door gonged, signaling nine o'clock. Ash shot from her chair and gasped.

"What are we doing? It's Friday! We have class in thirty minutes!"

"Oh, no! We'll never make it!" Marni wailed, shoving one last donut in her mouth.

"Nonsense," Fran said with a smile and a wink. "Francis can take you. *Francis!*"

In the backyard, the three animals had finally tuckered themselves out. They slept in a pile, soaking up the morning sunbeams. The big ape blinked open his tired eyes and yawned, stretching his four arms so much so that he pushed Mitzi and Flynn right off him. He scratched his head, his ear, his shoulder, and his rump simultaneously. Fran called for him again.

"Francis! Front and center!"

The gorilla lumbered toward his mother and readied himself for commands. Fran strapped a large, sturdy basket to the girallon's back and tugged it to ensure stability.

"We use this basket to carry picnic supplies, but you two should fit nicely."

The small, skinny girls climbed in awkwardly and wiggled until they were semi-comfortable.

The little, squat Fran stood face to face with her massive animal and shook her pointer fingers like a scolding mama. "Listen here. Take these girls straight to the Academy, drop them near The Shoppes, and then come straight home. Understand?"

The gorilla grunted.

"No side trips to the banana trees."

The gorilla grunted a second time.

"Thanks for the treats, Mrs. B!" called Marni as Francis rose to his full height.

"Won't you take some with you, dear?"

"No time!"

"We'll come back and visit, promise!" yelled Ash with a wave.

Fran patted Francis on the bottom. "Off you go!"

With Flynn and Mitzi keeping pace on either side, Francis sprinted, feet over fists, across the green countryside.

Though they were miles away, it seemed only a matter of minutes before the girallon screeched to a halt outside The Shoppes. He knelt down to let the girls slip out of the basket, then turned to leave.

"Wait!" Ash said.

She reached in her pocket, and sure enough, there was one carrot left. She handed it to Francis, who examined it before finally eating it and starting his journey home.

Wishing they had an extra set of arms to enhance their own speed, the two girls, flanked by their loyal beasts, ran down the main street of The Shoppes. They dodged and weaved through shoppers until they reached the entrance to the Academy grounds.

"Our books!"

"No time to grab them now," Ash said, glancing to the Academy's unrelenting clock. "We've got one minute!"

The four burst through the entry doors and rushed up stairs, down halls, and through corridors to Professor Thorne's classroom, just in time for Herbs and Healing.

They plopped down at the last two desks and pretended they weren't breathing as loudly as they most certainly were. Even Flynn and Mitzi were exhausted—a first for both animals.

Professor Thorne stomped in with her usual stern expression. She was closely followed by her beast, a small liger named Ruby. Normally, Ruby would be a cheerful addition to the classroom, helping Thorne pass out papers with her teeth and fetch items, while spending the boring times chasing balls and attacking loose strings on students' clothing. But today, Ruby rumbled with growls and glared at the children from atop Thorne's desk.

"Before opening your textbooks to Chapter Nine and fetching your ingredients for today's recipe, something of importance has been brought to my attention by Ms. Loomington. She found this while gathering classmates for a morning study group."

Thorne placed Ash's birdcage on her desk. Its contents?

One very, very upset ratatoskr.

"Uh oh," Marni said under her breath.

"Ms. Ridley and Ms. Mayberry, come with me."

As Ash and Marni rose from their seats and reluctantly followed Thorne to their impending doom, Ash glanced to Farrah, who returned a sinister smirk.

Thorne brought the girls into the empty hallway and crossed her arms, waiting for an explanation. They had no choice but to invent a cover-up story for their misbehavior. Marni explained that the ratatoskr had been tormenting Flynn, so *that's* why they had to cage it. Ash explained that Mitzi had been chasing a rabbit and run off. She had gotten lost, because she wasn't the brightest of animals, so they had to go find her, and *that's* why they had run into class that morning. Thorne argued that the stories were outrageous, but seeing as how Mitzi was a very particular kind of dumb, the recount seemed somewhat believable.

Marni was quite insulted by the part of the story Ash made up, yet not enough to object to the accusation and accept a much worse punishment for what they'd actually done. Ash felt awful about lying and somewhat guilty for using Mitzi's ditziness as a scapegoat, but Marni would get over it. It was certainly better than the alternative.

Their punishment for tardiness—and causing emotional stress to a ratatoskr—was to clean the indoor castle stables: three floors of hay, feed, and excrement to tend to, courtesy of the beasts belonging to the third-, fourth-, and fifth-year students. Nasty work, but Ash was relieved that the punishment wasn't expulsion, given her formal warning for the fire incident.

"So gross," Marni said with a cringe, shoveling some rather foul droppings into a bucket.

"Ugh. It's like being back at the circus again," Ash added, dealing with a smelly pile of her own.

The current stable's inhabitant was a gorgeous, white horse with a thick, silver mane, curly fetlock feathers, and a long tail that dragged through the hay. Its body, while soft, looked to have the texture of scales, and two horns spiraled out from its forehead.

"Kirins are pretty, but they sure make nasty dookies."

The horse whinnied near Marni's face.

"Oh, shut up."

Cleaning the first floor of the stables took all morning, and they'd just barely made it to floor two by lunchtime. It was hard enough to elbow big, uncooperative beasts out of their way to allow for proper cleaning, but now their stomachs growled with emptiness. To make things worse, it was Halloween. Through the windows, Ash and Marni saw all sorts of fun happening on the grounds. Students dressed their animals in costumes, carved pumpkins, and scarfed orange cookies. Dickon even ran around as a ghost, spooking unwitting passersby. It looked positively enjoyable.

Ash spent her shoveling time lost in thought. Her conversation with Draven hadn't even seemed real—and yet, she had the vials. Draven had offered her a choice: one favor in exchange for her father. It seemed simple and impossible at the same time.

"You know what really rubs me the wrong way?" Marni said, leaning on the butt of her rake. "How Thorne said that Farrah was looking for us for a study group. What study group? Who studies in the morning? What a load of..." Marni looked down at her overflowing waste bucket. "Well...*that*."

"Farrah was probably going to play some kind of horrid prank on us last night. She found the ratatoskr, sure, but who knows—we may have made out better than we know."

Marni snorted at the idea that anything would be worse than shoveling a hundred pounds of animal dung. On *Halloween*.

The fifth-year stables were the nicest of all. Each roomy slot was well lit, with top-of-the-line feed dispensers and constantly flowing water. The one they were currently in had two swinging wooden doors that allowed for easy access to a stone balcony, where Flynn and Mitzi had been sleeping. The two were still exhausted from their crazy night and active morning.

The flapping of large wings caused both girls to look out the opening. Hammond, with scarf, gloves, and knitted cap, hovered on the back of Hermaeus outside.

"Hiya, girls!"

Hermie perched on the balcony. Hammond hopped off, holding two cups with spoon handles sticking out.

"Hermie accidentally froze three vats of Halloween soup, so the cafeteria lady ground it up and made soup slushies! Here, I brought a butternut squash stew one for you, Marni, and pumpkin-tomato noodle for Ash."

An excited Hammond handed the girls their frozen meals.

"Thanks...?" said Marni, sharing a glance of apprehension with Ash.

After one taste, both girls burst out laughing, exhausted and kooky from their long day of work being topped off with the silliest of snacks.

"Well, I thought they were good," said Hammond to Hermie.

In the following three weeks, the red, orange, and golden shades of autumn gave way to the first snowfall. The first-year students with baby animals and those hailing from warmer climates found snow to be a brand-new experience. This led to a funny display of confusion, apprehension, and surprise for the young pets, while the veterans wasted no time. They rollicked and played with renewed energy as the year crept toward its end.

Mitzi loved the snow most of all. Hermie didn't feel a difference—he was already cold all the time. Flynn seemed to enjoy the look of it and the arrival of new snowbirds in the trees, but he was unaffected by the snow itself. Flakes melted instantly at the touch of his warm body.

Ash and Marni felt it best to keep their noses far from trouble after their detention. With finals quickly approaching, it was important to focus on studying and practicing. Flynn still hadn't fully mastered his acrobatic flying, and Talon had given her new flight patterns for him to commit to memory.

Training had become especially difficult. Ash's mind was far from her work, and far from Flynn. She felt time slipping away—every day she failed to make a decision regarding Draven's proposal was another day her father could be suffering. How could she possibly focus on trivial academics and silly flight patterns when more pressing things were at stake?

One moment, it seemed so easy. Deliver the king a synthetic poison and she'd get her father back. Simple as that. Plus, it was for the good of the entire country—a man who thinks he's dying would surely listen to his concerned brother, and Cascadia could be united again. This was for the greater good of peace!

...*Or would he even listen?* The next moment, it seemed hopelessly complex. What if she were caught administering poison to the king? Forget being kicked out of school, she'd be jailed for life—or have to become a fugitive on the run. How could she ever find her father then?

The decision weighed on her. She felt constantly exhausted and even snapped at Marni and Hammond several times. Flynn seemed to take on her agitation as well, acting strange and aloof.

After a full Sunday of snowball fighting and fort building with the other first-year students—save Farrah, who didn't want Fiona getting all wet and dirty—Ash and Marni stomped back up to their dorms in their big, heavy boots and oversized parkas. Even Mitzi was completely drained of energy from the day, which was a very rare sight.

The girls lumbered through the door to their dorms and into Ash's room to relax.

"Whew, snow really takes it out of you," Marni said with a big, satisfied smile emphasized by her bright, rosy cheeks. "I could sleep for a whole year after that."

Marni clumsily removed her parka. The coat sleeve knocked Ash's burnt jewelry box off her desk. It landed on the floor and the two vials from Draven rolled out.

"What are those?" asked Marni.

"They're nothing," Ash snapped, scrambling to pick them up and hide them in a drawer.

"Ash, you've been awfully odd lately. Are those vials from the nurse? You'd better take them."

"No, Marni. I'm fine," Ash shot back.

Off the concerned look of her friend, she sighed and calmed her tone. "I mean, I think I'm fine. I think I just...need to rest a bit. I'm tired from today."

"All right," Marni said politely. "We'll leave you alone."

She snapped her fingers at Mitzi, who was asleep and snoring on Ash's floor.

"But...just remember, I'm here. If you need me."

"Yes, yes, I know," said Ash, growing weary of the conversation. "I just need to sleep. That's all."

Nightfall came quickly with the shorter winter days. A new breed of owls had made their home in the beech tree. Their persistent hooting was calming for most, but irksome for Ash. She rested on her bed wide-eyed and awake, thinking. Flynn's gentle wheezing let her know he was asleep in his cage.

She saw things so differently now. She didn't see the professors as mentors; she saw them as liars. The king wasn't honorable; he was a prejudiced ruler who took advantage of the poor. Odetta and the Elders—they weren't trying to help her; they were just greedy for Flynn. Draven was the only one who had given her answers about her father when everyone else avoided the subject.

Two things were certain: She was getting her father back, and whoever wanted her bird, they'd have to deal with her first.

Ash had made her choice.

CHAPTER 17

THE PRINCE AND THE VALKYRIE

Ash waited for the scurries of the ratatoskrs to cease, noting fewer scratching sounds now that the weather was cold. She threw on her parka and boots, and slipped the two vials safely into an inside pocket.

She softly closed the door to Flynn's cage while he slept and locked it.

"I'm sorry, Flynny," she whispered. "But I have to do this. I have to know where my father is, and where we belong."

She'd be much stealthier without the others tagging along this time, plus the thick falling snow would act as a concealing veil.

She slipped unnoticed into the first-year stables and quietly located Fiona. Quickly, she picked the small lock with a safety pin she removed from a ripped portion of her parka lining. Before Fiona could awaken and protest, Ash held out a handful of carrot bits.

"You and I both know you're not bonded strongly enough with Farrah to care if I borrow you tonight," she whispered. "I don't even think you like her that much, and I'll join you in that club."

Fiona happily chomped the carrots as if it were the first time she'd had a treat in weeks. Farrah may have been acing exams like a model pupil, but the girl treated her beautiful unicorn more like a slave than a friend—and that was no way to enhance a bond.

"Plus, it's a travesty she doesn't let you play in the snow. She just grooms you all the time, huh?"

Ash stroked the unicorn's nose and admired her beautiful horn. She was thankful that Fiona had grown to the perfect riding size since their arrival at school several months back.

With a rope around the horse's neck and a soft pad as a saddle, Ash mounted up. The two crept out of the stables, and Ash was happy for the muffling snow.

Swiftly Fiona galloped, as if she'd never tested the limits of her own legs. Farrah, being so strict, never let the horse run at full speed and barely let her exercise at all. Between the snow and the open fields, Fiona was in heaven.

Ash's sense of direction took her due east, as she recalled her previous trip to the castle with Suarez and Diego. Years of traveling with Tilda had instilled in her effective methods of remembering landmarks, since the old witch would lose her temper if Ash couldn't navigate their caravan to cities in time for performances. Every time Ash got lost, it cost them money.

It was trickier in the dark, but keeping the ocean to her right, she eventually saw the towering spires of Castle Dragoon in the distance.

Ash led Fiona into Fir Forest. The trees whizzed by as they weaved their way through. They almost got lost in the continuous pattern, until up ahead they saw the castle walls.

They halted a safe distance away. Ash dismounted and took a deep breath. She carefully removed the two vials.

"Let's see...purple is Infizzible."

She popped the cork off the vial with purple liquid. It instantly fizzed with bubbles.

"Wow, it really is fizzy," she said. "Well. Here goes nothing."

She took one tiny sip.

Nothing happened.

"Hmm. Maybe it takes a while to—"

She looked at her hand holding the vial. It had disappeared up to her sleeve! She took another sip and the rest of her arm disappeared, clothing and all. A fit of giggles overtook her as her limbs became see-through.

She drank nearly the entire bottle before stopping, with nothing but her feet visible.

"Wait. You should have some, too, Fiona. So no one sees you."

Carefully, Ash poured the last sip onto Fiona's tongue and the confused horse swallowed.

"Um...well...at least your head is safe."

It was true. The only portion of the unicorn that was affected by the last of the bottle was from its neck up. Fiona was now just a headless white horse.

Ash led Fiona to a thick bush. After feeding her transparent mouth a few carrots, she convinced the horse to lie down in the snow. She tied the lead rope around a tree using a special knot she'd learned in Captain Bera's class.

"Stay here, all right? I've only got one hour—I'll be back."

Ash, a ghost in boots, jogged toward the castle's wall fortifications. Fearless of climbing and heights—an added bonus of growing up a farm girl—she climbed the tree nearest the wall, inhaling as she leapt. Gingerly she scampered along the top like a cat on a fence.

Far below to her right was a beautifully groomed courtyard. She saw structural art, beautiful lawn ornaments, and bushes shaped into all sorts of animals—each topped with snow that was being gently blown off by the wind like falling sugar. Near the wall was a tall statue of a former king that she thought perhaps she could jump onto and shimmy down. She wasn't quite sure where she was going yet, but getting inside the walls was step one.

With another deep breath, she leapt and clung to the statue's neck. Unfortunately, the head of the statue was loose. It wobbled.

A guard standing watch nearby whipped his head to the sound. He walked toward the statue and peered right at Ash, who hid her feet behind the statue's back. It was incredible—he was looking right at her face, but he couldn't see one bit of her.

The guard shook his head and returned to his post.

Carefully, Ash shimmied down the unpredictable statue and walked toward the main hold. Guards stood at every entrance—there'd be no way to sneak past them with such large, heavy doors.

Ash looked around at the many facets of the castle. There had to be some sort of clue as to where the king slept.

The front side of the main keep, facing north, featured one very large window. It was about three stories up and had a beautiful stone balcony. It would undoubtedly have the best view of any room in the castle.

That must be the king and queen's bedroom! she concluded.

With no time to devise a quiet way to reach the room from the inside, Ash knew she had to scale the wall. She examined the stones in the architecture—snow wasn't sticking yet, not with the wind. From her angle, there appeared to be enough cracks for hand and footholds all the way up, with thick crawling ivy for added grip and traction, should some stones be icy. Once she had gotten to the third level, there looked to be a ledge that would help her reach the balcony.

My father has done so many things for me, she thought. *I can climb one stupid wall for him.*

Ash found that seconds ticked by at double speed under the pressure of limited time. She'd climbed rocks and mountains her entire childhood for fun, but never with anything on the line.

Adrenaline kicked in and Ash scaled the wall, step-by-step, reach-by-reach, with only a few bobbles. When her fingers finally gripped the ledge and she was able to pull herself up, she only stopped for a moment to catch her breath. She knew most of her time had been spent on the climb, and she'd still have to descend back down at the end.

Leading out to the balcony from the inside were double doors that were thick, sturdy, and almost certainly locked. On either side were tall, narrow windows.

The blowing wind instantly erased every footprint Ash left in the snow as she walked along the ledge and onto the balcony. She peered through the window on the left. Inside she saw the king's enormous royal bed. Tiberius and Verna appeared sound asleep, with Tiberius lying closest to the window. Beside him on a bedside table was exactly what Ash needed: a goblet.

Ash examined the frame of the window. Where it would usually swing open, the hinges were frozen shut.

I wish Flynn were here, she thought. *He can heat up anything.*

She breathed onto the cold hinges, even knowing her own breath would take too many precious minutes to heat the metal.

To her surprise, it worked—much more quickly than she expected was even possible. First her hearing, now this. Perhaps, she considered, she was beginning to develop even more of Flynn's abilities.

Slowly, to prevent creaking, she swung open one side of the window. Invisible or not, she'd never fit through with her coat. She snagged the vial from her parka's pocket, then removed the coat and tossed it on the ground. It instantly became visible again.

Holding her breath and crossing her fingers that her head would fit through the frame, she slipped inside. The room was unnervingly quiet and Ash feared the beating of her petrified heart would wake the whole castle. Tiberius faced her, his eyelids closed and his breathing rhythmic. Water filled a pewter goblet near his bedside. Ash figured he drank from it throughout the night. At least, she hoped.

Ash uncorked the vial with the murky, green liquid. It was odorless, and as soon as she poured it into the water, it turned colorless.

The deed had been done. Draven had assured her the liquid was synthetic and wouldn't cause the king any real, lasting harm, but just the thought of tampering with his drink and toying with his health...it felt wrong.

Ash slipped out of the room, closed the window, put her parka back on, and began carefully descending the wall. It was much more difficult than climbing up, made worse by the panic that her time was nearly up.

Her foot slipped on a rock six feet from the surface below. She tumbled down the rest of the way, landing hard on her shoulder.

"Who's there?" said the deep voice of a nearby guard.

Ash sprinted. She found the courtyard with the wobbly statue and jumped for him. The crunch of footsteps in the snow signaled that the guards were close behind. She sprung off the statue and onto the curtain wall—a bit too hard. The statue's head tipped, and balanced. After what felt like a lifetime, it toppled into the snow in slow motion.

Ash gasped and covered her mouth. Her hands. They were visible again. The Infizzible Potion had begun to wear off. She rushed along the wall, much less carefully than before, nearly paying the price for it once or twice. The tall tree was in sight. She didn't look back to see how close the guards were, or if they'd even seen the random body parts running across the wall. All she knew was she had to jump.

Her fingers gripped tightly to the branches and snow plopped onto her face. She winced as a clump fell down her neck. She sat silently for several minutes before navigating her way down.

Both shivering from the cold and sweating from the caper, Ash returned to Fiona to find the horse lying in the spot where she'd left her. An exhale of sweet relief escaped Ash's lungs like a released balloon. She began to unknot the rope.

Ash froze—almost literally—when the unthinkable happened: she saw movement. She heard footsteps, too. Something—or someone—was nearby.

How could they have found me so soon? she thought, panic setting in.

Above her, she heard and felt the wind from flapping wings. She reached for some fan-like fallen branches to cover herself and Fiona.

"It's okay, girl," she said softly to a fidgeting Fiona. "Shh. Just stay quiet."

Peering through openings in the bush that masked her, Ash saw that the wings didn't belong to a beast—they belonged to a Valkyrie. Ash recognized her from the cave of the Half-Beasts. She was the small one, the youngest one of the Valkyrie trio.

Stepping out from behind a tree trunk was a man in a white cloak, which blended with the snow. He threw back his hood and Ash immediately identified him: Prince Victor.

"You waited for me," said the Valkyrie with a soft smile.

"I would wait a thousand lifetimes for you, Arielle," he replied.

Trailing behind Victor on a leather lead line was his loyal peryton, Vicky. Arielle extended a gentle hand to the winged stag's nose, but the animal snorted and turned away.

"Still a little jealous, are you, old girl?" teased Victor, patting Vicky's neck.

Arielle laughed. Her eyes sparkled. She seemed so much more...human than her rigid, obstinate older sisters.

"I'm afraid I don't bring you good news, Victor," she said gravely.

"You bring me joy just being here. That's enough for me."

"Victor, they're ready. Draven and General Gunnar have strengthened their offenses. Much quicker than we expected. I don't know how Draven's done it, but he's united every breed. He's even prepared to attack with mammoth beasts."

"What are you suggesting? Is this soon?"

"I'm not sure. Something has triggered it. Everything was quiet, simmering for so long, then suddenly they've readied themselves for battle."

Battle? Ash thought. *No, that's not right. Draven doesn't want a battle. That's the last thing he wants.*

"And the Valkyries? Your sisters?" asked Victor, grasping her hands in his.

"Gunnar and the others believe we're on their side, but we're still neutral, awaiting the next phase. We're not ones to be on a losing side of a fight, but the Valkyrian distaste for humans is palpable. They would not interfere should your race fall."

Fiona sneezed. Ash tensed up as the pair whipped their heads in her direction. Fortunately, the faint yelling of guard voices from the castle diverted their attention.

"I must go. I may have been seen."

"I will speak with my father," Victor assured. "Arielle, you must be careful. I can't lose you."

Victor and Arielle shared a kiss, made even more lovely by the delicate snowfall and the wooded backdrop.

Ash waited until the prince and the princess parted, Arielle rocketing into the night sky with a robust beat of her wings and Victor mounting Vicky for a quiet canter back to the castle.

With a steady pace and a head whirring with anxious thoughts, Ash rode Fiona home to the Academy.

CHAPTER 18

THE ATTACK

"Ridley! Nap on your own time or get off my battlefield!"

Captain Bera's ground-rumbling bellow instantly shook Ash out of her standing sleep.

"Sorry! Yes, I'm awake," she blurted, jerking so abruptly that Flynn irritably ruffled his feathers and wobbled on her shoulder. He tensed his feet and his talons poked into her skin harder than usual. As the bird grew, so did his toenails.

He was still rather grumpy from being locked in his cage for several hours last night. He liked to perch on the window-sill around midnight to watch the water skippers scurry upon the lake surface in the rippled reflection of the moon. Ash felt bad for upsetting her little bird's schedule and for quite literally ruffling his feathers.

Hammond, standing behind and to the left of Ash, per usual Combat class formation, subtly got her attention with a *psst*. "Uh, Ash, you've got a little..."

Ash wrinkled her forehead at the silly boy motioning toward his mouth at first, but the message was soon received. She wiped a bit of drool from her lower lip.

The sun had been abnormally warm all morning. It had melted nearly all the snow, save for big piles that hid from the rays under the protection of the Academy's goliath shadow. Normally, Ash would have welcomed the sunshine, but it was much too bright for her tired eyes on this particular day.

Between the long trip, climbing a tree, and scaling a frozen wall, Ash's bones throbbed with exhaustion. She'd gotten away with her deed. No tattling ratatoskrs or snitching blondes this time. Draven's request had been fulfilled and Ash was one step closer to finding her father. But, if the task was noble, why did she feel such guilt?

And that winged girl, Arielle.... What had she meant last night, saying Draven was *strengthening offenses*? She clearly didn't know about their plan and Draven's peace treaty. Everything was going to be fine.

As Ash relived the events of the previous evening, her eyelids drooped like stretched taffy and her chin dipped to her chest.

Flynn rapped his hard beak on the side of her head. She jerked awake for a second time.

"Yes! Hello! I'm awake!" she spit out, shooing away her cranky, feathered alarm clock. "Throw apples at my head and poke me with a walking staff, why don't you?"

Flynn squawked once to voice his disapproval. Ash returned his reprimand with an out-stuck tongue.

A soft, velvety nose nuzzled her left arm. Fiona had cozied up by her side, failing to hide her and Ash's newfound friendship in a most affectionate way.

"Fiona!" screamed Farrah at the sight. "What in all of Cascadia are you doing? Come back here at once! *Come!*"

The young unicorn looked like a deflated child as she gloomily turned toward her demanding master.

"What is wrong with you?" she scolded. Farrah's venomous gaze shifted from Fiona to Ash. "Have you been giving your disgusting carrots to beasts who don't belong to you again? Don't you dare give a morsel of anything to my Fiona!"

An ear-piercing whistle blow stunted Farrah's insult.

"Attack positions!" hollered Bera, lowering the whistle from her lips. "Time to run drills. Make sure you're spread out and staggered so no one gets hit...or frozen...again."

Hammond returned the others' accusatory glances with an innocent shrug.

Another whistle blow. "Block!"

Each child and their beast assumed a blocking stance, intended to deflect oncoming assaults.

"Attack!"

The children called out unique commands to their beasts, some in foreign languages. The animals thrashed, slashed, clawed, and reared—some spit acid and others shook the ground slightly with an earth-quaking attack. Ash always wondered what these drills must be like in the upper classes, where students and their beasts had even more advanced attacks.

Mitzi performed a small Shock Blast that sent sparks of lightning from her eyes, and Hammond called out "Shard!" to Hermie, who breathed frozen shards from his icy nostrils.

A few of the shards slightly nicked the rump of the student standing in front of him, who glared.

"Sorry!" Hammond said with a nervous grin. "His blast radius is surprisingly wide."

Farrah demanded an Energy Beam from Fiona, who stood at her right. The horse took a wide stance, lowered her head, and an ivory beam shot from her spiraled horn. It dented the grass and left it steaming with a white glow.

"Fireball!" Ash instructed as she tried to swallow a yawn. Flynn reared back and sent an apple-sized flaming sphere swirling from his mouth. Tired or not, Flynn was not going to let Ash's fatigue keep him from performing his favorite trick in the world.

Bera continued to call out instructions intermittently with whistles. "Attack! Block! Attack! Block!"

At the next attack command from Bera, Farrah voiced her strike command to Fiona, then looked in Ash's direction. Ash looked back at her. She saw Farrah's eyes narrow as the girl mimed an intense, forward-pushing motion toward her. The motion bent Fiona's Energy Beam and sent it straight into Ash's stomach. The blast propelled Ash backward, flying through the air nearly thirty feet. She landed hard, like a thrown ragdoll. She skidded along the grass far behind the last row of students.

Flynn let out an ear-piercing screech. He pinned back his wings and rocketed toward his master's limp body.

"Ash!" Marni shrieked, stiff-arming her way through gasping students to reach her best friend.

"It was an accident," Farrah blurted, looking just as surprised at her strength as her follow classmates.

"The heck it was!" Marni angrily eyed the blonde bully as she knelt with Hammond beside Ash, who was feeling dizzy and confused.

The midsection of Ash's tunic displayed a white, steaming circle where the blow landed. Flynn investigated the wound then flitted to Ash's face like a hyper hummingbird, as if to ask a million questions. *Are you hurt? Are you not hurt? Is your tummy all right? Why aren't your eyes fully open? Is your head okay? Do you need some berries? Do you know you have grass stains on your face? Are you hurt?*

Ash grasped her belly in pain, then rolled over and threw up on the lawn.

A collective "eww" resounded from the onlooking students, including from Hammond, whose boots had not been quick enough to escape the vomit.

"All right, all right! Show's over! Back to formation!" Bera sent sharp elbows into the arms of crowding children as she stomped her way through to Ash.

"Mayberry, Crump, back in your spots."

Marni and Hammond reluctantly abandoned Ash. Bera turned toward Farrah, who still looked shocked.

"Ms. Loomington, while impressive, we will not be practicing any magical attacks *on each other* until next year, is that clear? So, stop getting lessons from your brother and leave your classmates alone."

Farrah nodded her head rapidly and withdrew to her position. Ash may have had birdies flying around her noggin—or, maybe that was just Flynn—but she was alert enough to conclude that Farrah deserved a much worse punishment than a stern voice and a finger shake.

Marni's remark early in the school year was proving true once again. *"Like a Loomington could ever get in trouble."*

"You all right, Ridley?"

Ash sat up, rubbed her head, and nodded. Bera couldn't help but chuckle at Ash's grumpy expression and Flynn's unrelenting willingness to help.

"Well, now you know what it's like to get hit," Bera said with a wink, patting Ash a little too hard on the back. "Go sit down a while."

Ash spent her recovery time on the front steps of the school, thankful to have skipped the last half hour of class. Before Farrah's "accidental" blast to the gut, Ash could already tell that Flynn's attacks were escalating.

Nearly every class was the same: he'd start out with small fireballs, like he was supposed to, then spit out bigger fireballs, and then a Flamethrower attack, then an Ember Spin. Drunk with excitement, the firebird would become almost impossible to reel back. It was the pair's number one struggle, especially in Combat class. Flynn's enthusiasm would then excite Mitzi, who was already one squirrel sighting away from sprinting the length of Cascadia with Marni dragging behind on a leash. Then Mitzi would frighten the kid with the kelpie, who would rear back and irritate the kludde, whose roar upset the mngwa, and so on. As the dominos of destruction fell, the whole field was soon chaos. Until, of course, Bera would scare them all back to attention with one bellow and crack of a whip, followed by a head shake at Ash for instigating the whole thing.

Flynn caught a grape that had been flicked in the air. He gulped it down whole.

Ash would usually reprimand him for not chewing, out of fear he would choke and she wouldn't have the faintest clue how to relieve a small bird from suffocation. But she was too distracted.

She burped and groaned at her stomach pain, picturing elaborate revenge on Farrah. Maybe she could glue her butt to a desk chair. Or cut off a chunk of her dumb, curly hair with pruning shears. Spiders in her boots? Worms in her food? A precarious water bucket perched above the door of her dorm?

Her conscience eventually concluded that the pain was possibly fair karma for stealing Fiona and taking her for a joyride... an hour away...and then turning her head invisible. She'd call it even.

Gulp. Another grape launched from Ash's thumb down Flynn's gullet. He chirruped in hopes of praise for his grape-to-mouth coordination, but once again, she ignored him.

"Ash! Hey, Ash!"

Marni's voice vibrated as she trotted down the stairs from the school. Hammond tailed closely. Mitzi diverted from the duo to lunge at Flynn for some playtime in the sun.

She plopped beside Ash holding a dusty, torn, brown leather-bound book. Hammond sat on Ash's opposite side, his breathing much more labored than Marni's.

"You have some kind of stamina, Marni," he declared with an exhale.

"Ash, Hammond and I knew you've been feeling badly lately, so we did something in hopes of cheering you up!"

She placed the book on Ash's lap. It was much heavier than its small size suggested.

"After we talked with Mrs. Butterscotch, it got me thinking. Maybe, just maybe, we could find information about Flynn's master in his last life."

"Yeah, you know, perhaps we could locate him and he could teach you how to deal with Flynn better. How to control him," Hammond added, his breathing almost back to normal. "My family's responsible for building the library here and my sister works there part time. She has a key to the Professors Only room so I grabbed it from her dorm and we crept in!"

"And we nearly got caught," said Marni.

"Not because of me."

"Yes, because of you. Do you know how loudly you breathe? You sound like a congested wildebeest."

"I have allergies! I'm allergic to, like, half the animals at this school!"

"Anyway," Marni returned to the conversation. "We sneaked in—"

"*Snuck*," corrected Hammond.

Marni whipped her head to him. "Hey. Don't do the thing I do to you back to me."

"You're constantly correcting me!"

"Because you're constantly wrong!"

"Guys!" Ash interrupted.

It was clear by the bickering that her two friends had been spending a lot of time together. Without her. Had she been oblivious to that, too?

Marni cleared her throat. "We *snuck* in—"

"It was positively criminal, and so thrilling!"

"Calm down, you little garbage raccoon," Marni said to Hammond, rolling her eyes at his obvious adrenaline. "It's like you've never done anything bad before."

"It makes my lips tingly just thinking about it."

"That's...weird. But Ash, the only problem is...well, we don't exactly have good news. We couldn't find much. Just a small paragraph in here."

The cover and spine were faded, but displayed the letter "P" in gold. It appeared to be a very old book, too outdated to be of any real use to modern knowledge-seekers. For one, it was hand-written, which was quite crude compared to their current, printed textbooks. It must have come into being before the lettering press had been invented by a king's scholar three hundred years ago.

Ash paused momentarily to recognize that her history lessons had sinked in after all. Or was it *sunk*?

The title page was a bit more specific than the single letter on the cover:

> *The Bodas Bumble Academy of Beasts and Magic*
> *History of Notable Bonded Beasts and Regal Kin*
> *Volume P*
> *Year DCCIII of King Tyndareus*

"It means animals that start with the letter 'P,'" Hammond suggested, kindly.

"I think she gets it, Hammond."

Ash flipped through the aged, yellow pages, wrought with ink smudges and tears. It was almost impossible to navigate. Some pages had ripped out entirely. The animals were listed in alphabetical order, but there were no reference words at the tops of the pages. The pegasus section seemed to go on forever, followed by other animals Ash had never heard of, like a peluda (illustrated as some kind of hairy dragon) and a peng (a massive four-eyed, four-winged bird). The peryton section lasted for pages and pages, until Ash finally reached a chapter about some animal called a piatek.

That's too far. Where is the phoenix section? she thought.

She flipped the pages backward until she reached a single page titled "Phoenix."

Below the title was a description of the bird, including its appearance, wingspan, diet, and preferred habitat. The following paragraph described its attacks, going into great detail about the amount of fire the creature could expel and its temperature capabilities. It was mostly all information Ash had already learned and discovered on her own, if not a bit embellished by whoever had written it. The word *catastrophic* appeared, as well as the phrase *gravely destructive*. Her Flynn? He gazed at water skippers and liked grapes. Sure, he set the occasional student on fire, but *gravely destructive* was a bit of a stretch.

Though...she had only known him in two stages of his life: very young and very old. She wondered what he would be like in the years in between, during his maturity.

Finally, her finger reached the section titled "Notable Masters."

She tensed up. It was smudged, torn around the edges. The penmanship was difficult to decipher, but Ash could make some of it out:

> *M. Grevillea (born DCC– last seen DCCXXX)*
> *First recorded individual to bond to a phoenix bird.*
> *M. Grevillea…accepted into Bodas Bumble in the*
> *year DCCX of King Tyndareus, son of Sabastos*
> *the Second.*

Ash took a moment to calculate the math in her head. "That was exactly five hundred years ago," Ash muttered to herself. "The year this person bonded to Flynn."

> *Student showed great potential…high markings*
> *in the area of Combat…questionable acts…*
> *failure to graduate…*
> *Practicer of sorcery…incident…The rebellious*
> *act resulted in the fatality of sixty-four students,*
> *three professors, and twenty Kin.*

Ash felt a chill surge through her bloodstream. She came to the last readable sentence.

> *The phoenix was last seen departing M. Grevillea in*
> *DCCXXX as the first unbonding of a beast.*

"Unbonding?" Ash uttered as she read the word over.

Ash calculated some more. That was, in fact, over four hundred years ago, just like everyone had said. That's why people hadn't seen the bird in so long—it was the year it had departed its master.

"We've been taught unbonding is impossible," Marni said, placing a hand on Ash's shoulder. "This guy must have been so bad that Flynn—or the old Flynn—up and left him."

"No Bonded Beast has ever, in history, abandoned their owner," Hammond added.

"Except...Flynn," Ash said, the puzzle pieces shifting and linking together in her head. Her voice lowered. "Maybe that's why...they've kept this from me. Maybe...they don't want me to know what the bird is capable of."

She stared straight ahead. "What *I* could be capable of."

Hammond clapped his hands together, attempting to brighten the mood. "Good thing it was about a zillion years ago and that guy is long dead! Flynn is much happier with you."

Ash glanced to her bird. He was done playing with Mitzi, who'd moved on to digging a hole, and was now perched on a half-melted snowman in the shade. Two fuzzy bluebirds fluttered up, urging Flynn to join them for a fly. He irritably batted his wings until they left him alone.

Was he really happier with her? He had begun to grow just as moody and testy as she'd been acting. She never took him to the beach anymore. They never played or practiced their baton throws. In fact, she couldn't remember the last time they'd cuddled, or the last time she'd encouraged him in any sort of positive way.

"If Flynn left someone else...he could leave me," she said under her breath.

"No! Don't talk like that," Marni said, taking the book back. "It was silly of us to show you this. Let's just pretend it never—"

Suddenly, all three of the children's attention was diverted by loud, hurried footsteps. Professor Thorne walked briskly past them and up the stairs with an unmistakably horrified expression. She burst through the doors, ignoring everyone who greeted her.

Ash, Marni, and Hammond shared a glance.

"Stay, Mitzi," Marni said to her fox.

Ash opened her mouth to give the same command to Flynn, but seeing his inert expression, didn't bother.

The trio followed after Thorne.

Down halls and through corridors Thorne went, picking up her skirt and jogging whenever she was alone. She was too preoccupied with whatever had upset her that she didn't turn back once to see if she was being followed—an advantage to the clumsy trio, one of whom sounded like a congested wildebeest.

Ash recognized the path. Thorne was headed toward the High Council Room, where the Elders congregated.

Ash stretched out an arm that held her friends back before they turned the corner to the council chamber. They hid as Thorne pushed open the doors with alarming strength—a sobering racket in such a quiet section of the castle.

As the massive doors slammed shut, the three rushed forward.

"We'll never hear anything through this thickness!" Hammond whined, probably fearing his second scandal of the day would be thwarted by architecture.

Ash knew her hearing had been increased thanks to Flynn. She pressed her ear against the door.

"What is the matter, Rose?"

"Elders, the caladrius! It's refusing to look at the king!"

Ash quietly repeated the information to Marni and Hammond.

The two looked as though every drop of blood had been drained from beneath their skin.

"That's Elder Raleigh's bird," said Hammond, lips quivering. "Do you know what that means, Ash?"

"No?"

"The power of the caladrius is that it knows when someone is dying! It refuses to look at that person!" Marni blurted, anxious to return to the secrets happening behind the door.

Ash felt the blood drain from her face. It couldn't be.

"No.... It must be some mistake," she said, the words barely forming.

"The caladrius doesn't make mistakes," Hammond assured her.

Draven, Ash thought. *He tricked me! The poison was real!*

"Listen again," Marni urged.

"Then classes must be canceled. All students, first and second years especially, are to remain in their dormitories until further notice."

Ash, Marni, and Hammond rushed to the classroom where they were supposed to have been ten minutes earlier. Flynn and Mitzi, familiar with the routine after so many weeks, were already waiting for the girls inside. Flynn was perched on Ash's usual desk chair and Mitzi slept belly-up beneath Marni's.

There was no professor.

Just as Farrah opened her mouth to comment on their tardiness, Professor Suarez hastily entered the room. He had clearly received the news and it looked to be weighing on him heavily.

"Unfortunately, children, there is a pressing matter to which the staff and I must attend," he said in a severe tone, unusual for him. "I require all of you to lock up your beasts and head straight to your dormitories, do you understand? You will go immediately and stay there until further notice, without question."

"What happened? Is someone hurt?" Marni asked, both a feigned act of ignorance and genuine lust for answers.

"I said without question, Ms. Mayberry, and that was two. Everyone is dismissed."

Professor Suarez would have normally finished that command by saying "walk, do not run." The lack of those instructions seemed intentional, and the class sprung from their chairs and darted for the door. Something was wrong and everyone could sense it.

Students crowded the hallways in an evacuation, escaping through any exit possible. The message of danger had spread throughout the school and the tension was palpable.

Once outside, a snowy downfall covered the heads of students who walked and ran toward the stables and dormitories with their beasts in tow. Ash was knocked around as she searched the crowd for her friends. She held Flynn to her shoulder, less as a method of keeping him near and more as a reassurance that they were together.

"Marni!" Ash called out when she saw her friend chasing after a snow-bound Mitzi.

She crossed a sea of students to reach her.

"Marni, I've got a terrible feeling about this," she said as they hurried toward the treehouse. "I think I know what's happening. The Half-Beasts. They're going to attack. Their goal is to overthrow the king and now the king is dying!"

The two were only halfway to the treehouse before they heard it.

The growl.

The deep, earth-shaking growl that penetrated their insides. Slowly, they turned around.

High on the cliff—the same cliff Ash and Marni had climbed—stood an enormous, towering wolf, over a hundred feet from the ground to its haunches. Each sharpened tooth jetted up like a giant's spear, with black saliva dripping from its jaws. Its hair spiked up like a forest of spindly trees. Its ears were fringed with rips and tears, evidence of its past battles. Most unsettling of all, the beast's eyes were deeply golden and open wide, as if scanning the valley for the best place to begin his feast.

Ash recognized the creature in an instant. It was the wolf from the cave. The Fenris wolf.

There were screams and shouts of *"Run!"* as everyone in the vicinity scattered, even faster now, to their dorms.

"Hammond! Where's Hammond?" Marni shrieked.

Her words were lost as Ash remained fixated on the cliff. Through the snowflakes, Ash saw the Fenris wolf had company. An army of Half-Beasts appeared at the dog's feet, spanning the top of the cliff, edge to edge. They thickened every time Ash got a clear sight of them through the snowfall. With spears pointed up and swords wielded, there was no question—the school was about to be attacked.

No…no this can't be real. Did I—did I start this? she thought in horror.

A minotaur, probably General Gunnar, stepped onto a rock promontory beside the Fenris. He blew a horn that echoed through the valley.

Behind the Academy, a pink tentacle, the height and thickness of a redwood tree, shot up out of the ocean. It slammed down on the left wing of the school, crushing one of the castle's circular towers. The ground shook. The few students left on the grass fell to their knees.

The horn blow had signaled the attack. The Half-Beast army poured over the cliff like a burst dam. Flying harpies swooped down on the Academy, retrieving bricks with their taloned feet and projecting them through the many stained glass windows. They shattered in colored confetti.

It was clear to Ash now. This was happening because of her. The school that had saved her from an awful, abusive life was being destroyed because of the very acts she had committed, and it was happening before her eyes. She'd helped Draven. She'd turned her back on the Academy.

I'm a traitor, she realized, her body frozen with dismay.

But what could she possibly do to reverse her actions?

Like a dive-bombing kingfisher, Captain Bera, riding atop her Wyvern, Bertha, dipped from the sky and charged a harpy. Bertha's sharp claws grabbed the harpy in her midsection and flung her toward the ocean. With a battle cry, Bera charged at another. Professor Atlas followed close behind on his hippalectryon, a muscular red and turquoise horse with long wings and a hooked rooster beak.

"The professors! They're fighting back!" Ash exclaimed.

"Come on! Let's go!" Marni yelled, motioning toward the treehouse.

Glancing behind her as she ran, Ash saw the army reach the ground level. A second tentacle from whatever was in the sea smashed another castle turret. All the professors and Elders were now present with their beasts and retaliating.

On the ground, Thorne commanded her liger forward, who tore after a small group of satyrs with rabid speed and eager fangs. Suarez landed his fierce manticore before a charging centaur, and the two engaged in one-on-one battle. Elder Pyrrus galloped his three-headed cerberus dog across the field. It stomped toward enemies with boulder-sized paws and bit at them with each of its mouths.

The numbers were dramatically lopsided—upwards of five hundred Half-Beasts were invading the valley against only a handful of professors and Elders. Their beasts' powers were strong and they had magical attacks on their side, unlike the Half-Beasts, but even striking ten enemies at a time could prove to be insufficient. If only Ash had learned faster, if only she had gotten Flynn under control and they knew how to perform better attacks—then maybe, just maybe she could have helped.

Ash and Marni dodged debris and kept their balance as the ground shook. Their boots slipped on the wet grass and the air stung their cheeks. The treehouse was close. Just twenty feet away.

As they reached the treehouse entrance, Marni and Mitzi sped up the wooden stairs. Flynn zipped up beside Ash as she placed her foot on the first step.

She paused.

Spinning around, she faced the bay. The tentacles that had been waging war on the school were now creeping like underwater spider legs into the inlet. If the reinforced stonewalls of the Academy were no match for this creature's thick arms, then the treehouse would be splintered in mere seconds.

"Ash! That's a Kraken! Come on! Take my hand!"

Marni reached down for Ash from the false safety of the tree. Her eyes glanced to Marni only for a moment, then back to the inlet. The Kraken tentacles bubbled out of the surface like boiling noodles.

I can't—I can't just run away and do nothing, Ash thought. *The Half-Beasts are attacking because of what I did. I poisoned King Tiberius. And now my friends are in danger!*

She made up her mind. She couldn't escape her wrongdoing. It didn't matter if the threat was small or enormous, if she knew how to attack or not, she'd die before she'd let anyone harm her only friends.

"I love you, Flynn," Ash said to her companion, winging beside her. "I know I've been a terrible friend lately. I know you probably want to peck my eyes out sometimes. But I'm going to change that, I promise. Whatever happens, just stay with me."

Flynn resolutely voiced his agreement. He had a look of determination far beyond his years. He wasn't a baby bird anymore.

Ash stepped away from the treehouse and marched toward the water.

"Are you crazy? Ash!" Marni screamed behind her, but her pleas had already faded into the cacophony of sword clinks and beast roars.

Ash glanced to her right as she walked. The Fenris beast, the terrifying monstrosity, remained still. He hadn't moved from the cliff. Whatever horror he planned to bestow on his valley of prey, it hadn't come yet.

A tentacle exploded from the inlet and into the sky. If it fell forward, it would crush the treehouses. If it fell to the left, it would crush the stables.

Ash took a deep breath. She readied herself to command a fire attack from Flynn, knowing in the back of her mind that fire never worked effectively on sea-dwelling creatures.

But before her lips could utter the words, Arielle, the Valkyrie, dipped from the clouds. She stabbed the tentacle with her spear. She got in several deep stabs before a second tentacle batted her away. Arielle slammed hard into the rock wall to the right of the inlet, and tumbled onto the beach.

"No!" Ash shrieked.

She sprinted toward the girl's limp frame. Arielle's arms shook with weakness as she attempted to prop herself up. Another tentacle emerged from the water in front of her.

Ash hugged Arielle tight and rolled her out of the way just in time as the tentacle pounded the ground beside them.

The Valkyrie blinked her eyes with dismay.

"You've got to get up!" Ash shouted. "We're in danger and need to move, now!"

Arielle grimaced with determination. Ash helped her to her feet and Arielle shrieked as she put weight on her left leg.

The two hobbled up the paths of the cliff. They darted into an empty cave that hadn't yet been modeled into a student dwelling.

"Crawl to the back of this cave when you can. Try to stay out of sight," Ash instructed. "I'll send for help!"

The Valkyrie grabbed her leg in pain and weakly nodded.

Ash exited the cave and returned to the beach. A tentacle slammed hard in front of her, spraying cold sand in her face.

"Flynn! Fireball!"

Flynn, without hesitation, shot a large fireball at the Kraken's rubbery arm. He missed. Suddenly, seven more tentacles shot up from the water.

Ash and Flynn dodged the wriggling arms as they slammed against the ground. The earth was its drum to pound, and it quaked with every hit.

One tentacle smashed down inches in front of them. Ash barely hurdled it, landing in a somersault on the other side— another instance when the seemingly silly skills she had gained on the farm ended up being more valuable than she would have ever imagined.

"Fireball! Flamethrow! Flynn, just do *anything*!"

Flynn whizzed to the center of the inlet, where the tentacles originated. He launched a barrage of fireballs on each arm, his flames landing about every third strike. His small, red body pulsed as he rapid-fired.

Finally, the angry Kraken receded in scorched pain. A roar rumbled beneath the water, followed by a surge of bubbles. It wasn't a clean attack, but it had gotten the job done...for the time being.

The war heightened. The school grounds, which only hours before had been populated with laughing children and

frolicking animals, were now a terrifying and bloody battlefield. Minotaurs and centaurs fought with crafted weapons
and brute strength. Gargoyles terrorized the aerial defense.
Nagas slithered beneath the terrain and emerged for surprise
attacks. Arachnes dodged projectiles from Bertha's Wyvern
and werewolves lurched with claws out, hoping to take down
the cerberus.

Ash's fear escalated to hopelessness. They were incredibly
outnumbered. If the trained professors and Elders couldn't
even hold off the onslaught, what could the students do if they
were the only ones left alive?

The deep whinny of a horse resounded with tremendous
volume. Above Ash, soaring over the cliff, was the beautiful, white glow of Odetta on her fantastic pegasus. Shooting
white Energy Beams similar to Fiona's, but a hundred times
as intense, she began attacking the enemy ground troops.
Following behind her, both flying and galloping down the cliffside, were the Regal Kin.

The Kin were clad in purple and golden royal armor and
rode in on the most beautiful animals imaginable. Even more
so than the professors and Elders, the riders looked similar to
their beasts—hair color, body color, skin texture, eyes, ears.
Master and beast appeared as one.

The valley was alive with lightning and fire. Ice attacks
crossed paths with poison breath. Growls, grunts, howls,
hisses, and shrieks echoed against the cliff walls. Light beams
of every color from the magnificent array of shimmering dragons reflected off the white snow.

Ash wished the snowflakes weren't so thick so she could
see what was happening in the battle. If only she could get the

attention of one of the Regal Kin to help her protect her friends in the treehouse. The Kraken could be back at any moment.

Odetta landed on the ground in front of one man in particular. He looked human and was clothed in very little armor. In one hand, he held a spiked mace. He turned toward Odetta and smiled—a grin that even from Ash's distance was fear-inducing. He looked familiar.

The man from the cave...the one who read the book and spoke to the Valkyries, she remembered. *What was he called?*

The man clenched his hands into tight fists. His brow narrowed and he screamed, veins brutally popping from his neck and muscles flexing. He transformed, his body bulging and mutating to twice his size. Coarse fur sprang from his back, neck, and arms. His face formed into a snout. He looked half man, half boar—a wild, maniacal razorback hog with blood red eyes. The creature surged with anger.

Berserker! He's a Berserker!

Odetta unsheathed two scimitar swords. The blades were wide and curved, with sharp ridges like teeth. Outstretched to her sides, the swords resembled small versions of the silver wings of her pegasus.

She spoke a command to Odessus, readying the horse for the attack. The Berserker continued to scream, a heart-piercing battle cry that frightened Ash even more. The man sprinted toward Odetta like an enraged bull, a ball of red-hot fury charging across the field.

Odessus reared up and flapped his wings forward. A forceful gust of purple wind hit the beast mid-sprint. He shielded his face and dug his feet into the ground, refusing to be moved by the violent gust. When the wind ceased, the beast roared and sprung ten feet into the air, claws and mace ready to shred Odetta. The feathers in Odessus's wings instantly turned to knives and swiped at the creature in mid-air, slicing his arms deeply. He landed hard on the ground behind them and his mace flew from his grasp.

Professor Suarez was right that very first week in his class. The Wing Slice was absolutely incredible.

"Get off your horse and face me like the human scum you are!" he growled.

Odetta dismounted from her steed with grace and faced the wretched creature. Ash couldn't believe she would comply with his taunting.

The Berserker smiled and licked his fangs, bending his knees in preparation to pounce. Odetta crossed her swords on her chest as he ran toward her. She closed her eyes and her body glowed white—a blinding, hot light—and her swords began to magically grow. They grew to the enormous size of pegasus wings and surged with purple light. Odetta let out an unearthly scream—a woman's scream mixed with an angry, high-pitched horse whinny. The Berserker shrieked his own battle cry.

Odetta blinked open her eyelids, revealing glowing white balls instead of eyes. She reared back her gigantic swords. The Berserker lunged forward, claws first. The two clashed in a blinding ball of light.

Out of nowhere, a tentacle wrapped around Ash's torso. Like a limp child's doll, she was flung two hundred feet into the air.

Grasping at clouds and snow that couldn't stop her, Ash hovered momentarily in the sky before falling, plunging toward the ground.

She twisted around, looking below her as she plummeted. The Kraken emerged from the water, just enough to show an open and ready mouth full of sharp, machete-like teeth. It would devour her in one gulp.

Snowflakes whizzed by her face, accentuating her speed. Tears welled up in her eyes. Flynn grabbed at her sleeve with his beak, but he was too small to support her weight. She reached out and felt his velvety, hot feathers one last time.

This was it. No more school. No more friends. No more searching for her father. The teeth below wouldn't care about her excuses. This was how her adventure ended. Flynn would have to go on alone.

She incongruously remembered Marni complaining on their midnight escapade that hitting against hard objects when they were cold somehow hurt so much more than normal. And that was exactly the case when her body fell against Hermaeus's cold, scaly back.

"Woo! Yeah!" shouted Hammond.

Hammond and his dragon had scooped Ash out of the air moments before the Kraken could crunch her bones into a splintery paste. They ascended far above the reach of the Kraken, who was now dealing with a new enemy: a Hydra. Elder Mortimer, the oldest and frailest Elder, had raised his nine-headed sea serpent from the depths of the ocean. It was bigger than the Kraken and couldn't even fit in the inlet. One of its massive heads struck the tentacled monster and dragged it out to sea for a fair fight.

Hammond and Ash, with a delighted Flynn winging close by, evaded Kin and Half-Beasts in aerial combat, as well as soaring boulders, as they whooshed through the winter sky.

"I told you I'd repay the debt of you saving my life one day!" Hammond yelled, over the noise. "I hope we're even now, because I'm going to get in huge trouble because of you!"

"I can tell you're worried from that smile on your face!" she called back.

"What a rush this is—a real battle!"

Ash glanced behind them. Through the clouds and falling snow, the Fenris wolf could be glimpsed throwing back his massive head. He roared thunderously, so loudly that it somehow shook both the ground and the air around them. Ash tightened her grip around Hammond's waist as she prepared for the monster to strike.

Before the Fenris could lurch forward, an enormous eagle, twice the size of the biggest dragon on the field, dove from the sky. It grabbed a chunk of the dog's skin with its sharp talons and he howled in pain.

"Looks like Professor Talon's Roc will give that big dog an even fight," Hammond said. "That bird is magnificent!"

Ash breathed a sigh of relief. Somehow, at last, the war seemed winnable, now that the two biggest enemies had enemies of their own.

Ash knew that she'd done all she could at the Academy, but a thought struck her. *If all of the Regal Kin were here, who was defending the castle?*

King Tiberius was dying and only she knew why—Draven was planning something. She had to act. Now.

"Hammond, will you take me to Castle Dragoon? I'll explain on the way."

Hammond nodded. He voiced a command to Hermie and they sped toward the kingdom.

CHAPTER 19

THE TEST

H ammond lowered Hermie onto the roof of the castle—the same tower that Ash had scaled to reach the king's bedroom. Things looked hectic here, as well, even more so in aftermath. Soldiers and guards lay motionless around both the exterior and interior of the castle walls. It appeared as though any and all Regal Kin had been called to the Academy, leaving the castle vulnerable.

"This looks bad, Ash," Hammond admitted. "It's too quiet here."

"Hammond, go make sure Marni and everyone is all right. Do you remember the cave below yours with the mold problem?"

"Yes."

"There's a girl in there—she has wings. She's a Valkyrie. She's on our side. Please make sure she's all right, but be discreet if you can."

"You mean...like a secret mission?" he said, trying overly hard to come across as casual.

Ash couldn't help but grin. "Yes, Hammond. A secret mission."

"My lips are tingling again!"

Hammond mounted Hermaeus, but paused before commanding a takeoff.

"But...what about you, Ash?"

Ash's heart warmed at his concern.

"I'll be all right," she said. "Just take care of the girl—her name is Arielle. Go!"

She shooed him off. It would be no good dragging Hammond into her mess—a mess that could get her not only expelled, but exiled...or worse.

The boy and his dragon disappeared into the clouds, leaving Ash to wonder if she really would be all right. As Flynn trilled a goodbye to his big, icy pal, the warmth in Ash's chest faded. Her heart plummeted. Hammond's optimism had brightened her spirits, but it was back to cruel reality.

Ash peered over the roof's ledge for an opening into the castle. There was a broken window right below her. She swung down, gripping the cold edge with her fingers, and thrust herself inside.

She was in some sort of study, with overturned chairs and books scattered everywhere. She heard the clanging of sword against sword, as well as voices. It seemed that some sort of battle still raged on in rooms below her.

The castle was still mostly foreign to her—she'd visited only twice. It would be impossible to navigate.

Ash grabbed a framed painting of the royal family off the wall. She showed it to Flynn and pointed to the faces.

"Flynn, remember the king? The queen? Victor? Evan?"

Flynn examined the picture and perked up at the names, seeming to recognize them.

"Go find them!"

She pointed a finger down the hall. Flynn, focused and sharp, comprehended the request and zoomed out of the study.

Ash stepped out of the room, into an open hallway with a railing. Over the railing, she could see below to the first floor. Guards lay lifeless, scattered around like something had blown through the place without warning. Walls displayed scratch marks and wooden furniture was broken and splintered. A coat of armor was toppled to the ground and dirty footprints—too large to belong to a man—dotted the marble floor.

The distant sound of swords ceased with a deep growl. Half-Beasts must still be in the castle, terrorizing the floors below. She'd have to move quickly and quietly. She hoped Flynn would be clever enough to avoid them.

Ash gasped to herself as she remembered her father. Draven had mentioned that he was imprisoned—could he be imprisoned here in the castle? Locked inside a dingy, cold, rat-infested cell in the depths of the basement? Perhaps a dungeon?

In all the chaos, no one would even notice her sneaking around. She could break him out, and they could run away together, far from this nightmare. They could return to Oatsville and rebuild their lives. They could have their farm again, and their farm animals. She had so many stories to tell him!

It was so very tempting. But...was he even in the castle? There were prisons all throughout Cascadia—he could be miles and miles away. The time it would take to determine if he was in the building could be the difference of life or death for King Tiberius. But was he already dead?

The overwhelming decision seemed to fall on Ash like a thousand-ton weight.

No, I can't search for my father now, she thought. *I have to right my wrong first, or at least try.*

Flynn returned at lightning speed.

"What is it, Flynny?"

He chirruped once and sped down the spiraled stairs. Ash followed.

He descended two floors with her to a very prestigious looking hallway. One door, the first on the left, was open. It looked like a bedroom fit for a small prince—it had to belong to Evan, though he was nowhere in sight.

"Hello? Can you hear me? Please, I need help!"

Down the hallway on the left was a second door. It hummed with a green, unearthly glow. Flynn landed on the ground and peeked through the inch-wide gap between the floor and the door, indicating he recognized the person inside.

"Prince Victor? Is that you?" Ash shouted.

"Don't touch the door! It's under a spell!" Victor exclaimed.

"Do you know who did this? Where is the king?"

"It's my Uncle Draven. He's a powerful sorcerer. I've been trapped in here and I don't know what has happened. But, my father is very sick and they've been keeping him in the infirmary in the west wing—if Draven knows of his illness, he'll undoubtedly check there."

"Flynn, go find King Tiberius. Don't be seen," she whispered to her bird and pointed down the hall to the west. He took off once again.

Ash's mind raced with plans, all of them seemingly impossible.

"I can't free you! I don't know how to break spells!" she said, pounding a fist against the wall in frustration.

"If only I could get out of here and contact the Regal Kin," Victor said. "I don't understand why they haven't come."

"There was a red herring—they were sent to defend the Academy from an army of Half-Beasts and leave you defenseless," she said. "Wait. Victor, do you have a window in there?"

"Yes," replied his muffled voice.

"Is it under the same spell?"

"No, but I'm several stories up. I can't jump or climb down from here—I'd slip and die for sure."

"What about your peryton?"

"She's tethered in the stables. Plus she'd never hear me call her from this distance."

Ash closed her eyes. She remembered her days in Tilda's circus with Perry the peryton. Escaping a tethered rope would be simple—perytons could easily use their strength to snap leather in two, but something had to prompt them. Flynn would have never left her side during turmoil, but Victor wasn't bonded to his beast in the same way. He didn't attend the Academy, therefore Vicky was essentially a glorified pet. But there had to be a way to get Vicky to come to him.

That's it!

"Victor! Do you have any instruments in your room? Anything that plays music at all?"

Ash could faintly hear the prince rummage through drawers.

"No...no, there's nothing here."

Ash momentarily gave up hope. She couldn't touch the door, so picking the lock with some sharp trinket or something from her pocket was out of the question. But the thought triggered her to reach for her pocket anyway.

The pan flute.

She withdrew the purple pouch.

"Hello? Are you still there?"

Ash ignored him. She removed the pan flute from the pouch. She once again pictured the day her father had given it to her and taught her how to play it.

That one-inch gap under the door was just enough to slide the flute through and avoid the spell on the door itself. But... letting go of the flute felt like she was letting go of her father. It was as if he embodied the instrument.

"Hello?"

In an instant, Ash took a deep breath and slid the flute into the room.

"I hope you can play a pan flute," Ash said. "Perytons respond to music. Especially high-pitched tones—they become almost hypnotized. Victor, play a tune out your window on the small pipes. Vicky will come, I know it!"

Through the door, Ash could hear him play a beautiful melody. The sound brought her back to the days when she would sing and play for Perry. That and her singing were the only ways to calm the beast down and get him to obey her commands.

She never thought her miserable time spent shoveling manure and getting backhanded by Tilda would provide her with knowledge that would one day assist a prince.

Sure enough, after a minute or two, the distinct sound of large, flapping wings could be heard. Hooves clomped against the wooden floor as Vicky sped through the window and landed inside the room.

"Thank you—wait, who is this? Who am I speaking to?"

"It's Ash, Ash Ridley. But that's not important—you must listen," she said. "Go to the Academy. Send the Kin here. Then, find a boy named Hammond with an ice dragon. He's with Arielle in the caves. She's hurt."

"How do you know—!"

"I just know. Hammond and I won't tell anyone. You can trust us."

"Don't do anything until reinforcements arrive! We'll bring an army to save my father!"

Vicky snorted as Victor mounted up. Ash didn't wait to hear them lift off before running down the hall. Flynn was speeding toward her in a terrified fluster. He whipped around immediately, leading her to the infirmary.

The entrance to the infirmary was chilling to behold— deep claw marks and blood streaked the floor. Some living thing had been attacked here and then dragged off. The walls were spotted with black singe marks from what Ash assumed were magic attacks. Someone had fought their way forcefully into this room, and anyone who had tried to oppose them was now long gone.

Ash's palms sweated profusely while the rest of her body shivered. The hair on her arms and neck bristled. She could hear her heart pounding against her chest, harder than the Kraken had shaken the earth by her feet not an hour earlier. She narrowed her brow and marched toward the door. There was no time to succumb to fear, and no time to wait for the Regal Kin.

She flung open the doors with a grimace, Flynn by her side, with red, angry eyes, ready to attack.

"Don't...move."

Draven spoke in a calm voice. That same gentle tone from the cave where they met.

Ash's grimace turned into a look of terror. The room was circular, with a high cathedral ceiling no doubt intended to make its royal patients feel less confined. And there, in a white medical bed, lay a shriveled and weak King Tiberius—pale, eyes sunken, lips cracked. His outstretched hand gripped a feather quill, outlined by a magic green glow that controlled his motion.

Draven stood over him, wielding his snakelike staff in one hand and a single sheet of unrolled parchment paper in the other. Like the arm of a puppet, Draven was manipulating the king's hand to write on the page.

Coiled in shadow beneath the wrought iron of several more medical beds was Diabolos, the scitalis serpent. The beast's gaze was locked on Ash with a bloodlust for the taste of her flesh.

"He's very fragile now. Grasping the last thread that holds his existence together. See how quickly the poison you administered has taken effect?"

Ash's throat went dry. Her eyes refused to blink. The motion of Flynn's wings as he hovered in the air was the only evidence that time had not frozen.

"Let him go," she said, voice shaking.

Draven chuckled merrily, a bright contrast to his dark demeanor. His open mouth showed off his serpent's tongue, split down the center.

"Yes, of course! I will be delighted to let him die in peace," responded Draven with a smile. "But first, I need him to sign the bottom of this."

King Tiberius quivered his lips in protest as Draven flicked his staff, but he was too feeble to form words. The king's marionette arm pressed the quill to the paper and began slowly to sign it.

"Is that...the peace treaty?"

Draven nearly jolted the king's entire body as he snorted a laugh.

"Peace treaty! You daft, stupid girl," he snarled.

With such a simple insult, Ash instantly felt like a helpless child again. Abused by Tilda, far from her father. Nowhere to run.

"This document will decree to Cascadia that I, Draven, am no longer banned from the castle, and will humbly take the throne once my poor, poor brother passes away," he explained, feigning sorrow. "Once it's finalized with a signature, of course."

"What happened to talking to him? You said all you wanted was an audience!" she cried.

"This is so much more efficient."

Draven concentrated on the king's hand motion. The signature was almost complete.

Ash zeroed in on the staff.

She lunged forward and snatched it from Draven's hand. It instantly shrank to its smaller, foot-long size. Flynn soared toward the ceiling. Ash flung the stick to him, rolling it off her fingers just like they'd practiced with the relay baton. Flynn caught it in his talons and snapped it in two. The halves tumbled to the marble floor.

Ash whipped her head to Draven, but her burst of confidence waned when his reaction was nothing more than pursed lips.

"Oh, look what you did," Draven said with a pout, examining his contract. "Now I only have a half-signature from my brother. Oh well. Close enough."

He casually rolled up the paper and tucked it inside his jacket.

Off Ash's stunned silence, he picked up one of the wooden halves of his broken staff that rolled to his feet.

"You do realize that things like staffs and wands are simply instruments to make magic more precise, don't you? I may not be as graceful without it, but I can still do this."

While the magic from Draven's staff had been delicate and controlled, the shock that streamed from his outstretched hand was a wild blast of green lightning. It lit up the room and struck Flynn hard in mid-air.

Flynn's body froze, wings still spread. Ash screamed in horror as gravity pulled him earthward. She jumped forward to catch him, but like the release of a compressed spring, Diabolos struck. He wrapped around her, rendering her immobile.

Flynn's limp body slammed hard against the marble floor.

Tears instantly welled in Ash's eyes. Flynn wasn't moving. But why? No spell could hold him. It had to have been the force of the blow that knocked him out cold.

Her bird's half-open, golden eyes were cloudy. They were comatose. There was no life in them.

The thick serpent body of Diabolos bound her from feet to neck. Tighter the beast squeezed—tighter every second.

"*Tsk, tsk, tsk,*" Draven uttered. His eyes intensified with one blink, matching the bloodthirsty stare of Diabolos. He licked his sharp fangs with his lengthy split tongue. "This is what the Academy has to boast? How could they possibly enroll a girl so exhaustingly dense?"

The king let out a raspy moan, like the dusty exhale of a corpse.

"Oh, her?" Draven said to him in condescending response. "Why, that is Ashtyn Ridley. Don't you recognize her? She's the girl who murdered you."

"No!" Ash shrieked, squirming to loosen her arms. "You said the poison wasn't real!"

"What are you worried about, Ash? That he knows the identity of his killer? He'll be dead any minute."

Draven took three slow, deliberate steps toward the trapped Ash. Her breath shortened. Her vision was spotty. Little gasps kept her conscious. A tear rolled down her cheek as she eyed her motionless companion on the ground.

She couldn't sense Flynn's presence anymore. Since they had bonded, he had become almost an extension of herself. She'd begun to intuit his emotions and share his feelings. Suddenly, there was a painful void—a hole in her heart.

Was Flynn dead? Stunned? Would she ever be with him again?

"Please," she whimpered. "Wake him up. Please. Please, wake him."

"You have the chance to choose, Ashtyn," Draven whispered. "What to do, what to do...what does the peasant girl do?"

He circled her, running his fingers along the scaly body of his scitalis as he walked.

"Join the Half-Beasts, Ash. No one at that rich, pretentious Academy cares about you. When I rule Cascadia, everyone will be equals. Rich, poor, beast, or human." He leaned in close. "I'll spare you as a reward for your help and loyalty. We'll find your father. Together. Just say the word and I'll release you."

Ash could feel her face turn purple. Her entire body throbbed like the beat of an executioner's drum.

Father. Just the word on his split tongue made Ash cringe with fury. He had already broken his promise once about divulging her father's whereabouts—how many more hoops must she jump through for him? He was a liar. He had lied about the poison. He had lied about the attack. He had lied about everything.

She remained silent.

"Fine!" he erupted in response to her refusal to speak. "Idiot child! Fool!"

He spit as he spoke. His eyes shone bright yellow with black slits, like needles cutting through amber stones. He uttered a foreign command to Diabolos. The serpent's grip grew even tighter. Ash's throat gurgled with pain.

"I've had just about enough of you," he said, his tone calming.

He grabbed the paralyzed Flynn by his stiff head.

"But your phoenix.... Are you in there, little birdie?" Draven rapped on Flynn's skull. "I'm afraid I'm going to have to take him from you. You see, his previous master is a friend of mine and would very much like to have him back."

"Flynn...would...never leave me!" Ash barely squeaked out from her tightened throat. "He's...bonded to me!"

Draven smiled. "Yes. But only while you're still alive."

Diabolos obeyed Draven's snap, and his fangs plunged into Ash's shoulder, sinking deep.

She was too numb to scream.

Her eyes flashed wide. Her skin felt like it was shrinking around her skeletal frame, her insides shriveling, her blood thinning.

"The bite of the scitalis is one of my favorites when it comes to poisonous beast bites," Draven explained with a velvet voice. "It's nothing like the concoction you gave Tiberius. You see, this one takes effect in mere seconds."

Ash choked and lurched from the pain. She lost the energy to gasp for air. Her teeth clenched so hard she felt they might shatter.

Tunnel vision closed in. She saw only Flynn, his tiny, red-feathered body in the grasp of a madman. He must have been terrified. He needed her, she knew it.

With everything, every ounce of will left inside her, she sang their song.

The road is long, for my darling dear
The wind is cold, the sun's disappeared
But don't be 'fraid, for this, too, will pass
We'll lie soon down on green, silky grass
We'll lie soon down on green...silky...

Flynn blinked his eyes.

Everything went quiet. Ash entered into a state that was devoid of all outside forces.

In the peace, Ash didn't hear Flynn as much as she simply sensed the words, saw them in her mind:

May I attack him, master? Do you approve?

Ash's face brightened. With the last of her strength, she looked to her bird and nodded.

"Why aren't you dying!" Draven shouted with a rage that shook the floor.

"Because...we can't," whispered Ash. "But *you* can."

An all-encompassing light engulfed the room. Flynn burst forth from it with an almighty cry. He broke free from being paralyzed—a spell that could never hold a phoenix.

A massive fireball erupted from Flynn's belly and swallowed Diabolos and Ash whole. The serpent's skin bubbled, sizzled, and finally disintegrated. It let out a final shriek as it shriveled into a pile of charcoal.

The fire felt like nothing more than a warm summer day to Ash. She rose to her feet and stepped out of the flame.

She walked with purpose toward Draven, who recoiled before her like a pitiful, frightened garter snake. Engulfed in Flynn's fire, Ash was no peasant girl—she was strong, reborn in the flames.

With a push of her hands, the fire swept over Draven. His clothes instantly ignited and his flaming, screaming silhouette ran off, crashing through a window to the unforgiving depths below.

As the fire subsided, Ash went limp. She crumpled to the floor and rested her head on the marble. She gasped for breath, her body overwhelmed.

Slowly, her eyes closed.

CHAPTER 20

ASH'S FATE

sh had never known any kind of sleep to be more peaceful than tree-sleep beneath a Cascadian Apple Tree. A warm September night, springy grass as a mattress, and a breeze that carried the most delectable aromas of fruits and flowers. Perhaps, though, it would be better if it weren't ruined by the occasional pungent stench of manure from the kludde's cage, or projectiles being flung at her noggin from those menacing monkeys. But it was probably for the best—she couldn't sleep all day. She had chores to do.

Ash blinked open her eyes. There were no animal cages... no Cascadian Apple Tree...just the scent of warm vanilla and a hint of cinnamon.

In place of springy grass was a real mattress—silky and spongy, it hugged her body. Velvety red bed sheets wrapped her in a cocoon and her head sank deep into a feather pillow.

She gasped and sat up. Where was she?

"I thought perhaps you would like to wake up in a royal bed after performing a royal deed."

The room was lit only by lamps and slivers of light peeking in through closed curtains. King Tiberius, clad in burgundy robes, swayed to and fro in an elegant rocking chair with a book on his lap.

She was in the king's bedroom! She was napping in his enormous bed!

"Sorry, your majesty?" she said, clearing her throat.

The king closed his book and set it on a small table. He rose from his chair and sat beside Ash on the bed.

"You did save the king of Cascadia from an evil sorcerer who planned to take his crown, did you not? That seems like a most royal deed to me."

All at once, like a crashing wave on the peaceful beach of her mind, the memories returned. Draven. The infirmary. The poison.

"But...you were dying. From poison. Draven tricked me, I didn't—"

"Shh, child," he said softly. He placed a loving hand on her arm. "I may have been dying, but I heard every word. And not to worry—Professor Thorne had just the healing herbs I needed for the poison's antidote. And Flynn is safe with Elder Raleigh."

Flynn! At the sound of his name, Ash looked around for him frantically. Was he all right?

Tiberius gently kept her from leaping out of bed. "Calm down, my dear!" he said with a chuckle. "Your little friend is right here."

The king placed his index finger and thumb between his lips. Quite loudly, he whistled a three-note tune.

Like a sparkling, red firework, Flynn zoomed in from the hallway through the cracked door. He circled Ash's head and hovered face-to-face. *Are you hurt? Are you all right? Do you know you've got a bump on your head? Why is your shoulder bandaged?*

"He barely left your side long enough for my physicians and Professor Thorne to treat you."

"He's a little protective, I guess," Ash said with a smile. Flynn landed on her right, uninjured shoulder and pressed his head into her cheek for an affectionate nuzzle.

"A little!" responded the king with a hearty laugh. "He singed a nurse on the rear with a fireball just for giving you a shot!"

Ash smiled. She stroked Flynn's warm body and massaged his neck. He cooed and purred—a most comforting vibration.

"Thankfully, he made friends with the caladrius bird. Between you and me, I think he's got a little crush," he said with a wink. "Oh, and I will teach you that whistle, if you'd like."

"About that," Ash asked hesitantly. "How do you know how to befriend a magical beast? You don't have one of your own, do you?"

Tiberius paused a moment, and sighed. He walked to a dresser and slid open the top drawer. He removed a small, framed painting and handed it to Ash.

"This was Timothy, my sphinx."

The picture was of a young Tiberius in a Beast Games competition uniform. His arm was wrapped around the neck of a gorgeous beast—a lion with a face resembling a man. Tiberius was smiling and Timothy looked at him with faithful eyes—it was clear they were best friends.

So the sphinx was his Bonded Beast! Ash realized, remembering Draven's lies about his brother.

"I loved him very much. We did everything together, Timmy and I. We had a very strong bond," Tiberius lamented. "But...my brother was jealous of me. Draven and I were quite different. I strove to make our father proud, with leadership and strength. Draven wanted nothing to do with us. He was moody and ill tempered, spending most of his time alone practicing dark magic against my father's will.

"During the javelin throw at the Beast Games one year, he used his sorcery to send my javelin straight through the heart of my Timothy. There was nothing anyone could do. I lay there beside him as he died moments later."

Ash's heart broke as she listened. Flynn murmured sadly, reflecting his master's emotions.

The king took a deep breath and continued. "My parents banned Draven from ever being king. In spite, he lied to the Half-Beasts of Cascadia, telling them I killed my sphinx on purpose because the creature's face resembled a man. Preposterous! He told them I hated all Half-Beasts and they should be executed—a radical belief that many of my grandfathers strongly agreed with. Quite sadly, the turmoil between humans and Half-Beasts is not a new one, and with Draven uniting all of their races against us, peace seems further away than ever."

"No thanks to me," Ash admitted, guilt still weighing on her conscience.

"Nonsense," he responded. "Draven manipulated you to do his dirty work. You and Flynn were trapped like flies in his web of tyranny. And clearly, his attack was planned long before you ever even spoke to him."

Flynn hopped down to Ash's lap and found a cozy spot to curl up.

Tiberius spoke in an intimate, low voice. "Ashtyn, you must know by now that your phoenix is very, very powerful, and extremely dangerous. Many people will desire to use the pair of you for their own agendas, because of what you're capable of. You must never let anyone persuade you. You must be strong in your decisions. Do what's right for you and Flynn."

Ash nodded earnestly. The king spoke with such wisdom and cared so much for her and Flynn...when he didn't have to.

"One more thing, about Timmy, sir," Ash said. "You're the king. Can't you have another Bonded Beast?"

"Unfortunately, no," he said, returning the picture to his drawer. "Every person can bond to only one beast in their lifetime, and vice versa. Sure, I could have one as a pet, but with the inability to bond, I could never control a dangerous animal. Maybe I'll get a gerbil instead."

Ash glanced to Flynn, now napping in her lap. There was still so much about magical beasts and bonding she had yet to learn.

"Well, your majesty...I know it's not the same, but you can see Flynny any time you'd like. He really likes you, I can tell."

Tiberius laughed and scratched the little bird's head. "I would be honored."

The door to the hall swung the remainder of the way open as Professor Thorne barged in with hands on hips.

"Tiberius! Are you smothering the poor girl when she's just woken up?"

"I'm sorry, I'm sorry!" Tiberius raised his hands in defense and left the girl's side.

Ash never thought she'd be so happy to see her stern teacher. Thorne felt her forehead for a fever and inspected her shoulder bandages. She adjusted Ash's tunic and smoothed her hair.

"I do believe it is time for you to get some fresh air," she said with a grin.

Thorne and Tiberius helped her out of bed. It took several moments to regain her balance. Flynn watched his master hobble with curiosity and perched himself on her shoulder. Two maids threw back the heavy curtains that concealed the double doors leading out to the balcony. Both Ash and Flynn winced from the bright sunshine.

Opening the doors, Tiberius and Thorne led Ash onto the balcony.

Gathered below were several warriors of the Regal Kin with their beasts, many students, even the professors and Elders. They were silent. Ash couldn't read the mood of the crowd, and wondered what was in store for her.

The king raised his hand to address the onlookers.

"The acts of my brother are unforgivable," he began. "He plotted against us. Led an attack upon our beloved Academy. Even drafted children to be his puppets."

The crowd murmured. Ash looked at the ground with shame.

"Rumors run through Cascadia more rampantly than our many rivers. Whatever you may hear about the events of yesterday and those leading to it, one thing must be made clear."

The king grasped Ash's hand.

"This girl has saved us."

Ash looked up from the ground.

"Ashtyn Ridley stopped Draven from becoming a tyrannical ruler and in turn, helped save Cascadia. I pardon her from her trespasses, and she will be revered as a hero."

The king raised Ash's hand in the air. The crowd erupted in cheers. All of them, student and professor, Elder and Kin, clapped and smiled at the king's mercy and Ash's heroism.

"See? I'm the king. I can do that," Tiberius whispered to Ash with a wink.

Ash grinned from ear to ear and her eyes sparkled.

An unmistakable hoot, followed by barking, reached Ash's ears as Marni, Mitzi, Hammond, and Hermie celebrated from atop a stone wall.

Flying beasts circled in the air, prompting Flynn to joyfully take wing. To the far left, Queen Verna grinned in delight beside an annoyed and bored Prince Evan. Prince Victor stood apart from them, his golden crown gleaming in the sun. He caught Ash's attention, held up her pan flute, and nodded a thank you.

Ash smiled and blushed. For the first time, she truly felt special.

ONE WEEK LATER

he Academy was still being cleaned up and restored, thanks to about a thousand carpenter elves sent for by Dottie and Donnie. The duo was a comical sight as they organized and instructed the elves while struggling to keep their smilodon cubs from causing even more destruction.

There was over two feet of snow on the ground, which provided an added hindrance for the elves, who were only a foot in height. The sky salted down even more flakes. Students packed their belongings, frolicked in the snow, and greeted their parents as they arrived in sleighs and carriages to transport their children home for the winter holiday.

In Professor Thorne's spacious private study, which had remained mostly unharmed, the professors, as well as Elders

Odetta and Pyrrus, sat in a circle around Ash and Flynn. It was much less intimidating than the High Council Room. Some of them had decent chairs to sit in, but Professor Talon and Suarez sat awkwardly in small student chairs. It was comforting to feel as though her superiors were on her level, if only for today.

Ash explained what happened with Draven and the king in great detail. She began with the notes from Irving and the sirens. She tried her best to speculate as to the location of the Half-Beasts' lair. Recounting her morning with Mrs. Butterscotch brought a grin to her face. Reliving the moments before Draven's downfall made her certain that nightmares were in her future.

She even included how she had left school premises after hours, but excluded Marni from every story. This was Ash's responsibility, and hers alone.

The professors and Elders returned a mixture of intrigued and disapproving looks. The king of Cascadia may have pardoned her wrongdoings against him, but there were still plenty of Academy rules she had blatantly broken.

When Ash finished her story, the professors shared heavy glances.

"This was...obviously not a typical experience for a first-year student," Thorne said with a sigh, sitting behind her ornate desk. "We understand you were unfairly targeted, but you did commit many infractions that we cannot overlook. You will be held accountable."

Ash nodded bravely. She would accept the consequences.

"We will discuss the length and form of your punishment over the winter break, and have it prepared for you when you return in January."

Ash's eyes brightened. "You mean, I can come back?"

Thorne's stern lips softened. "Yes, you can come back."

Elder Pyrrus spoke up. "Also, please note that Odetta has kept her word to you and gathered information about your father. He is a prisoner, in a penitentiary in far East Cascadia."

Ash's throat tightened and her heart rate increased.

Draven was right after all, she thought. *My father really is in prison.*

"At this point it is a royal matter and out of our control," he continued. "But King Tiberius has assured us that it is a priority and he will look into the matter at once."

Ash swallowed her protest with a loud gulp. Yet again, she felt like a helpless pawn in the adults' chess game. She'd been brushed aside once more.

"In the meantime, you begin your break today," Thorne informed her.

"What about finals?" Ash blurted, followed by realizing she should have just kept her big mouth shut.

"Thought you'd never ask," said a satisfied Thorne. "Professor Atlas will be delivering your written finals to you in exactly one week."

"Deliver to me...where? In the dorms?"

Thorne shared a subtle look with Odetta.

"If it's all right with you, Ash," began Thorne. "Odetta has arranged a place for you to stay in Rosedale City with the

Loomington family. We thought you'd appreciate staying the holiday with a familiar face: your classmate, Farrah."

Ash gulped again, even louder than before. Forget formal punishment—this was going to be torture enough.

She glanced at Odetta, who smiled knowingly at her.

"It...sounds wonderful," Ash said, as appreciatively as she could manage.

A knock came from the door and Thorne beckoned them in. Dottie stood in the doorway and gave a meaningful nod to Professor Suarez.

"Please come with me, Ash," he instructed, rising from his chair.

Ash and Flynn followed. He led them silently through what was left of the school corridors, which were scattered with debris and layers of sawdust from the Carpenter elves' repairs.

Professor Suarez paused before opening the door to Talon's Avian classroom.

"Perhaps Flynn should stay here."

Ash pointed to a bookshelf, saying "Perch." Flynn obeyed and flew over.

Suarez took a deep breath.

"You only have ten minutes," he said, his kind tone communicating sympathy.

Ash returned a confused look.

"You can thank Tiberius later," he whispered.

He swung the door open. Inside the shadowy, empty classroom were two muscular guards in uniform. They both had swords at their hips and one had a chain attached to his arm. On the other end of the chain were shackles, one on each wrist of a prisoner sitting in a seat beside a desk. The man was dressed in disheveled rags and his brown hair was messy and unkempt. It fanned over his wrinkled eyes.

"Dad?" she said.

Landon Ridley looked up. His eyes saw his beautiful daughter. The chains rattled as he stood to his feet.

"Ashtyn!"

She ran across the room to him, weaving through desks and chairs. They embraced—a hug that had been so many months overdue. They could feel each other's hearts pounding. Ash never wanted to let go.

"Where have you—I mean how have you—"

Landon laughed at her stuttering and his wet eyes sparkled. "I'm all right, I'm okay."

He sat back down in the chair to meet her eye line. He swept wispy strands of hair behind her ears.

"Taxes?" Ash asked.

He nodded. Her smile began to fade.

"I told you they'd get me one day," Landon said with a wink. "Ridleys are rebels. But it seems you already know that."

A red flash burst into the room and flew circles around their heads. Flynn chirped wildly before perching on Ash's shoulder.

"Ha ha! Who is this little handsome fellah?"

Ash shared a glance with her bird and couldn't help but grin again. "This is Flynn, Dad. He's a phoenix."

Flynn chirped once more.

"I mean...he's *my* phoenix."

Landon held out his hand and whistled a merry tune. Flynn perked up and immediately hopped over to him, his little feet curling around his fingers. "I remember you telling me about

Flynn from the circus. But you described him as old, molting, and ugly." He leaned in to whisper to Flynn. "No offense."

Ash giggled. Her dad and Flynn, the two most important things in the world, were right there in front of her. Nothing in the past few months even came close to the bliss of this moment. A warm, happy tear trickled down her cheek.

Flynn hopped up Landon's arm and onto his right shoulder.

"Wow. A student at the famous Academy with a Bonded Beast of her own. More beautiful than ever. I couldn't be more proud of my daughter," Landon said softly. But his tone quickly shifted to a playful one. "And what's this rumor I'm hearing about you helping the king and saving the world from utter destruction or something like that?"

He punched her arm gently and she smiled. "It's...a long story."

Suarez chimed in politely. "About two more minutes, Ash."

Ash nodded to her professor, then turned back to her father.

"I'm going to get you out of that prison," she whispered to him.

Landon shook his head. "You let me worry about that, I'll be just fine. You focus on school. This is an amazing opportunity and I won't have you taking it for granted."

The two shared one more hug as their brief time together came to an end.

Landon turned to the bird on his shoulder. "You going to take care of her for me?"

The bird whistled a reply.

"Is that a yes?"

Flynn tilted his head to the left and let out an abrupt chirp.

"Okay, I believe you."

Ash was delighted by this adorable exchange. Landon nudged the red bird and he flew back to Ash's shoulder.

"I love you so much, Dad."

"I love you, Ash."

Their hands locked together for a final few seconds. Landon let her go and she backed toward the door. He gave her one last smile and wink before she and Flynn turned to leave.

Suarez placed a gentle hand on her back as he guided her through the door and shut it behind her.

They walked away in silence. Suarez spoke up after several minutes.

"I meant to ask you, Ash," he said brightly, in a clear attempt to lift her spirits. "If there happened to be—and I'm not saying there is currently—but should an opportunity arise to, perhaps, play on Jeffrey's relay team in the Beast Games this coming spring...would you and Flynn happen to be interested? Just as a backup player, of course. At least come to the first practice. What do you say?"

Ash grinned and looked up at him. "I'd say...we'll race you there."

Outside, the snow blanketed trunks and suitcases with a layer of white, as families loaded up their vehicles. There were hugs, waves, and final snowball attacks as everyone said goodbye.

George and Vivian Loomington finished loading Farrah and Edmund's belongings into their exquisite green sleigh with golden trim, which was obviously brand new. They called for Edmund, who was getting in one last aerial race with his rivals, Jeffrey and Rebecca.

Ash gratefully handed Flynn's birdcage and a small bag of her things to Mr. Loomington. He loaded them in the sleigh.

"I can't believe *you* are coming with us," scoffed an irritated Farrah, shivering inside her expensive parka. "You better keep that flea-ridden bird of yours out of my things."

Odetta stepped near the two girls. "That's a rather rude thing to say to a girl who has a portable heater. It's a long, cold journey home."

Odetta winked at Ash. Farrah grunted with frustration and stomped off.

Ash looked around to make sure no one was nearby, then motioned Odetta to lean in close. The elegant woman's long white hair brushed the snowy ground as she knelt down.

"Odetta, in the castle, when Flynn and I faced Draven...I... communicated with Flynn. Somehow. I didn't hear a voice... more like he put the idea in my mind. I saw images. I knew what he was trying to tell me. I don't think I was hallucinating, though I was losing air..."

Odetta placed a hand on Ash's good shoulder. Flynn perched himself on Odetta's outstretched arm. "Ashtyn, telepathy is a very, very special power—a power that your classmates will not experience for several years, and some of them, not at all."

She swept hair from Ash's face, gently tucking it behind her ear.

"You and this bird are very special, and you have the potential to do incredible things."

Ash smiled and promised herself she would remember those words.

"Ash! Hey, Ash! Over here!" yelled Marni.

Odetta urged Ash to go to her friends and Ash took a few steps toward Marni. But she stopped and turned back to Odetta.

"So, what happened with you and the Berserker?" she asked.

Odetta raised her eyebrows, and her ever-tranquil expression morphed into a mischievous smirk.

"I kicked his butt," she said quietly.

Ash laughed as Odetta turned and walked away. She watched her go, then trotted over to her friends.

Marni sat in the driver's seat of a slick, aerodynamic sleigh, with Hammond beside her. Pulling the ride was an animal Ash had never seen fully grown: a cockatrice, a two-legged dragon with a big rooster head. The beast crowed and flapped its wings, eager to take off.

"Look, Ash!" Marni exclaimed with the reins gripped and Mitzi panting over her left shoulder. "Father said I can take you and Hammond up in our new sleigh before we pack up! I've never driven, of course. You up for it?"

Marni, Ash, and Hammond let out a collective scream as the sleigh dipped and swerved through the clouds. Mitzi's tongue flapped in the wind like a pink flag out of her open, smiling mouth and Flynn squawked as Ash gripped him tight. Beside them in the air, Hermie struggled to keep up with the reckless cockatrice and clueless driver.

The cockatrice dropped downward, and they sped straight toward the ground. At the last minute, the beast veered up and they skipped across the snowy Academy field. The last skip before they returned to the sky sent a wave of snow spraying right into Farrah's face. They cringed at her humiliated squeal behind them as they lifted off.

"Sorry, Farrah!" Ash yelled. She looked to Flynn and shook her head. "She is definitely not going to like me as her new roommate."

Steadying the cockatrice, the three released their tension with an exhale.

"Well, you can't do better than me, that's for sure!" Marni said confidently.

The friends screamed again as the cockatrice ditched the smooth ride and dipped steeply downward. Flynn lifted out of Ash's lap and joined Hermie in the air. The two winged beasts weaved to and fro, up and down playfully. Ash laughed when Flynn tucked in his red wings to charge headfirst through a cloud.

With some help from Ash's good arm, Marni steadied the ride once again, and there was another shared sigh of relief.

Just when Hammond looked to be finally enjoying the flight, Hermie, up ahead, sneezed and sent a burst of snow and frozen snot right into his face.

"Oh, just once I'd like to be warm."

Ash placed her index finger and thumb in her lips, and whistled the same loud three-note tune that King Tiberius had taught her.

Flynn sped to her side. She pointed at Hammond and Flynn coughed out a small burst of fire. Hammond's chill turned to singed hair and a charcoal face.

"Thanks," he replied, looking down at his burnt scarf and jacket.

They ascended even higher. Over the sides of the sleigh, the three admired the beautiful valley where their Academy was nestled, and the cliffs that embraced it.

"Ash, Hammond," Marni said. "I think this might just be the best year ever."

Ash nodded. She couldn't wait to come back in the spring.

ACKNOWLEDGMENTS

O n the bumpy coaster of writing, where one minute you think your story is awesome and the next you're convinced it's garbage, my husband, Shawn, kept me from flying off the rails with his love and support. Thanks to Stuart Newsom, Ben Borthwick, and Lyn Cloninger for being the first ones to read the (very) rough manuscript, my parents, Steve and Dawn, for teaching me that grammar is cool, Ashley Eckstein for inspiring me to never give up, and my rockstar editor, Natasha Simons. Finally, the people who brought my book to life, the Permuted Press team: Michael L. Wilson, Anthony Ziccardi, and Heather King. Telling this story has been my dream since I was a little girl, and you all helped that dream come true. Thank you.

ABOUT THE AUTHOR

Photo by Brooks Ayola

Lisa Foiles is an actress and content creator, best known as a former series regular on Nickelodeon's award-winning sketch comedy show, *All That*. She writes, hosts, creates music, and plays with her two small children, Chloe and Calvin—all while making time to craft fantasy worlds for the daydreams of young readers. *Ash Ridley and the Phoenix* is her first novel.